THE SLITHERS

by Philip Caveney

The Slithers
Philip Caveney
© Philip Caveney 2017
The author asserts the moral right to be identified
as the author of the work in the accordance with the
Copyright, Designs and Patents Act, 1988.

Cover illustration:
Kylie Tesdale

Published by:
Fledgling Press Ltd,
First published 2017

www.fledglingpress.co.uk

Printed and bound by:
Martins-the-Printers, Berwick upon Tweed

ISBN 9781912280056

This book is dedicated to Scotland – my new home.

ONE

THE POND

'Zach! Time to get up! Come on, it's nearly ten o clock.'

Dad's voice came echoing up the stairs, sounding distinctly annoyed. Zach reluctantly pulled his head out from under the covers and gazed around the unfamiliar bedroom.

'And good morning to you,' he said sourly, to nobody at all.

He'd been here less than a week and the summer holidays seemed to stretch before him like a life sentence. He hated this place already, hated the fact that it was out in the middle of nowhere, that he didn't know anybody. Back in England, he'd been due to start Sixth Form College after the summer break. Now he'd learned that it was different in Scotland, that he'd be expected to enrol at a local school, where he would sit his Highers and continue on to what everyone called 'Advanced Highers'. He wasn't exactly looking forward to that.

Most of his stuff was still in big cardboard boxes

stacked around his bed and he hadn't yet summoned up the energy to unpack more than a couple of them. The very idea made him feel weary. Ever since he'd arrived, he'd harboured the dim hope that Dad would change his mind about Scotland, that he'd suddenly announce that he'd made a terrible mistake. They'd call it quits and the two of them would head back to London; a familiar bustling place that came complete with friends and clubs and cinemas and coffee bars and all the things that made living without Mum bearable. But it seemed that Dad was determined to stick it out.

'Zach!' Dad's voice again, louder now. 'I really mean it. I have to head off soon. At least come down and eat something.' Zach noticed that though they'd only been here a few days, Dad's natural Scottish accent was already becoming more pronounced. Like he was settling in.

Zach sighed. He threw back the covers, got out of bed, and paced to the window, where the morning sun was already streaming into the little white-painted room, making him squint. Peering down at the back garden, he could see that it was going to be another scorcher. The lawn looked brown and dry, the few flowers in their ramshackle beds withered on their stalks. In the very centre of the garden, the pond resembled a big, malignant wound, oval in shape, some twenty feet across, thick with mud and clumps of dead weed. As far as Zach could tell there was nothing living in there, not so much as a solitary tadpole. It seemed to sum up this place perfectly. Dead boring.

Cliff View cottage had belonged to Granddad Alistair, a strange solitary man who Zach could barely remember, since he'd died when Zach was six years old. As the name suggested, the cottage was perched on the top of the cliff, commanding a stunning view of the Moray Firth. After the old man's death, Mum and Dad had rented the place out for several years to anybody who fancied a 'picturesque holiday home in beautiful Aberdeenshire'; it had been, according to his dad, a 'nice little earner.' But then two years ago, the family's world had been blown apart. Mum had fallen suddenly and mysteriously ill and after a rapid decline, she'd died. Dad's career had pretty much died along with her; he'd been unable to face work and eventually, he'd lost his job. The only option was to sell the apartment in London and move up here, where they could live mortgage-free and where Dad thought he might have some chance of finding freelance work. Zach didn't get any say in the matter. He'd been packed up with all the other possessions, driven out to a place called Portknockie, but which Zach preferred to call 'The Back End of Nowhere,' and simply told to get on with it. But he didn't feel much like doing anything right now. He couldn't even be bothered to shower.

He peeled off his pyjamas, pulled on a pair of jeans and a T-shirt and padded barefoot down the rickety wooden stairs to the kitchen, where he found Dad making coffee and filling two bowls with cereal.

'Come on,' he said. 'Shake a leg. We'll get nothing done if we just lie around all day.' He ushered Zach to a seat at the kitchen table.

Dad had taken to being relentlessly cheerful lately. It was his new thing. But Zach wasn't fooled for a minute. He could see that it was all an act and that Mum's death had taken so much out of Dad, he was like a shadow of himself. She'd been gone a year now and there were still dark rings under his eyes, his long fair hair peppered with streaks of grey. Back in London, Dad had been the MD of an advertising agency, handling accounts for important clients. But Mum's long illness seemed to have taken away all of his confidence. When Mum was first diagnosed, Dad's partners in the business had been supportive, they'd assured him that they would take care of everything until he felt ready to return. But losing Mum had taken all of the fight out of him. When he finally did manage to drag himself back to the office, he was like a different person, vague, unable to make a decision about anything. Eventually, his partners had got fed up with it. They'd gone behind his back and voted him out, offering him a paltry sum of money by way of compensation. Shattered as he was, he hadn't even tried to fight it. The family savings had all gone on an expensive last-ditch medical treatment for Mum, which she hadn't even lived long enough to complete. Now Dad was bereft and here he was, exiled to the sticks, chasing jobs in small agencies at a fraction of the salary he used to command.

'Got a tip-off about an opening at an ad agency in Cullen,' he told Zach, setting a bowl of cereal in front of him. 'Heading up there for an informal chat with them in a bit.' He winked, as though sharing a confidence and slipped into a chair on the other side of the table. 'I've got a really positive feeling about this one. Fingers crossed, eh?' He removed the lid of the milk, sniffed hopefully at the contents and seemingly satisfied with the results, poured some over his cereal. 'What do you want to do?' he asked Zach. 'You can come in with me if you like and we'll have a look around the town, once I've had my meeting.'

Zach scowled. 'I'll stay here,' he said. He picked up the milk and poured some into his own bowl. Then he pushed the cereal around for a while, but didn't actually lift any of it to his mouth.

'I could do you a bit of bacon if you prefer,' offered Dad.

'No, this is fine,' Zach assured him.

'But you're not eating anything.'

Zach lifted a spoonful dutifully to his mouth and crunched the tasteless flakes between his teeth, his face expressionless.

'Look, I know it isn't easy for you. But... we've got to give this our best shot. There's no point in just hanging around here feeling sorry for yourself. You need to get out and make friends.'

'What friends?' snarled Zach. 'I had friends back in London. Loads of them. Good friends. I don't know anyone here. Not a living soul.'

'Yes, and you're not likely to if you don't make some effort.' Dad chewed thoughtfully for a moment. 'Maybe...'

'Maybe, what?'

'I was thinking, maybe you should look for a summer job. There must be stuff you could do around here. The herring fishermen down on the quay, they always need help with their catches…'

'Oh yeah, that'd be good. Stinking of fish all day.' Zach pushed his bowl away in disgust. 'Yeah, lead me to it. Where do I sign?''

Dad frowned. 'Well, there must be *something* you could do. Stacking shelves at the supermarket… stuff like that.' He caught Zach's scornful expression and came right back at him. 'Yeah, I know it doesn't sound enticing. Christ, do you think I like chasing after the dead end jobs I'm going for? Knowing that they'd rather pay some spotty teenager, cos they can get him for a fraction of the price? But… we have to suck it up, Zach, because if we don't, we may as well just lie down and die.'

There was a long silence, before Zach said, 'Like Mum did.'

There was a terrible silence then. Zach slurped at his coffee, which seemed to taste of nothing at all, while Dad concentrated on finishing what was in his bowl. Finally, he seemed calm enough to say something else.

'If you're intent on staying here, at least help me out with something.'

Zach sighed, shook his head. 'What?' he said, wearily.

Dad got up from the table. 'Come with me,' he said.

He walked out through the open french windows and Zach followed, aware of the intense sunlight on the back of his neck. Dad led him across the lawn until they were standing beside the pond. This close, it smelt awful, a concentrated stink of rotting vegetation and something distinctly fishy.

'We need to get this eyesore drained,' he said. 'And filled in.' He indicated a large mound of turf off to one side of it. 'That's what your Granddad dug out in the first place.' He smiled grimly. 'It was his pride and joy, the pond.'

'This?' Zach looked at it bleakly.

'Yeah, he put it in all by himself, wouldn't let anyone help him.'

'Didn't you give him a hand?'

'Oh, it was long after I'd left for London. A bit of a hobby for him, I suppose. Of course, it was different back then. There were frogs and newts and dragonflies… lots of stuff growing in the shallows. He really went to town on it, you know? Mind you, he was a bit paranoid about it. Whenever we brought you to visit when you were a toddler, he would insist that you weren't to be allowed within twenty feet of it. It was almost as though he was afraid of it…'

'What did he do?' asked Zach. 'For work, I mean.'

'He was a fisherman, originally. Ran a little trawler out of the harbour here. But that went belly up and he worked out on the oil rigs right up until his accident in the late 80's.'

'Oh yeah, he had a dodgy leg, didn't he?'

Dad nodded. 'He had a bad fall, meant he couldn't work on the rigs any more. He got a bit

7

of compensation from his employers and he had a small private pension. He did the occasional bit of part time work around the village, you know, odd job man, painter and decorator, that sort of thing. And…' Dad smiled, as though remembering, '…one time I came up to visit him… this was just after he put the pond in, and… he told me that he'd found some kind of treasure.'

'What? Get out of here!'

'No, I'm serious. He'd never tell me exactly what it was, only that he'd found it near here and that he'd never have to worry about money ever again.' Dad chuckled. 'Well, whatever he thought he had, he must have spent it all because he didn't leave me anything in the will apart from the house… but thank God he did, otherwise I don't know where we'd be now. Sleeping on the streets, I shouldn't wonder.' Dad shook his head, as though attempting to shake off the past. He pointed to the mound again. 'Anyway, you'll need to shovel all that back in to the hole,' he said. 'I can't afford to hire somebody and… well, I'm busy chasing jobs, so...' He looked at Zach. 'I'm not expecting you to get it all done in one day, or even in a week, but it would give you something to occupy yourself. And you'd be helping me out, big time.'

Zach stared into the stagnant olive green depths and thought they mirrored the way he felt.

'How would I drain the water?' he asked.

Dad kicked at a rubbery black layer that bordered

the edges of the pond. 'That's a liner,' he explained. 'I guess if you just pierce it a few times, the water should drain straight through into the ground. It could take a while, obviously. Then you can pull the liner out and start filling in the hole. '

Zach scowled. 'Why not just leave it where it is?' he muttered.

'If we do that, the ground will get boggy every time it rains and nothing will grow. I was thinking we could put a vegetable patch here, something useful. It's weird because the old man once told me that's what *he* was initially planning to do, but he must have decided to put the pond here instead.' He gazed once again into the water. 'You know, for about ten minutes, I did have this crazy notion about trying to restore this, get it back to its former glory, but… I think it's past saving, don't you? Somebody should have taken it in hand years ago.' He looked at his son warily. 'So, what do you think? I know it's a big ask but…'

'I'll do it,' said Zach and Dad smiled. 'For a tenner,' he added.

Dad's smile faded. 'Come on, son, that's not very helpful,' he said.

'A tenner,' replied Zach, looking at him. 'Or I don't lift a finger.'

Dad glared at him, but got no reaction. For a moment he seemed on the point of walking away but must have thought better of it.

'OK,' he said quietly. 'I'll pay you when it's all done. Not before.'

Zach shrugged. 'Fine,' he said. 'Deal?'

Dad sighed. 'Deal,' he said. 'Let's hope I get that bloody job.' He indicated a small, moss-covered shed at the top of the garden. 'You'll find tools in there,' he said and walked back to the house, his expression grim.

Zach watched him go, hating himself as he did so. Why, he wondered, did he have to be like this? He didn't even have anything to spend the money on. Couldn't he for once have just said OK? Would it have killed him? He nearly ran after Dad to say he'd only been joking, but somehow couldn't bring himself to do that. No, he'd wait until he actually handed him the money and then he'd say, 'No worries, that one was on me.' Make a big gesture of it. Except that he even doubted that he'd do that. Because Mum leaving the way she did had left something hard and cold inside him and he doubted he would ever be rid of it.

Dad disappeared inside and Zach turned his attention back to the pond. He looked once again for some signs of life in the reeking shallows. Surely there ought to be *something*? Frogs, toads... insects? But the water looked poisonous, as though it would kill anything that was reckless enough to venture in there.

Zach sighed. The sun was gathering strength and he could already feel the heat surrounding him like a blanket. This was going to feel suspiciously like hard work, he told himself. But a deal was a deal, so with that in mind, he turned and walked back towards the house to change his clothes.

TWO

A DISCOVERY

Zach found some old clothes in one of the boxes up in his room - a paint- spattered T-shirt and some jeans that were gone at the knees. He put on a pair of black wellies and then clumped to the bathroom to slather sun tan lotion on his face and neck. When he got downstairs again Dad was back in the kitchen, dressed in his best suit and having a last coffee before leaving. He already looked uncomfortably hot.

'All set?' Zach asked him and Dad nodded, forcing what he probably hoped was a confident smile.

'It's only a small agency,' said Dad, almost apologetically. 'They're looking for a junior. I don't exactly fit the bill but… well, I'm prepared to take a low wage to start with. Until I find my feet.' He looked so heartbreakingly hopeful that Zach felt obliged to give some encouragement.

'Dad, you used to run the biggest agency in London,' he said.

'Yes.' Dad nodded. 'Yes, I did, didn't I? I need to remember that.'

'So you'll be a big fish in a small pond.'

'Hmm. Well…' Dad put down his coffee cup. 'Better get going I suppose.' He glanced towards the french windows. 'Talking of ponds, you be careful,' he said. 'We don't want any accidents.'

Zach snorted. 'It can't be more than two foot deep,' he said. 'And I'm not a toddler any more.'

'Even so. A man can drown in an inch of water. I read that somewhere.' Dad picked up his Italian leather briefcase, a souvenir of better days and went out through the french windows. Zach followed and watched him climb into the battered old Volkswagen parked on the drive. Dad opened the windows because the car's air conditioning had stopped working months ago and he couldn't afford to get it fixed. 'See you later,' he said. He started the engine and drove off towards the open gate that led to the lane. Zach watched until the car was out of sight, then turned and strolled up the garden to the shed.

He unlatched the rough timbered door and swung it open, peering warily inside. Judging by the thick mantle of cobwebs that swathed everything within, nobody had entered the place for years, but after a bit of poking about Zach located the tools he thought he'd need – a spade and a garden fork. He looked around and noticed a rusty old Stanley knife lying on a battered wooden workbench alongside a large Yale key. As Zach reached to pick up the knife, he noticed that some words had been scratched into the surface of the bench, in a series of jagged, angular capitals. He was obliged to brush away some dust and strands of old webbing in order to read them properly.

WE BURY LOVE

FORGETFULNESS GROWS OVER IT LIKE GRASS

THAT IS A THING TO WEEP FOR, NOT THE DEAD.

Zach frowned, puzzled. He had no idea what it was supposed to mean. On impulse, he lifted the Stanley knife and pushed the button to expose the rusty blade. He held it against the W of 'We' and saw that it fitted perfectly. He wondered who had taken the trouble to cut the words into the old bench and why they had chosen those particular ones. Granddad Alistair, he supposed. It seemed most likely. From what Dad had told him about the old boy, he was a bit of a weirdo. Grandma Mary had died when Zach was just a baby and the old man had lived alone out here, keeping himself to himself. Dad had told Zach that Granddad Alistair used to go into the nearest village once every two weeks to stock up on provisions. Other than that, he stayed at home and never spoke to a living soul. On the few occasions that Dad and Mum braved the long drive up to visit him, they hadn't stuck around for long and never chose to stay overnight, preferring a hotel. Mum in particular had hated coming here. She used to tell Dad that she felt as though the place was haunted and though Dad didn't believe in any of that nonsense, he never put up much opposition.

The awful thing was that because they heard from Granddad Alistair so rarely, they didn't find out he was

13

dead until weeks after it had happened. A postman had called with a parcel for the old man and got no response. He'd gone around the back of the house and noticed that the french windows were open. It was a fine summer's day and Granddad Alistair was sitting in a chair by the windows. At first glance the postman had thought he was wrapped from head to foot in a black blanket. Then he'd gone a little closer and the blanket had begun to buzz and stir…

Zach couldn't suppress a shudder. He noticed a large bluebottle, trapped in a spider's web in the corner of the shed and his skin crawled. He turned away, dropped the Stanley knife and the gardening tools into a rusty wheelbarrow. He noticed a pair of old canvas gloves lying on the bench and threw them in too, then pushed the squeaking barrow back out into the garden. It was somehow a relief to be in the sunshine once more.

He trundled the barrow laboriously back to the pond and, selecting the garden fork, he stepped to the edge and thrust the sharp-pronged head under the surface and down through deep layers of sludge, until he felt some resistance. He pushed on the wooden handle with all his strength and felt the spikes pierce the liner. There was a glopping sound and a couple of bubbles rose to the surface. They popped, releasing an eggy stink. Zach grimaced, pulled the fork out and repeated the exercise, with the same results. He did this another half a dozen times and then stood back and looked expectantly at the surface of the water, but the level didn't seem to have dropped at all.

He threw down the fork and thought for a moment. The only solution he could think of was not an agreeable one, but he told himself, it ought to speed matters up a bit. He inspected the gardening gloves, shaking them vigorously, wanting to be sure that nothing had taken up residence inside them before he put them on. A couple of earwigs dropped out, but nothing more threatening than that, so he put the right glove on. He picked up the Stanley knife and then stretched himself on his stomach at the edge of the pool. With his left hand, he turned back the short sleeve of his T-shirt until his right arm was completely bare. He steeled himself for a moment and thrust his hand down under the surface. The glove instantly filled with shockingly cold water. He'd known this would happen but somehow couldn't bring himself to stick his bare hand in there. His first impulse was to pull it out again, but he resisted that. Another inch or so down he entered a thick layer of what he assumed was mud.

He gritted his teeth and kept pushing, nervous for some reason that there might be something moving down there, but it would have been a hardy creature indeed that could have survived in these conditions. Finally, when the surface of the water was lapping at his armpit and he was beginning to think he would never reach the bottom, the blade of the knife stabbed into the liner. Zach made an extra effort, pushing the blade through the fabric and then he drew his hand sideways, making a long slit.

The effect was dramatic. There was a gurgling

sound and a whole flurry of bubbles rose to the surface, releasing a stink that almost made him retch. The water level began to drop rapidly, so Zach kept his arm where it was, moved his hand a few inches to the right and performed the same action again. The thick plastic liner came apart easily beneath the sharp blade. It made Zach feel strangely powerful. Almost without thinking he began to stab and cut and slice, relishing the way the liner yielded to his power. Now the water level was dropping at an alarming rate and Zach finally withdrew his bare arm, which glistened beneath a layer of fine chocolate-coloured mud. He used his other hand to scoop up handfuls of the receding water to splash the worst of the mud away. It smelled abominable, like something that had died.

Finally, he got to his feet and took a couple of steps back, watching in fascination as the last of the brown water slipped through the lacerated liner, leaving only a black, oily sludge. Zach examined it carefully, still amazed that nothing appeared to be living in it. Shouldn't there be worms, grubs, *something*?

He dropped the Stanley knife and peeled off the sodden glove, then returned to the edge of the pond and started removing the big stones that held the ends of the liner in place. He staggered a short distance with each stone and dropped it out of the way, before returning for the next one, making a large untidy pile on the lawn. He was uncomfortably aware now of a thick sweat pooling on his brow and trickling down his spine beneath the T-shirt, and he considered taking a break to get his breath back, but somehow couldn't bring himself to do it. He carried on, working his way around the oval pond and lifting every stone. When he had removed the last one and piled it with the others, he chose a spot where the liner looked the least embedded in the turf. He wrenched the edges free, having to use considerable effort to do so and now found that he was obliged to repeat the process, going all the way around again until he had loosened all of it. Once this was achieved, he returned to his starting point, stooped to take a firm grip and pulled with all his strength.

For a few moments, nothing happened. The liner, still heaped with a thick layer of mud, seemed determined to cling tenaciously to its former home, but Zach renewed his efforts and finally managed to move it a few inches towards him. Encouraged, he pulled again, gritting his teeth with the effort and this time the liner moved more easily, relinquishing the space it had covered for so many years, the far edges of it dropping into the hollow. Zach paused, took a couple of deep breaths, aware that he was now sweating from every pore, but nevertheless determined to pull the liner free. He made a last titanic effort and the torn black fabric came completely away. It slid towards him and squelched up the near side of the pond, revealing what lay beneath.

Zach stopped and stared, open-mouthed in astonishment. There was a large, metal grille set into the bottom of the pond, through which the water must have spilled. The grille was set in a stout frame and Zach could see that it could be opened like a door. Except that at the moment it was secured by a heavy padlock. Which was pretty weird in itself.

But infinitely more troubling was the fact that from somewhere far below the level of the pond, a pale green light was shining and radiating upwards through the grille. And in that instant, Zach knew that whatever else happened, he would have to find out where that light was coming from.

THREE

GONE

'That's weird.'

He heard himself say the words aloud and then actually looked around to ensure that he was alone. He wasn't sure why, but there was something in him at that moment that didn't want to share this discovery with anyone. He stepped forward and jumped down into the hollow that had so recently been filled with stagnant water.

His wellingtons sank to the ankles in mud, but he took no notice. He squelched over to the grille and peered down through it. Underneath it, he could see that there were two flat grey boulders with a wide gap between them. He felt a strange stirring in his gut as he saw that a narrow shaft led straight down into the gloom.

It was hard to see much more with the grille in his way and he examined the padlock, which looked really strong. His first thought was to go and get a large rock so he could smash it open, but then an image appeared in his mind, an image of a Yale key which he was sure he had seen only recently. But where? He concentrated for a moment and it came to him. The workbench in the shed...

In an instant he was back on his feet and trotting up the garden to fetch it. There it was, lying on the workbench, right where he'd pictured it. Of course, he couldn't be sure it was the right one, but for some reason he had a strong feeling that it would be. He grabbed it and hurried back to the pond, jumped into the basin, trudged back to the centre and crouched down beside the padlock. The key fitted easily. It was a little stiff and he had to wiggle it around a bit, but after a couple of attempts it snapped open with a click and Zach was able to slide it out. He took hold of the grille and lifted it. It opened with a creak of protest. He was now looking into a vertical shaft that dropped straight down between the flat boulders.

Now that he had a better view he noticed a detail he'd missed before – a series of rusted metal rungs had been hammered into the stone at regular intervals and they led straight down the shaft. It was apparent at a glance what they were. Handholds.

'No freakin' way,' he murmured. He leaned closer, trying to ascertain where that weird green light was issuing from, but wherever it was, it was far below the ground. He reached forward and gripped the nearest rung, gave it an experimental pull. The metal was old and corroded and bits of rust flaked off beneath his hand but it seemed strong enough, rooted as it was, deep into the bare rock. Now Zach was assessing the opening, trying to gauge whether it was wide enough to allow him access...

Something cut into his thoughts, the sound of a car engine approaching. He lifted his head and looked towards the gate. Dad's car was coming up the lane! Zach glanced at his watch and realised with a dull sense of shock that two hours had passed since he started work, though it only seemed like minutes. He reacted instinctively, unsure of why he was even doing it. He slammed the grille shut, jumped upright, scrambled out of the hole and grabbing the mud-covered liner, flung it back across the hatch, just as Dad's car came in through the gate. Zach turned and lifted one hand in greeting. He noticed the padlock lying beside his foot, the key still attached and he stooped to grab it and shove it under the nearest edge of the liner, out of sight. Standing back up, he saw Dad's glum face regarding him through the windscreen. The car slowed to a halt and the driver's door opened. Dad got out, looking like he'd just returned from a beating.

'Hey, how did it go?' asked Zach, but he already knew the answer. It was right there in Dad's disappointed expression.

'Waste of time really. Same old thing. The guy I spoke to said I was too qualified for the post. Which means, he didn't want to pay any more than the minimum wage. He *did* give me a tip-off about something else though, another agency…' Dad's voice trailed off. He had just noticed the pond. 'Hey!' he said, sounding delighted. 'You didn't waste any time, did you?'

Zach shrugged his shoulders, hoping he didn't look guilty. But why should he? He hadn't done anything

21

wrong, had he? He just knew that he wasn't going to tell Dad about what he had found. Not yet, anyway.

'It wasn't too difficult,' he said. He waved a hand at the crumpled liner. 'I thought I'd let that dry out for a bit before I do any more. It'll make it easier to move it.'

Dad frowned. 'If you want, I'll put some old clothes on and give you a hand.'

'No! No, that's OK. I kind of… you know what, I enjoyed working on my own. I'll get on with it tomorrow. You… you'd probably like a cup of coffee, wouldn't you? I could murder one myself.'

Dad looked at him suspiciously. 'You're offering to make me coffee?' he murmured.

'Yeah, sure, why not? Come on, you can tell me all about the interview.'

'OK…' Dad locked the car and followed Zach towards the french windows. 'You… haven't been in the sun too long, have you?'

'Very funny.' Zach kicked off his muddy wellingtons before going inside. He walked across to the kettle and switched it on. 'So, what's this new hot tip the guy gave you?'

Dad dumped his briefcase and took a seat at the table. 'Oh well, it'll probably come to nothing.'

'Tell me anyway.' Zach spooned instant coffee into two mugs and took the lid off the biscuit tin

'Well… there's this other agency in Aberdeen. Bigger, much more successful. They've managed to pull in some surprisingly prestigious clients. The guy told me they're expanding and the MD is looking for an assistant...'

'You could do that job with your hands tied behind your back,' Zach assured him and Dad gave him a strange look.

'Zach, have you swallowed a bottle of happy pills since I went out?' he asked. 'Only, you're like an entirely different person.'

'Oh, I guess it's just... having something to do. It makes you feel different about things. So er... what kind of stuff would an assistant be expected to do?'

Dad started to tell him, at length, but Zach wasn't really listening. In his head there was the vivid image of a tunnel leading down into the ground and a pale green light at the end of it...

'Zach? The kettle.'

He came back to himself, to find the kettle bubbling away, throwing clouds of steam into his face. 'We need a new one of these,' he said, clicking the button off with his thumb. 'It's supposed to switch off automatically.'

'I'll add it to the list,' said Dad, flatly. 'I'm still hoping we can get a telephone engineer out here to install a landline, one of these days.'

'We've got our mobiles,' Zach reminded him.

'Yeah, but you can't always depend on them, can you? Be useful to have one in case of an emergency.'

He watched as Zach made the drinks and brought them to the table, together with the biscuit tin.

Zach spooned a couple of sugars into his coffee and stirred it.

'So did it give you much trouble?' asked Dad. 'The pond?'

'No, not really. I got stuck in with a Stanley knife. It drained pretty fast after that.'

'Yeah, Dad's old tools are all out in that shed. I'll have to get out there some time and sort them.'

'Tell me more about Granddad Alistair,' said Zach.

Dad looked surprised. 'I'm not sure you *want* to know any more about him,' he said.

'What's that supposed to mean?'

'It means that your Granddad was... well, let's just say he was *unusual*. That's probably the polite way of putting it.'

'You know that thing you told me before? About the treasure. What do you suppose that was all about?'

Dad laughed bitterly. 'Probably the first signs of madness,' he said. 'I mean, he was my dad and I loved him, but he *was* peculiar.'

'Peculiar how?'

'Where would I start?' Dad seemed to ponder the question for a moment before continuing. 'He was a real loner, for one thing. Secretive sort. Never wanted to go anywhere or do anything. That's why there's no telephone line out here. Made it near impossible to keep in touch with him. You had to write him a letter if you were planning to visit! And he was downright unfriendly to strangers, wouldn't give them the time of day. He led Mum a dog's life before she...' He broke off. 'In many ways, though, he led a charmed life. Never a day's illness, right up to the end. Not

24

even a cough or a cold. Like I told you before, he had that accident on the rig, but it didn't slow him down one bit. Your Grandma was the same. Perfect health, all her life.' He smiled. 'You know, the old man told me once that a 'higher power' was looking after them both. Which is odd, because he wasn't at all religious. And then of course, towards the end, he started seeing things…'

'What kind of things?'

'Erm… oh, various barmy visions. It was probably some kind of dementia. Used to tell me that he'd seen things creeping around the garden at night.'

'Like… what?'

'Oh, God knows. Elves or pixies, I suppose. Some such nonsense.'

Zach tried not to laugh. 'Your dad thought there were fairies at the bottom of the garden?'

'Yeah. Only the way he described them, they didn't sound anything like as cute as that. What did he call them once? Oh, yes. The Slithers.' Dad rolled his eyes. 'I can't blame it on alcohol. He was a teetotaller, never touched a drop. No, I think he must have had what's called 'early-onset Alzheimer's'. I mean, he was only in his seventies when he died.'

'You don't think maybe…?'

'Maybe what? That he really *had* seen fairies? It's superstitious nonsense, Zach. Though mind you, there's still plenty of people round these parts who believe in that rubbish. Some of the older fishermen out on the harbour, whenever they bring in a catch,

25

they still leave a few fish on the beach for the 'sea devils'. Sort of a tribute type thing.'

'No way!'

'I'm serious. Oh, they love that kind of thing here. One reason why I was mad keen to move away as soon as I could.'

'OK, so you're saying that Granddad Alistair was a bit of a head-the-ball?'

'That would be putting it mildly.' Dad raised his eyebrows, then pointed to the french windows. 'You ever notice anything strange about those windows?' he asked slyly.

Zach looked at them. 'Like for instance?' he asked.

'Well, you ever clocked how many locks and bolts are on them? It's like Fort Knox here.' Dad pointed to a selection of keys hanging on a row of hooks beside the french window. 'Everything had to be kept in the right place, he was very particular about that. And I'll show you something else.' He got up from the table and walked over to the windows. He reached in behind some curtains and pulled out a long wooden pole that must have been propped against the wall. The pole had a metal hook on one end of it. Dad reached up and slotted it into a fitting on the outside of the windows, just above the lintel. He pulled and a steel shutter came sliding smoothly down. Dad only lowered it a foot or so, but it was clear it could descend to floor level if necessary. 'He had these things fitted to every entrance on the ground floor, a couple of months before Grandma Mary... went.'

'Went?' Zach caught Dad's discomfort. 'Don't you mean, died?'

Dad looked uncomfortable. 'No. I mean 'went'. It's a weird story, actually.'

'Weird, how?'

'I mean, what happened to her. Grandma Mary.'

'What *did* happen to her?'

'That's just it. Nobody knows.'

'Dad, what are you talking about?'

Dad took a deep breath. 'She went missing, Zach. Disappeared without a trace.'

'Are you trying to be funny?'

'I wish I was. I've lived with the knowledge of it for over twenty years. It was so long ago it feels like it didn't really happen. Except that it did. Let me see now… it must have been…' Dad thought for a moment. 'Nineteen ninety-five? I was long gone by then, working in London. I'd just hooked up with your mum and we'd got our first place together. The story is…' Dad paused for a moment as though reluctant to continue.

'Go on,' Zach urged him.

Dad sighed. 'Granddad Alistair woke up in the middle of the night and the other side of the bed was empty. At first, he thought Mary must be in the bathroom, or something, but she wasn't there, so he came downstairs.' He waved a hand. 'These windows were open and the shutters had been raised. The key was still in the lock and there was no sign of her. She'd just… opened up and wandered off into the night.

27

Didn't even bother to change out of her nightgown. And she was never seen again.'

'Oh come on, no way!'

'Way. Trust me, I wouldn't lie about something like that.'

'But that's… weird.'

'Isn't it, just? Your mum reckoned that she'd simply got sick of the old man and done a runner, gone off to start a new life somewhere else, probably with some fancy man in tow, but… who leaves without changing their clothes and packing a suitcase? Besides, she'd never have done that. She loved Dad, for all his failings.'

'So… did they like… search for her?'

'Of *course* they did. There was a big campaign. Nationwide. "Have you seen this woman?" kind of thing. And of course there was a police investigation. I think for a while the cops actually thought that your granddad might have, you know, done away with her, but that all came to nothing. He insisted that somebody had come into the cottage in the middle of the night and taken her, against her will, but that didn't really add up either. There were no signs of a struggle, or a break in. No, it looked as though she'd just unlocked the windows, opened the shutters and wandered out into the garden. Of course, we were hopeful at first that she'd be found, but months passed… then years… and there was nothing.'

Dad strolled back to the table. He selected a ginger biscuit from the tin and dipped it into his coffee.

'How come I didn't hear about any of this before?' asked Zach.

'It happened when you were tiny. We weren't going to tell you about stuff like that until we thought you were old enough. And then, I don't know… it just got put off and put off and other things got in the way. But you're old enough to know about it now. And you *did* ask me to tell you more.' Dad managed to bite the dipped biscuit just as it began to droop. 'Thought you might have noticed the shutters though.'

'How would I if we never use them?'

'Good point. Anyway, Alistair must have felt threatened by something. He had them fitted a couple of months before Mary disappeared and he locked them, every night. Another reason why your mum hated staying here. Made it feel like a prison visit.'

'Maybe they were put there to keep the fairies out?' suggested Zach and Dad laughed.

'Oh yeah, now there's a theory. Your Grandma was abducted by pixies. That's one thing the police force didn't consider.' He gave Zach a concerned look. 'I hope all this isn't worrying you too much,' he said. 'You know, we rented this place out to holidaymakers for years after your Granddad died and not one of them ever reported anything out of the ordinary. Oh, and before you ask, he died from a heart attack. No suspicious circumstances.'

'It was horrible though, wasn't it?' muttered Zach. 'Him sitting there in the chair for all those weeks.'

Dad took another biscuit. 'Who told you about that?'

'Mum did.' Zach gave his Dad an accusing look. 'She used to tell me lots of things, rather than keep me in the dark the whole time.'

Dad ignored the taunt. 'Well, like I said. He was a strange guy, my old man. And Grandma Mary disappearing like she did, it clearly affected him. That's when he started talking about things lurking in the garden at night. Seriously, I considered many times putting him in some kind of a home, but he was too stubborn to allow that to happen. Said that this place was his castle and he wanted to be here to defend it. And...'

'Yes?'

'To be here if Grandma Mary ever came back.'

'Wow. That's... incredible. Not much chance of that happening now, I suppose?'

'Well, I'm not holding my breath.'

Zach thought about that for a moment, imagining the old woman wandering in out of the night, still dressed in her nightgown. For some reason, the thought gave him the creeps. He made an effort to push the thought from his mind. He got to his feet, collected the mugs and carried them to the sink. 'Well, I'm pretty bushed,' he announced. 'I'll carry on with the pond tomorrow,'

Dad gazed after him for a moment. 'I've enjoyed this,' he said.

Zach looked at him quizzically.

'Enjoyed what?' he muttered.

'Talking. Weird though the conversation was, it's

ages since we sat down and had a good old natter. We should do it more often.'

'Yeah,' said Zach. 'Sure. We can do that.'

Dad drained the last of his coffee and then glanced at his watch. 'I need to make a phone call,' he said. 'See if I can line up an interview for that other job. Or at least, another 'informal chat.' If you hear me scream, you'll know what they've said. "Too qualified." You OK to put the tools and stuff back in the shed?'

'Sure,' said Zach, but once again, his mind was elsewhere. He was thinking about the narrow opening between the two rocks and the tunnel, leading down towards that mysterious green light. He had to know what was down there.

Tomorrow, he thought. *I'll find out then.*

FOUR

DOWN

Zach pulled the liner back from the pond. Most of the mud on it had dried now, making it much easier to move. He kept pulling until the opening was just about exposed and he left the liner lying half in, half out, so it could be easily pulled back over the entrance to the shaft if necessary. He jumped down into the hollow and walked across the liner, clods of dried mud crumbling under his feet. He swung open the grille, went down on his knees and studied the opening, deciding pretty quickly that yes, it was just about wide enough to take him. He pulled his mobile phone from his back pocket, switched on the torch app and shone the beam down the shaft, but it wasn't powerful enough to show any kind of a floor. Clearly it was a long way down.

'OK,' he muttered. 'I can do this.' He switched off the torch and returned the phone to his pocket. Then he turned himself around onto his hands and knees and backed towards the entrance. He lowered his legs through the opening until his feet found purchase on the first rung. He steadied himself, one hand on either side of the hole and swung his legs down to the next rung and then the next and bit-by-bit he went down, twisting his body from side to side, in order to fit. It was pretty tight and he thought to himself that a bigger guy would have trouble getting down here, but the photographs he'd seen of Granddad Alistair showed he was a skinny old man and Zach was pretty sure that he must have known all about this shaft, must have put the pond where it was in order to hide it. But why make it so difficult to get back in there? Why not just a trapdoor or a hatch of some kind? To put a pond there suggested that he had never wanted anybody else to know about it.

Now Zach's hands were on the first rung and only his head was above ground. He went down, slowly at first, questing with a foot to find the next rung and hanging on tight with his hands. It was gloomy down here, but not completely dark, because of that unearthly green glow which seemed to grow gradually stronger as he descended.

It was cold too, but the action of swinging hand over hand still caused a sweat to form on his brow. He continued his descent for what seemed like ages and as he went, the green light grew stronger, so that he was finally able to make out details scratched into the stone shaft in front of him. He noticed that there were pictures etched into the smooth, grey rock, crude depictions of men and animals. Here, he recognised what looked like a deer and a bit further down, some kind of a buffalo or bison? It put him in mind of pictures he'd seen on a history website of Stone Age cave paintings.

He kept on moving and just when he thought that he had to be nearing the bottom of the shaft, his questing foot hit solid ground and he was able to step back from the rungs. He gazed up and the rectangle of light that was the sky looked shockingly tiny, making him realise that he really had descended a long way. He turned and looked around. Ahead of him stretched a horizontal tunnel, the roof just a few inches above his head. It went straight on for a short distance, before angling sharply to the right. The source of the light, Zach thought, was emanating from just around that bend. He took a deep breath and began to walk.

A powerful feeling flooded through him. He felt as though he was on the verge of a major discovery. He had no idea what it might be, but he felt elated, excited, almost breathless with anticipation. He turned the corner into the brightly lit section of the tunnel and stopped in his tracks. He stared. He couldn't help but stare.

She was sitting on a rock just a few feet away from him. Her head was bowed but he recognised her instantly, the shape of her, the long black hair which cascaded over her shoulders. She was dressed casually in an old sweater and a pair of jeans and her hands rested on her knees.

'Mum?' he croaked.

She lifted her head to look at him and her face was white and wasted. There were dark circles under her eyes and sores around her mouth. She let out a breath, which clouded on the air.

'Hello, Zach,' she whispered.

'What are you doing down here?' he asked her.

She smiled, a slow smile. 'Waiting for you of course,' she whispered. Then her tongue slid from between her lips. The tongue was black and forked and it kept sliding out until it had dropped down past her chin.

He woke in his bed with the last echoes of a shout escaping from his open mouth. He was sitting bolt upright, soaked in sweat, the cotton sheet clutched in his hands. He was trying to catch his breath, which was spilling out of him in a series of hoarse gasps. The illuminated dial of the digital clock on his bedside cabinet told him that it was 3.11 a.m. He heard the sound of footsteps on the floorboards outside and the door opened. Dad stood there in his pyjamas, looking concerned.

'You OK?' he asked.

Zach nodded. 'Sorry,' he whispered. 'Had a… nightmare.'

Dad looked at him helplessly. 'You want to talk about it?'

'No! No, I'm… I'll be fine. Go back to sleep.'

But Dad came into the room and sat on the edge of the bed. 'I wasn't asleep anyway,' he said. 'Nervous about the interview, tomorrow. Can't believe I managed to get another one at such short notice.'

Zach lay back against his pillow and waited for his breathing to return to normal. 'You'll be fine,' he said.

'Do you really think so?'

'Sure.'

'What was the dream about?' asked Dad. 'I hope it wasn't caused by what we talked about earlier. Your Grandma's disappearance and everything.'

Zach shook his head. 'No,' he said. 'No, I dreamed about Mum.'

'That's understandable,' said Dad. 'I have some of those myself. Guilty dreams, mostly. Thinking that maybe I could have done more for her. But I tried everything I could think of and none of it worked. We… we've never really talked about it, have we? About what happened to her.'

Zach shrugged. 'What's there to say?' he muttered. 'She got sick and she died. End of.'

Dad looked at his hands, the fingers interlaced. 'It was so quick. There was barely time to say goodbye.'

Mum had been diagnosed with cancer, right out of the blue. Lung cancer, which was weird because she'd never smoked a cigarette in her entire life. The first intimation that something was wrong was when she went down with a hacking cough. It persisted no matter what medication she took, so she'd finally gone to the doctor to get it checked out. He'd sent her to the hospital for an X-ray and for some reason that had taken weeks to organise. Finally, the awful truth had been revealed. The cancer was already well established and was deemed inoperable. The hospital estimated that she had a year left but as it turned out, it was less than eight months.

'I miss her so much,' said Dad. 'So much it hurts. I used to think... I used to think that when she was with me, I could do just about anything I set my mind to. And now she's gone...' He spread his hands in a gesture of helplessness. 'I don't feel capable of very much at all. Sometimes, Zach, it's all I can do to get myself dressed in the morning.'

Zach looked at him. 'And there was you saying *I* was feeling sorry for myself.'

Dad smiled awkwardly. 'Yeah, you're right. I need to snap out of it. Pull my socks up. Isn't that what they tell you?' He started to get up from the bed. 'We'll get through this,' he said. 'The two of us. We'll find a way.'

'How did Granddad Alistair get through it?' asked Zach.

Dad paused, frowned. 'What do you mean?'

'Well, after Grandma Mary disappeared. That must have been hard for him, don't you think?'

Dad sat down again. 'Why all this sudden interest in Granddad Alistair?' he asked. 'You've never shown any before.'

'You've never talked much about him. And well, I suppose it's just that now we're living here in his house and everything... after what you told me, I feel I'd like to know more about him. Is that so wrong?'

'Of course not. Maybe I should have made more of an effort to tell you when you were younger. The truth is, me and Dad, we weren't very close. Not as close as

37

a father and son ought to be. I kind of made my escape from here. Went down to London and started my own life and forgot all about my parents. I hardly ever came back to visit them, only when I absolutely had to. I'm not proud of that. And it's good that you're taking an interest.'

He considered for a moment. 'You know, all of Dad's paperwork and old photographs are still stored up in the attic. If you're so interested, maybe you should have a look at them. I keep telling myself I'll go through them some time but I can never seem to work up the enthusiasm.'

'Yeah, maybe I'll have a look tomorrow,' said Zach. 'Dad?'

'Yes?'

'Do you think... do you think Mum is like... still aware of what's happening to us? Do you think she can see us?'

Dad looked uncomfortable. 'Zach, you know how I feel about all that stuff. I've never been religious and neither was your mum.'

'So what do you think happens to us when we die?'

Dad sighed. 'Nothing,' he said. 'I'm sorry, Zach, I know that sounds miserable, but it's what I believe. I think we just go down into a dark... pool and... that's your lot. I'm sorry. I'd love to think that your mum still has some kind of afterlife or whatever you want to call it, but for that, I'd have to *believe* and the truth is I just don't. What about you, Zach, what do you believe?'

There was a short silence. 'I believe I need a glass

of coke,' said Zach and he pushed back the sheet. 'You want one?'

'No thanks.' Dad got up from the bed. 'Don't stay up too late. You must be tired after all that hard work you did today. Did I thank you for that?'

'No. And don't forget, you're paying me for it.'

'Oh yeah, right.' Dad smiled ruefully and headed out of the room. 'Goodnight, Zach.'

'Night.' Zach followed him onto the landing and went down the stairs in the semi-darkness. He padded barefoot into the kitchen, relishing the cool touch of the tiles under his feet. He didn't bother switching on the main lights. He opened the fridge and pulled out a can of cola, the glow from within temporarily illuminating the kitchen. It made him think about the green glow that had emanated from under the pond. He closed the door, snapped the can's ring pull and turned to face the french windows. He moved closer, taking a swig of coke as he did so.

There was a nearly full moon, which illuminated the garden, picking out the dark shape of the empty pond and the darker cluster in its centre that was the discarded liner. Zach was thinking about tomorrow, about descending the real shaft, wondering how similar it would be to the one he saw in his dream and hoping against hope that his dead mother wouldn't be waiting for him down there.

He was about to turn away from the window when the liner moved. He froze rigid, feeling a thrill of terror jolting through him. It had only been for an instant, but he was sure that the black layer had ballooned briefly upwards, as though something was pushing it from below. He stood watching intently, hardly daring to breathe, but nothing more happened and he told himself it must have been his own imagination, fired by the stories his dad had told him. Again, he was about to turn away, when the liner moved a second time and now he was sure, quite sure that something *was* moving beneath the black fabric, making the heavy folds stir.

Dread pulsed through him, making his heart thud like a drum in his chest.

Then a plastic bag went whirling past the window and he realised that a wind had got up out there. He took a step closer to the windows and as he watched, the edge of the liner, hanging over the far side of the pond, lifted briefly as the wind got under it. A ripple of movement ran the whole length of the fabric. Zach remembered to breathe and turned away with a shake of his head.

'I'm losing it,' he whispered and went back up the stairs to his room.

FIVE

TOYS IN THE ATTIC

After breakfast the next morning, Dad showed Zach the hatch outside the main bedroom that led up into the attic. There was a pole with a hook on the end of it, leaning against the wall in one corner and Dad reached up with it, pulled down the hatch and then unlatched the sliding loft ladder that was fixed to its topside. It slid smoothly down into position.

Dad flicked a switch on the wall and a light came on up there.

'There you go,' he said, gesturing. 'Knock yourself out. I'd come up with you but I need to go and make myself pretty for the interview.'

'Yeah. Good luck with that,' said Zach. He put a foot on the bottommost rung and climbed. It only took a few steps to get up there. He saw that the steep-sided room had been properly floored with thick wooden boards, so there was no danger of putting his foot through the ceiling below – and when he got himself upright, there was just enough head height for him to stand. He paused for a moment, looking warily around.

There was a real jumble of stuff up here.

To his left, stacked against one wall was a series of big old paintings, landscapes mostly and some black and white photographs in frames, most of which showed stern-looking people in old-fashioned suits and dresses. There were a couple of rusty metal filing cabinets and a battered wooden writing bureau, its roll-top closed. A bentwood chair stood in front of it. There was a huge stack of old newspapers beside the bureau and a litter of shabby exercise books were piled on the floor nearby. Against the right wall were some grotty old toys – a couple of scabby-looking marionette puppets slumped in a corner, an ancient board game called *Monkeys and Coconuts* and a really hideous Mister Punch Jack- in-the-box. The box was open and Mr Punch drooped out of it, his grinning painted face dulled by a layer of grime. Some of Dad's old toys? wondered Zach. If so, it was no surprise he'd been in such a hurry to get out of here.

Zach walked across to the bureau and tried the roll-top. For some reason, he'd expected to find it locked, but it slid upwards with little more than a faint squeak of protest. Inside, there were a series of upright slots that were packed with books. Zach sat down on the chair and selected one at random. He studied the dust jacket for a moment. *The Myths and Legends of Scotland* by Professor Angus McVeigh. It didn't sound very exciting, so Zach pushed it back into its slot and looked for something else.

He pulled out a larger scale volume than the others and saw that it was an old-fashioned scrapbook.

In case he should be in any doubt, it had the word 'Scrapbook' printed on the cover in a lurid red font. Zach opened it to the front page and drew in a breath. A colour photograph was gummed to the facing page and it showed something familiar – an opening in the ground between two grey boulders leading to a vertical shaft. All around it was evidence of some kind of work in progress – a wheelbarrow full of earth, some trays of plants and a spade, which looked exactly like the one Zach had used yesterday. Underneath the photograph, somebody had written a date in scratchy capitals. APRIL 1985. Zach turned the page and now there was a closer shot, looking directly into the hole, showing the faint green glow from underground. Zach was pretty sure that something was different from what he'd found, though. As far as he could see, there were no metal rungs leading down.

He turned the page. The next picture was a shot of Granddad, dressed in overalls and wearing a strange helmet that was fitted with some kind of lamp. He was standing by the opening, into which a couple of lengths of stout rope trailed. He was grinning confidently at the camera and brandishing some kind of tool, a short handled device with a sharp pick attached to it. The next picture showed him lowering himself through the opening and giving the photographer (Grandma Mary?) a cheerful 'thumbs-up'. Heaped beside the hole were a whole stack of metal rungs and beside them a metal headed mallet. Once again, there was a date. APRIL 1985. So clearly, it *was* Granddad who'd installed those metal handholds back in the day, obviously to make it easier to climb in and out.

A gurgling sound made Zach lift his head. It was coming from an old metal water tank off at one end of the attic and Zach realised that Dad must be in the shower directly below it.

Zach turned his attention back to the scrapbook and turned another page. The next photograph showed the same bit of garden, but now, the hole and the two boulders had been covered by the metal grille, which was secured with the large metal padlock. Granddad, dressed in normal clothes, was standing beside it with one foot resting on the hatch. Zach noticed that he wasn't smiling anymore. The date inscribed under this photograph was AUGUST 1985.

Zach paused to consider this. It seemed as though Granddad had, at first, decided to make the opening more accessible, presumably so he could return to the shaft whenever he wanted to. But something must have happened between his first descent in April and this picture, four months later, something that persuaded him that it was not such a good idea to leave it open. An accident perhaps? Or did Granddad Alistair really think that fairies were going to come up from underground and dance around in his garden?

He turned the page and found two smaller photographs, both of them taken at night, but it was impossible to tell what they were actually pictures *of*. Zach could only make out vague shapes, grey smudges against black, but each photograph was dated: the first,

OCTOBER 1985, the next, FEBRUARY 1986.

Another page, another photograph. It was dated APRIL 1992 and it showed work beginning on what was to become the pond. In the first photograph Zach could see the metal hatch. A series of shots showed the pond's progress over several days: the hatch covered by the liner, the liner secured by a ring of stones, the pond being filled with a hosepipe, a shot of Granddad Alistair planting something in the shallows. The final shot, which was dated MAY 1992, showed the finished pond, but it looked very different to what had been there until yesterday. The water was clear, plants were blooming in the shallows and Granddad Alistair was standing proudly beside his creation, smiling once again.

Zach turned another page, expecting more photographs but the next thing he found was a clipping from a newspaper.

LOCAL WOMAN MISSING!

blared the headline and it was accompanied by a black and white photograph of Grandma Mary, looking directly at the camera, her face rather grave. Zach began to read the accompanying article.

Local resident Mary Hamilton of Cliff View Cottage, Portknockie, was officially declared missing on Tuesday night. Mary, the wife of local resident Alistair Hamilton, is sixty-four years old and apparently walked out of her house in the early hours of Sunday morning. Anyone who thinks they may have any information as to her whereabouts are asked to phone this special emergency number...

There was more, much more. Article followed article, all pretty much saying the same thing and Zach found himself skimming through them, though he did linger over a clipping that showed a worried-looking Granddad Alistair on the steps of the local police station.

Local resident quizzed over disappearance of wife

read the headline and the article explained how the police had cast doubt on Granddad Alistair's story, that somebody had broken into the cottage and abducted his wife.

'There was no sign of a break-in,' said Detective Inspector Campbell, 'and no sign of any struggle. Despite the fact that the house was fitted with metal shutters to the ground floor doors and windows, there was no damage to any of them.'

But the next clipping, which showed Granddad Alistair shielding his face in the back of a police car was titled,

LOCAL MAN RELEASED AFTER POLICE QUESTIONING.

The gurgling in the water tank stopped and Zach reminded himself that Dad would be out of the shower and dressed in a matter of moments. He flipped hurriedly through the rest of the press cuttings until he found something different; another colour photo. This was a real puzzle, because it showed work being carried out on the pond *again*. There was the empty basin, drained of its water and there, the metal grille, the door open. To one side, a torn and shredded black liner lay crumpled in a heap and beside it, a new one, folded into a neat square, waited to take its place. The date was MAY 1997 – two years before Zach was born.

Under it were scrawled four words.

I GAVE IT BACK

Zach frowned. He didn't have the first idea what this was supposed to mean. On the landing below, he heard Dad coming out of the bathroom and walking back towards his bedroom.

'You OK up there?' he shouted.

'Er… yeah, fine.'

'Need me to come up and help with anything?'

'No, that's all right.'

A pause and then Dad's footsteps continued on to his room. Zach turned another page and there was the pond once again, returned to its former glory and dated JUNE 1997. There was no picture of Granddad standing beside his creation, but Zach realised that was hardly surprising. Mary would no longer have been there to take the picture.

Zach turned the page again, expecting to see more but there was nothing else in the book, just a load of blank pages. Zach leaned back in his seat and thought about what he had seen. OK, so this was the sequence of events, as far as he could figure it. Granddad had been digging a vegetable patch in the garden, had found the hole and had gone down to investigate it – had even hammered in a series of rungs to make it easier to get in and out. Then, for reasons known only to himself, he'd put a lockable cover over it. But something had happened to make him want to cover it more completely by installing the pond, and it must have been something to do with those murky night photographs…

Zach thumbed back and examined them again. He couldn't make out anything he recognised, though he did think, in the last shot, there was a vague indication of something odd down in one corner… a rough, wet surface reflecting moonlight… but nothing you could put a name to.

Anyway, Granddad had installed the pond. And it must have been around then that he'd fitted the shutters on the ground floor doors and windows. But then Grandma Mary had gone missing. After which, for reasons best known to himself, Granddad had drained the pond and opened up the hatch again. Zach turned to the relevant page and read the words once more.

I GAVE IT BACK

What did that mean? *What* had he given back? Something he'd found under the ground? The treasure he'd told Dad about?

48

'Zach, I'm going to have to make a move.'

'Er, yeah… coming now.' Zach was about to get up from his seat, when he noticed something lying in the corner of the open bureau. A small brass key. Zach picked it up and pulled the roll-top back into the closed position. He tried the key in the lock and it fit perfectly. It turned with a satisfying click. When he tried to open the bureau again, it stayed shut. Without even wondering why he was doing it, he slid the key into his jeans pocket and then got up and walked to the hatch. He turned himself around and descended. Dad was waiting on the landing, dressed once again in his best suit.

'Find anything useful?' he asked.

'No,' said Zach, perhaps a little too quickly. 'It's junk mostly. Old papers, notebooks, stuff like that.'

Dad nodded. 'He was a real hoarder. I think his old bureau is up there, isn't it? That's where he kept his most important stuff.'

'Yeah, that's locked,' said Zach, turning away in case his expression betrayed his deceit.

'Hmm. Well, the key must be around somewhere.'

'I'll have a look for it,' Zach told him. He slid a hand into the pocket of his jeans and touched the key with his fingers. 'There are some of your old toys up there,' he added. 'Some puppets? And a really mangy-looking Jack-in-the-box.'

Dad grinned. 'Oh, I remember Jack! Used to play with him for hours.'

'Really?'

'We didn't have X-Boxes and PlayStations then,'

Dad told him. He held out his arms. 'How do I look?' he asked.

'You look fine,' Zach assured him. 'I'll come out with you. I want to do some more work on the pond.'

'You take it easy,' Dad told him. 'You've got all summer for that.'

'Just the same, I'll make a start,' said Zach. He followed Dad down the stairs and stood watching impatiently as he collected his briefcase and checked he had everything he needed. They went out through the french windows and Zach thought about the hole in the ground waiting for him, waiting to show him its secrets. Dad walked to the car and seemed to hesitate.

'I don't even know why I'm doing this,' he muttered. 'I've got no chance of swinging this one.'

'Of course you have!' Zach assured him.

'Hey, maybe the two of us should just take a drive out somewhere. It's a lovely day and…'

'Remember what you said yesterday,' Zach interrupted him. 'We need to pull our socks up.'

Dad sighed, nodded. 'I suppose you're right,' he said. He unlocked the car and got in behind the wheel. He started the engine and slid down the windows. Tiny beads of sweat were already in evidence on his brow. He looked out at Zach. 'Be good,' he said and for reasons he couldn't fathom, Zach suddenly felt incredibly guilty.

'Dad!' he said, urgently.

'What?'

'I just… I just wanted to say good luck.'

'Thanks, son. I appreciate that.'

Zach watched as the car trundled towards the gate and then on up the lane. He waited until it was out of sight and then he was running to the shed to get the tools, because he didn't want to waste any more time.

He needed to find out what was under the ground.

SIX

DOWN AGAIN

At first, it was exactly like the dream. He pulled back the liner to expose the grille. He walked across to it, opened it up, kneeled beside it and took his mobile phone from his pocket. He switched on the torch app and sent a beam of light down into the shaft but it simply wasn't strong enough to reach the floor.

'OK,' he said. 'I can do this.' He returned the phone to his pocket, flipped around onto his hands and knees and backed towards the hole. He lowered his legs through the opening until his feet found purchase on the first rung. He steadied himself, one hand on either side of the hole and swung his legs down to the next rung and then the next and bit-by-bit he went down, twisting his body from side to side, in order to fit through.

He descended, rung by rung, slowly at first but increasing the speed as his confidence grew. He began to notice that some things were different to the way he'd seen them in his dream. For one thing, the shaft wasn't the eerily smooth cylinder he'd encountered there, but a more natural opening, comprising layers of rocks, piled one atop the other. In some places, it widened out, in others it became precariously narrow, obliging him to twist his frame this way and that in order to slip through. The rungs however, had been inserted with precision at regular intervals and hammered deep to create a secure hold.

There was no sign of the cave painting images of his dream, but some distance down, he did make a strange discovery. Etched into a flat piece of grey stone in front of him, a foot above one of the rungs, somebody had paused long enough to scratch a name and a date.

A. Hamilton. 1985

Well, here was confirmation, should it ever be needed, that Granddad Alistair really had discovered this shaft and that whilst installing the metal rungs, he'd paused long enough to carve his own name. It felt weird to be so literally following in his Grandfather's footsteps and he tried to imagine what it must have been like for the old man, hanging onto a length of rope, without the secure metal rungs to cling to.

By now the green light was surprisingly powerful, illuminating the shaft all around him. Just as Zach was thinking that surely it couldn't go down much further, his questing foot found solid ground and he was able to step off the last rung. He took his mobile from his back pocket, hit the torch app and examined the ground at the bottom of the shaft. A couple of rusted metal rungs lay where they had fallen, along with the remains of a broken mallet. Zach stooped to examine this. The wooden handle had snapped as though the force of repeatedly driving the handholds in to the rock had been too much for it. Zach set it down again, stood up and looked back towards the surface. The rectangle of blue sky was bigger than it had been in the dream. He estimated that he was maybe twenty or thirty feet below the ground. He turned and saw that a low-roofed, horizontal tunnel led off ahead of him for a short distance before angling sharply away to the right. He realised he didn't need the torch here so he switched it off and slipped it back into his pocket. He started walking.

In the dream, this was the part of the exploration where he'd been filled with excited anticipation. But he felt a quite different emotion flowing though him now, a feeling of apprehension. He remembered what he had found around the next bend and the thought of it terrified him, because this was no dream, this was really happening. If he stepped around that corner and found his dead mother waiting for him, he didn't know what he would do. Run screaming, he imagined.

He kept going, steeling himself as he drew closer and closer to the bend. The green light was emanating from around there and he found himself holding his breath, ready to run if he needed to. He reached the corner. He hesitated for a moment, his heart thudding in his chest. He counted to three and then, letting the breath out, swung around the corner.

He stopped and stared, trying to figure out exactly

what it was he was looking at. He had to lift one hand up to his forehead to prevent himself from being dazzled by the glare.

It was resting on the ground, alongside one wall; a large glowing oval object, about the size of a rugby ball, pale green in colour but mottled with patches of darker green which appeared to be swirling and changing even as Zach looked at it. It was clearly the source of the unearthly light and he thought it looked as though it was made from some kind of smooth stone, like marble. It resembled more than anything else a large egg or the kind of fantastically coloured boulder that you might find beside the sea, washed smooth by thousands of years of tidal movement, but it was also translucent and the light was definitely emanating from deep within its core.

Zach remembered to breathe. He took a step closer to the thing, then another and now a feeling of exhilaration started up within him, he felt suddenly incredibly alive, more alive than he could ever remember feeling before, as though each of his individual atoms had been removed, scrubbed and carefully replaced. He moved closer still and crouched beside the stone, basking in its aura. It didn't appear to be threatening in any way. On the contrary, that weird pulsing glow was welcoming, comforting, like the presence of a friend. Zach reached out the fingers of one hand to touch it, worried that the glowing stone might be giving off some kind of heat that would burn through his flesh, but when his fingers were just inches away, there was no impression of any heat whatsoever, so he gathered his courage and touched the stone with his index finger.

Two things happened then. An incredible surge of energy rippled through his entire body, bringing with it an uncanny feeling of wellbeing. At the same time, the stone changed colour, the green mutating instantly to yellow, then to orange, and finally a deep blood red. Encouraged, Zach placed the flat of his hand against the stone.

Another thing happened. He seemed to momentarily drift outside of his own body. The world shimmered, shuddered, rippled before his astonished gaze and for a while, he wasn't sure how long, he floated in a kind of ecstatic trance. Then darkness pooled into his consciousness and he seemed to sleep. It might have been just a few minutes or even a few hours, he didn't know which, but suddenly an image loomed out of the murk ahead of him. A man materialised; a stranger dressed in a white linen suit, his black hair slicked back on his head with gel. He was sitting on the other side of a desk and he smiled at Zach, a kind of superior smirk and he said, 'So, what makes you think you have something to offer us?' and Zach smiled back, feeling cool, confident, more confident than he'd ever felt in his life and he said, 'You'd be a fool not to take me on. I'm the best in the business.' Only that wasn't Zach's voice, it was somebody else's, a voice he thought he recognised...

And then the world seemed to melt, slide, drift for a moment, before Zach came fully back to his senses and found himself crouched in front of the oval stone, the flat of his hand still resting against it. He removed the hand and was aware of every atom of his body tingling with a new awareness. The stone turned pale green again, lighting up the tunnel in which it rested and Zach looked around, seeing it properly for the first time, noticing that it was actually a large bowl-shaped cavern, the roof hung with multi-coloured stalactites, the walls bulging with glittering crystal formations. It was incredible, like a completely different world that he had stumbled into. A little further on, he could see that the light was reflecting from what appeared to be a large pool of still water. From away to his right there came the powerful scent of salt air and he realised that off in that direction must be the sea. Hadn't Dad once told him about some amazing caves that honeycombed this part of the coast?

Zach returned his attention to the oval stone, realising that he wanted it. He couldn't say exactly why but he wanted it more than he had ever wanted anything in his entire life and here it was for the taking. Impulsively, he reached out to try and pick it up. He'd expected it to be really heavy but it seemed to have no more weight than a piece of pumice stone, it came up easily into his arms and seemed somehow to belong there. He could feel warmth coming off the stone in waves and flooding through him, a slow pulsing kind of energy and he knew in that instant that it was going to be his and nobody was ever going to take it away from him.

He stood up and stared around the chamber as though challenging some unseen person to stop him, but the place was deserted. He turned and hurried back the way he had come until he reached the shaft, then stood for a moment, wondering exactly how he was going to get the stone back up to the surface. An idea came to him. He set it down for an instant and pulled off his long sleeved top, used it to improvise a kind of sling, tying the arms across one shoulder and keeping the swathed stone in front of him, swaddled like a baby. He glanced back once more but there was nobody to stop him from doing this, so he set his foot on the bottommost rung and began to climb. He went quickly back to the surface, without pausing for breath, the effort wrenching sweat from every part of him and within minutes, he was clambering out into the open sunlight with his precious bundle held against him. Once out, he lowered the grille behind him and as an extra measure, he found the padlock, slid it through the hasp and clicked it shut. He pulled out the key and slid it into his pocket. Then he stood for a moment, getting his breath back.

He understood now that whatever this thing was he was clutching against him, it was the same thing that Granddad Alistair had found down under the ground and he realised too that something must have happened to make him return it, but at this moment in time he thought that nothing would ever make him do that because the stone felt as precious to him as treasure. And wasn't that what Granddad Alistair had told Dad all those years ago? That he'd found treasure?

Zach glanced at his watch and was shocked to discover that he'd been underground for nearly an hour. Dad would surely be back before long! Zach ran in through the french windows and went straight up the stairs oblivious to the trail of muddy footprints he was leaving on the carpet. Once in his room he opened his wardrobe and hid the stone, wrapped in his T-shirt, at the back of it. Green light was filtering through the thin material so he draped a denim jacket over it, wanting to be sure that somebody glancing in there wouldn't notice anything odd. He found himself another T-shirt and pulled that on, then hurried downstairs to the garden, aware that time was ticking away.

He grabbed the spade and was about to start digging up the mound to the left of the pool when he realised that if he started throwing soil into the hole now, most of it would just go trickling down through the grille, so he dropped the spade and went to the pile of rocks he'd removed earlier. He found a big flat one, wide enough to bridge the gap between the boulders and laid that carefully across the opening.

Satisfied that no earth was going to fall through the grille, he climbed out, grabbed the spade and started digging, flinging clods of black earth into the hole. He wasn't exactly sure why he wanted to cover up the evidence of what had been hidden under the pond; he only knew that he would not rest until it was done. He worked dementedly, sweat pouring down his face, and he didn't stop until his hands were blistered and the pond basin was filled to the brim with soil. Then he strode out onto the levelled ground and tamped the dirt down with the back of the spade, thwacking it again and again until it was all compacted.

Only then did he allow himself a breather. He threw the spade aside, dropped to the ground and lay there panting for breath, thinking about the shaft that only he knew of, hidden now beneath a deep layer of earth. He felt so much better knowing that it was hidden from the sight of others. For the time being at least, he wanted to be the only person who knew about it.

As he lay, exhausted, he became aware of a distant sound, the rumble of a car engine gradually getting closer, but it seemed to him that his hearing must have improved beyond all recognition, because it was a good ten minutes before the Volkswagen came into view down the lane, moving fast, much faster than Dad generally drove. Zach lay there, allowing his breath to return to normal and he watched as the car came steadily closer, raced in through the open gateway and slewed to a halt. The door swung open and Dad got out, his face a picture of astonishment. He was wearing a grin that threatened to split his face in two. Zach stared at him and he stared back and somehow when Dad finally spoke, Zach wasn't surprised at all, even though he pretended to be.

'Zach! You won't bloody believe it. You'll never guess what's happened. I only went and got the job. They want me to start on Monday!'

SEVEN

NO RESERVATION

They sat at the kitchen table, Zach with a glass of cola and Dad with a can of lager. He hardly ever drank in the daytime, but today he explained, was different. Today he was celebrating. He was acting like a man who'd just won the National Lottery. He couldn't seem to stop grinning but Zach had to admit to himself it was good to see him so happy for the first time in ages.

'It was just the weirdest thing, Zach. I arrived at the place and I had no confidence, no confidence at all. Well, you saw me when I set off! Even you had to give me a pep talk. And then I was shown into this conference room and it was just me and Gerry…'

'Gerry?'

'The MD, the guy whose assistant I'm going to be.' Dad scowled. 'He struck me as a bit of a twerp to tell you the truth, really his own biggest fan, but he's the head honcho there, so I've got to keep on his good side.' He winked, took a swig of lager. 'And I sat down and he asked me the age-old question, you

61

know, the one they always ask at these things, 'What makes you think you've got something to offer us?' And for a moment, I was just flummoxed, I didn't know what to say…'

Zach nodded. He knew what came next. Of course he did, because somehow, he didn't really understand exactly how, he'd been *there*, he even knew exactly what 'Gerry' looked like, right down to his crumpled linen suit and his nasty gelled hair.

'… and then suddenly, out of the blue… I was the most confident guy in the world and I don't know where it came from, I just said to him, "You'd be a fool not to take me on. I'm the best in the business!" Seriously, that's what I said!' Dad laughed at the sheer outrageousness of it. 'I don't know what got into me. I mean, I could have blown it, right there and then, he could have just told me to sling my hook and I wouldn't have blamed him but… the look on his face! I could see he was impressed by what I'd said. He just kind of leaned forward and said, "Tell me more," and then I was off, wasn't I? Off and running. Oh, you'd have been proud of me, Zach! I outlined a plan to double his agency's profit within two years. Right off the top of my head.' He thought for a moment. 'Weird thing is, I think some of it could actually *work.*'

Dad took another gulp of lager. 'Anyway, it did the trick. He must have gone for it, because I'm starting Monday. I'm on a month's trial at a basic wage, but assuming I don't mess up too badly, they'll take me on full time with proper pay.' He looked worried now as something occurred to him. 'Zach, I appreciate this probably isn't what you want to hear, right now. I *know* the plan was to spend some quality time together this summer, but… well, I don't see how I can say no to this, buddy. It'll mean long hours and I might have to go in to work some weekends, but…'

'That's OK,' Zach assured him. 'I get it.'

'Really? Because I don't much like the idea of leaving you cooped up here all by yourself.'

'It's no problem. I'll be fine.'

'You're making it easy for me. Thanks.' Dad glanced towards the open french windows. 'I can't believe how much work you've done here in just a couple of days,' he said. 'I appreciate it. Hey, I haven't forgotten, by the way.' He reached into the breast pocket of his jacket and took out his wallet. 'I think we said a tenner, didn't we?'

But Zach waved him away. 'Don't worry about it,' he said. 'I enjoyed doing it. It's my treat.'

But now Dad was looking at Zach with evident concern. 'Zach, your hands!'

'Huh?' Zach looked down in surprise. The palms of both hands were a livid red and there were raised blisters on most of his fingers. He shrugged. 'Not used to digging, I guess. No worries. I'll stick some Savlon on them.'

'Really, you need to take it easy,' said Dad. 'I know I got on your case the other day, about pulling your weight and all that, but it *is* supposed to be your holiday, so… don't overdo it.' He frowned. 'Well,

63

look,' he said. 'We need to celebrate. What say we go out to eat tonight? There's an Indian restaurant in Cullen, I think we can just about afford that.'

Zach shrugged. 'Whatever,' he said.

'You're not keen?'

'Yeah, sure I am. I love curry.'

'Well, why don't you go and get yourself cleaned up? I can put the tools back in the shed.' He glanced at his watch. 'We'll head off around six. I don't think there'll be any need to book.'

'OK.' Zach got up from the table. Now he thought about it, a shower would be welcome. His body felt sticky with sweat. He went up the stairs, noting as he did so the trail of drying mud trodden into the carpet, but he told himself that Dad was probably in too good a mood to make anything of it. Zach went into his bedroom and closed the door. He went straight to his wardrobe and rooted around in the back of it. He wanted to check on the stone, make sure it was all right. He pulled off the jacket and unwrapped the T-shirt from around it. It was still glowing pale green but when he picked it up, it changed colour again, going to yellow and then to deep red. Zach grunted, as he felt a strange tingling sensation in the palms of his hands. He let one hand go and looked at it. The blisters appeared to have decreased in size. He sat down on the bed, cradling the stone in both hands, feeling the soreness in his palms receding. After a few minutes, he checked them again. Both hands now looked perfectly normal.

'No way,' he murmured. The stone had healed him.

He remembered something that Dad had told him about his grandparents. 'The old man told me once that a 'higher power' was looking after them both. Which is odd, because he wasn't at all religious…'

Was this it? Was the stone the higher power that Granddad Alistair was talking about? Zach stood up, and walked to the window, still holding the stone against his chest and he gazed down at the patch of freshly dug earth where the pond used to be. Dad was wheeling the barrow back towards the shed looking slightly overdressed in his suit trousers and immaculate white shirt.

Zach thought about taking the stone downstairs and showing it to Dad, telling him exactly how he had come to find it, but he realised he couldn't do that. Dad would ask too many questions, ones that Zach couldn't even begin to answer. And he'd have to say, 'No, Dad, you didn't get that job. *I* got the job for you. *I* did the talking.' No, he needed to find out more about the stone first. He needed to find out exactly what it could do. Only then, would he consider telling Dad about it.

He carried the stone back to the wardrobe, wrapped the T-shirt around it and hid it away in a dark corner, covered by the jacket. He took another look at the palms of his hands. There was now no indication that there had been any problem with them.

'Mint,' he murmured to himself and headed off to the bathroom to have that shower.

*

They drove into Cullen and Dad immediately noticed that Zach's hands were looking better. 'What happened to the blisters?' he asked incredulously.

Zach shrugged. 'They kind of… washed off in the shower,' he said.

'Mustn't have been as bad as it looked,' said Dad, clearly mystified.

'Maybe just gunk and stuff from the pond,' offered Zach and Dad seemed to accept it.

The town was surprisingly busy. The good weather had brought out the crowds and there seemed to be a lot of holidaymakers in a mood to spend money. Dad parked up the car, fed coins into a meter and led the way to the restaurant. They pushed through the swing doors of the restaurant and were surprised to see that despite it being so early, the place was absolutely heaving with customers. Standing by the door, they couldn't see a vacant table in the whole establishment. The owner hurried over, looking harassed, his lean face shining with sweat.

'You have a booking?' he asked.

'Er… no,' said Dad, looking apologetic. 'Sorry, I didn't realise it would be so busy. Is it worth us waiting?'

The man shrugged his shoulders. 'Maybe half an hour, forty minutes?' he suggested. 'We're very busy today.'

Dad looked at Zach. 'Perhaps we should order a takeout?' he suggested.

But having come all the way here, Zach didn't feel inclined to change his mind. 'I'd rather sit down,' he said. He looked decisively around the crowded restaurant and focused on one particular table by the window, where a young man and woman were sitting with their drinks, chatting happily. It came suddenly into Zach's head that this was the table he wanted and at the same moment, there was the absolute conviction that he could get it. He pointed to the table. 'I think those two are just about to leave,' he told the manager.

The man followed his gaze and shook his head. 'No, they just got here,' he assured Zach. 'They're still waiting for food.'

Zach concentrated all his attention on the table. He felt a redness welling up in his mind. 'No, they're definitely going,' he repeated and quite suddenly, the man stood up from the table, as though he been jabbed with a cattle prod. He grabbed his jacket off the back of the chair and shrugged it on. His companion stared at him blankly for a moment and then she too stood up, collecting her handbag as she did so. The pair of them left the table without hesitation and made their way towards the manager, their expressions blank. Seeing there was a problem, he left Dad and Zach and went over to them.

'Is something wrong?' he asked them.

The man leaned close to him and spoke urgently into his ear. He pointed at Zach and Dad and then moved across to the counter, to where a woman stood at a cash register. The man took out his wallet as he did so.

The manager looked completely bemused, but he turned to Dad and Zach and pointing at the newly vacated table, indicated that they should sit there. Dad looked at Zach, bewildered, but the two of them walked across to the table and sat down. The manager followed them and removed the other couple's half-finished drinks.

'I don't understand,' said Dad. 'What's happening?'

The manager's expression suggested that he didn't understand it either. 'The gentleman says he will pay for your meal. He's already ordered a special banquet for two.'

'What?' Dad turned and looked towards the counter in alarm, but the man had already finished paying and he and his partner were leaving without looking back. 'But that's... crazy,' said Dad. 'I don't even *know* them.'

The manager's expression seemed to say that he'd seen all manner of crazy things here. 'Must be your lucky day,' he said. 'You want drinks?'

'Erm... I'm driving so I'll just have a coke. Zach?

'A lemonade please.'

The manager moved off in the direction of the kitchen. Dad stared at Zach. 'What just happened?' he asked.

Zach spread his hands in a universal gesture. 'Search me,' he said. He studied the menu. 'The special banquet,' he murmured. 'Wow. That's the most expensive thing on here.'

Dad started to get up. 'There must be some mistake,'

he said. 'I'll have to go after them. I can't let them pay for our food.'

'Sure you can.' Zach took his arm and pulled Dad back down into his seat. 'Just relax.'

'How did you know?' Dad asked him, accusingly.

'How did I know what?'

'That they were going to leave.'

'It was just a feeling, I suppose.'

'But… it was almost as though you said it… and they… did it.'

'Yeah, like that could happen.' Zach forced an unconvincing laugh. 'I wish.'

'It doesn't make sense,' insisted Dad. 'Why would two complete strangers…?' He broke off as a couple of waiters approached the table with a huge platter heaped with samosas, bhajis, tandoori chops and other delicacies. The first man set the platter on the table in front of them, while his companion supplied a couple of heated plates.

Dad looked at the selection in dismay. 'We can't eat all this,' he said.

'You'd better pace yourself,' said Zach. 'There's another three courses yet.'

'Well, it's… barmy. But, it *does* look delicious.'

The two of them started eating and as Zach devoured an onion bhaji, all he could think was, *I did this. I made it happen.*

And as he chewed, an interesting question occurred to him. He began to wonder what else he might be capable of.

69

EIGHT

LUCKY

Zach let himself out of the front door of the cottage. He locked up, then wandered to the gate and out onto the lane, slipping on his new Ray Ban sunglasses as he went. He took his time, because he was in no great hurry. It was another baking hot day, Dad was at work and Zach had been feeling bored sitting around the garden. It was time to have a little fun.

Over the past five days, he had learned what the oval stone could do – or rather, what it would allow *him* to do – and after some early trial and error, he'd rapidly become more confident in his abilities. He kept telling himself that anything was acceptable provided nobody got hurt. That was important.

He wandered along the quiet lanes, heading downhill towards the sea and eventually came into the village. He had already discovered that there wasn't much here to occupy him, but he didn't feel up to travelling to one of the bigger towns today and there were a couple of local calls he wanted to make. His first stop was at the CostCutter that doubled as the village's Post Office.

More importantly, as far as Zach was concerned, it was the only place in the village that was licenced to sell scratch cards. As he stepped inside, the usual guy, a tubby balding man, dressed in a fleece jacket despite the sweltering heat, eyed him suspiciously through a pair of thick-lensed spectacles.

'You again,' he said ungraciously, as Zach approached the counter.

Zach grinned. 'That's a nice welcome,' he said. 'Anyone would think you weren't pleased to see me.'

The man sighed. 'What can I do for you?' he asked.

Zach pulled a two-pound coin from his jeans pocket and proffered it. 'I'll have a scratch card please,' he said.

The man hesitated, looking reluctant.

'Need to see my ID again?' Zach prompted him.

The man sighed, shook his head. 'No,' he said flatly. 'I've already seen it.' He indicated a whole row of brightly coloured cards, hanging on strips from their reels. 'Any particular sort?' he asked.

'*You* choose,' suggested Zach, brightly. He watched as the man's chubby hand wandered across the display, as though he was trying to decide which card had the least likelihood of winning. Eventually, he selected a strip that was predominantly green. Zach noticed that it had a picture of a leprechaun on the front. The little bearded man was holding a crock of gold, from which twenty pound notes were protruding. The man tore a card off and handed it to Zach, who took a pound coin from his pocket and still standing at the counter, scratched off the silver panel, revealing the results. He smiled and handed the card back.

'That's a hundred pounds please,' he said politely. The man looked weary. The first time Zach had done this, five days ago, he'd been astonished, jubilant even. He'd punched a fist in the air and congratulated Zach and told him how delighted he was, because it was the very first card he'd sold that had won more than ten pounds. But Zach had been in every day since and had won exactly the same amount each time.

'How are you doing it?' growled the man in exasperation.

'I'm just lucky,' Zach assured him.

'Nobody's *that* lucky!' The man leaned closer. 'After you left yesterday, I scratched fifteen of the bloody things and I didn't win a penny.'

Zach looked suitably sympathetic. 'I suppose you'll still have to pay for them?' he asked.

The man gritted his teeth. He opened his cash register and regarded the contents forlornly. 'You'll be cleaning me out,' he observed. 'That's pretty much all I've taken today.'

'You get the money back from the scratch card people, don't you?' said Zach. He continued to stand there, one hand extended. The man muttered something under his breath, but he pulled five twenty-pound notes from the drawer and handed them over. 'Thanks.' Zach gave him a pleasant smile. For a moment, he considered buying another card, but didn't really have the heart to do it. Best to keep it to just once a day in each store. He'd already visited most of the newsagents in the surrounding area, travelling out by taxi when he needed to. He'd been on the internet to find the locations and had marked them all down on a map. At the back of his wardrobe, beside the stone, he had already deposited a thick stash of money. He wasn't sure how much was there, because he hadn't actually got around to counting it yet. But he always took a couple of hundred out with him. He reached into his back pocket, pulled out the thick bundle of notes and added the new ones to it. As an afterthought, he handed the man the pound coin he'd used to scratch off the foil. 'I'll have a pack of gum, please,' he said, pointing to the confectionery display and watched as the man selected a pack and handed it over. Zach gave him the pound. 'Keep the change,' he said.

The man's face was a picture. He looked like he wanted to punch Zach, really, really hard.

'When I find out how you're doing this' he said, 'I'll…'

Zach waited, interested, but the man's voice trailed away. It was clear that he didn't have the first idea *what* he'd do if that situation ever arose. But then, it never would. Zach had bought the cards fair and square. Was it *his* fault if he kept on winning?'

He turned away and strolled out of the shop, leaving the man to deposit the pound coin in his nearly empty till. From here, it was a four minute walk downhill to the esplanade and the amusement arcade.

Actually, 'arcade' was far too grand a term for it. It

was essentially a couple of two storey flats that had been knocked together. A garish red banner hung across its front, spelling out the word AMUSEMENTS and there was a amateurish picture of a pirate chest emblazoned with the image of a skull and crossbones. To hammer home the point, there was also a colourful life-sized figure of a one-legged pirate posed beside the door, complete with beard, eye patch and a hook for a hand.

As Zach approached the building, he noticed that the usual gang of kids were sitting on the low wall outside the 'arcade,' two oafish-looking lads and three girls. They all watched him with interest as he approached. They'd seen him come and go over the past few days and were aware that something out of the ordinary was happening. The heaviest of the boys, a shaven-headed youth in a khaki jacket and combats, said something to his friends and they all laughed raucously, in the way that weaker kids always laugh at a tougher kid's jokes, loudly but unconvincingly. Zach didn't take any notice. If the truth were told, he was kind of interested in one of the girls, a punky-looking teen in torn jeans and a tie-dye T-shirt, who he thought looked a year or so younger than him. There was something about her dark eyes that he liked, but he hadn't yet decided whether or not he was interested enough.

He walked past the kids, taking off his Ray Bans and hooking them onto the neck of his T-shirt as he did so. He went into the gloom of the arcade, a fizzing, jangling labyrinth, its aisles lined with a mix of neon bright electronic games and old-fashioned one-armed bandits. He strolled over to the booth where a bearded guy in a *Megadeath* T-shirt stood inertly, looking at his mobile phone. Letters were tattooed on the fingers that held the phone, spelling the word BAD2. Zach couldn't help looking at the fingers of the other hand, splayed on the counter top, which completed the message: BONE. Zach suspected there was supposed to be a 'the' somewhere in there, but the guy had just run out of fingers. He also had a name badge pinned to his T-shirt which announced to the world that he was called 'Beefy'. Zach couldn't help feeling that wasn't his real name. He hadn't encountered Beefy before, which was good, because the guy who usually watched over the place had already grown wise to Zach's abilities and tended to head him off before he could even get close to a machine. Zach reached into his pocket, took out the roll of cash and peeled off a twenty. He slid it across the counter.

Beefy took the twenty-pound note and held it up to the light for a moment, as though he was some kind of expert in forgery. For that, Zach glanced at Beefy's phone, lying on the counter top, and stopped it from working, though of course, Beefy didn't know that yet. Seemingly satisfied with the note, he pushed a stack of one-pound coins across the counter. Zach picked up several of the large polystyrene cups that stood beside the hatch, then turned away and wandered the room for a moment, looking for the best prize money on offer.

There were only a couple of other people in here. A skinny older woman with dyed ginger hair sat on a stool, her waxy face expressionless as she fed coin after coin into a machine called ALIEN CASH ATTACK! A short distance further on, a man with a ruddy complexion was doing pretty much the same to a game called SUPER FRUITERAMA.

Zach came to an old-fashioned fruit machine with a pull-handle that offered a top prize of fifty-pounds in exchange for three golden bells. Zach studied the machine for a moment, then pushed a pound into the slot. He pictured the three golden bells in his mind's eye and then pulled the handle. The cylinders span around with a brassy clattering sound. After a moment, they stopped one after the other, delivering one, two, three golden bells. There was a brief silence followed by a satisfying clatter as twenty-five two pound coins spilled into the tray.

Beefy was prompted to stop messing with his lifeless phone and actually step out of his booth. He came over, his mouth hanging open as Zach collected his winnings and dropped them into the polystyrene cup. It was evident from the bemused expression on Beefy's face that the machine had never paid out the top prize before. Zach turned to Beefy and handed him the full cup. 'Would you mind cashing that up for me?' he asked politely and moved on. Beefy stood there, looking down at the cup in bewilderment.

Zach walked over to the woman, who was looking at him as though he'd just stepped out of a spaceship. She was frozen in the act of putting a one-pound coin into the slot. Zach smiled at her. 'May I?'

he asked. He took the coin from her, pushed it in, decided what outcome the woman most probably wanted and pressed the button. He moved on, the electronic wheels chittering as they span, but he'd only taken a few steps when he heard the clatter of more money spilling into a tray. The woman gave a weird squawk of astonishment and started gathering up her winnings.

Zach continued towards the only other customer, thinking that he'd help him out also, but was brought up sharp when Beefy hurried around to block his path. 'What do you think you're doing?' he cried.

Zach shrugged. 'What does it look like?' he murmured. 'I'm playing the machines.'

Beefy gave him a cold smile. 'You're that kid, aren't you? The one that wins. The boss warned me about you. He said I wasn't to let you play.'

Zach looked from side to side. 'You can't do that,' he said. 'This is an amusement arcade, right? It's where people come to play the fruit machines. And I won fair and square.'

'How are you doing it?' snarled the man. 'Is it magnets? Is that what you're using? Got hidden magnets in your pockets have ye?'

'I'm just lucky,' Zach assured him. He was aware now that the kids from outside, alerted by the shouts from within, had gathered in the open doorway and were watching with interest. 'You can't ban me from playing,' said Zach.

'Wanna bet?' Beefy was pretty adamant that he

could do what he liked, but had clearly failed to see the irony in his words. 'Look, no offence kid, I could lose my job over this.'

'All right, well give me the money I've already won and I'll go.'

'I ain't giving you nothin'! The boss said you wasn't allowed to play.' He glanced towards the woman who was still piling her winnings into a paper cup, as though unsure what to do about her. 'People ain't supposed to *win*!' he added, by way of explanation.

Zach looked at him, telling himself that he could hurt the man badly if he chose, but he really didn't want to do that, not unless he had to. So he stared directly into his eyes. 'Get my money,' he said quietly.

Beefy seemed to be about to argue but a blank look came over him and instead, he turned on his heels and walked over to the booth. He went in, opened the cash register and took out five ten-pound notes. He came out again, his face expressionless and handed them over. 'Thanks,' said Zach, brightly. He pulled the wad of notes from his back pocket and added his latest haul to it. Then he turned to head for the exit but the kids were still blocking the door.

'Excuse me,' he said, but Shave-Head clearly wasn't about to step aside until he was good and ready.

'We've been watching you,' he said.

'Have you? Why's that? Can't you afford a telly?'

'You was in here two days ago and you won money then.'

Zach pretended to think about it for a few moments. 'You're right,' he said at last. 'I'd forgotten.'

Shave-Head sneered. 'You're a funny man, aren't ye?'

'I'm not a professional,' Zach told him. 'I just do it in my spare time.'

Shave-Head leaned closer and Zach could smell the stink of cheese and onion crisps on his breath.

'How do ye do it?' he asked.

Zach shrugged. 'I put a coin in and I pull the handle,' he said. He reached into his pocket and took out a pound. 'Here, have one on me,' he said and pushed it into the top pocket of the youth's camouflage jacket.

Shave-Head stared at Zach in open-mouthed astonishment.

'You cheeky little… How would you like a punch in the face?'

Zach considered for a moment. 'That's what I get for giving you a pound?' he muttered. 'Remind me never to give you a fiver.'

The other kids laughed out loud at this, astonished perhaps by Zach's sheer recklessness but Shave-Head clearly didn't find it very amusing. 'I could flatten you,' he announced.

Zach smiled at him and looked straight into his eyes. 'I doubt it,' he said. 'You can't even stop wetting your pants.'

Shave-Head's eyes widened as he registered the

insult and he actually lifted a hand to strike, but then his eyes snapped downwards in shocked dismay. Zach followed his gaze. A dark stain was spreading slowly across the front of the youth's khaki combat trousers.

'Oops,' said Zach.

Shave-Head gasped. He looked around in panic, his face flushing bright red. He turned and pushed his way roughly past his companions, then ran straight out of the arcade, his heavy boots clumping on concrete. The others kids trailed out after him.

'My phone won't work!' snapped a voice behind Zach and he turned to see Beefy tapping helplessly at the screen of his mobile.

'Some days are like that,' said Zach and he followed the other kids outside. They were staring up the street at the already distant figure of Shave-Head, who was running full pelt, presumably in the direction of the nearest toilet.

The punky girl looked at Zach, a half smile on her lips.

'How did you *do* that?' she murmured.

'Do what?' replied Zach, feigning wide-eyed innocence. He followed her gaze. 'Oh *that*. I didn't do it. *He* did.'

'You want to be careful,' she warned him. 'Cameron will be after you for this.'

'Cameron? Is that his name? You'd think by his age he'd be house-trained, wouldn't you?'

The girl smiled again, deeper this time. 'You're

weird,' she said, but the way she said it sounded like a compliment.

'You're not so bad yourself.' He took a breath. 'Well, I'm heading home now,' he said. He looked into her eyes and waited for a moment. 'You coming?'

She gave him a scornful look. 'No I'm not,' she snapped. 'Christ, you must think you're *it*.'

Zach felt a surge of disappointment. He was already so used to getting his own way, it was a shock when something didn't work.

'Suit yourself,' he said flatly. He put on his *Ray Bans* and started to walk.

Behind him, he heard the scornful shouts of the other kids.

'The weirdo so fancies you!'

'Does not!'

'Does too! I reckon you fancy him, as well!'

'Don't be daft!'

There were catcalls and whistles after that.

Zach was at the top of the street when he glanced back and saw that the girl was following him anyway. He paused, waited for her to catch up with him. She clumped closer in her heavy Doc Martens boots, her hands in the pockets of her jeans.

'What took you so long?' he asked her.

She shrugged. 'Playing hard to get,' she said.

There was a silence. Up at the top of the street, outside the arcade, the other kids were standing in front of the arcade, watching them.

'What about your mates?' Zach asked her.

She looked down the street at them, as though she'd already forgotten who they were. 'Them?' She gave a snort of derision. 'They're a bunch of losers,' she said and she turned back to look at him. 'So, where we going?'

'This way,' said Zach and they started walking.

NINE

PEPPER

They wandered uphill along the sun-drenched lane. For a long time, neither of them said anything. After a while, Zach decided that he would have to be the one to break the silence.

'You got a name then?' he asked.

She smiled. 'Might have. Who wants to know?'

'Me. Er... that is, Zach. Zach Hamilton.'

'Like the football team.'

He stared at her. 'What?' he asked.

'Hamilton Academicals. It's a footy team. One of my uncles used to support them.'

Zach thought about this for a moment.

'I don't think there's any connection,' he said. 'So... what do they call you?'

'Her Majesty.'

'No, seriously.'

She seemed to consider for a moment before replying. 'Pepper.'

'What?'

'That's my name. Pepper.'

Zach stifled a smirk. 'Don't tell me, your second name is Potts!'

She adopted a weary look, as though she'd heard the joke a thousand times. Perhaps she had. 'No, it's not Pepper Potts,' she said. 'Neither is it, Pepper Grinder or Pepper Pig. It's Pepper Murray.' They walked on for a bit, before she said, 'I like your *Ray Bans*.'

'Do you? I've got some you can have, if you like.'

She gave him an odd look. 'What's that supposed to mean? "You've got some I can have?"'

He shrugged. 'There's this machine in the arcade in Cullen. One of those grabber things? There's watches and sun glasses in it. I've won a few pairs of *Ray Bans*, you can have some if you like.'

She stared at him. 'But nobody *ever* wins on those things,' she said.

'Well, I think they must do,' he corrected her. He showed her the watch he was wearing. 'I got this the other day.'

'On the grabber?'

'Yeah.'

'I must have put a fortune into those machines over the years. Never won a thing.' She looked ahead. 'Where do you live?'

He pointed uphill. 'Up the top of this road,' said Zach. 'It's called Cliff View. It's up on top of the er... the cliff. Hence the name.'

'Oh yeah, I know that place. My dad says...' She broke off.

'Go on,' Zach prompted her. 'What does your dad say?'

She looked uncomfortable. 'He says something happened there, back in the day. A... murder.'

Zach laughed. 'It wasn't a murder,' he said. 'It was a disappearance. My Grandma went missing.'

'Oh, is that all?' Pepper grimaced. 'You talk about it as though it's nothing. Isn't it a bit weird living there?'

'You've no idea,' Zach told her. 'But it happened years ago.' He thought for a moment. 'So, where do *you* live?'

In Portknockie. In a house with my mum and dad. It's boring but it's OK.'

Zach nodded. 'And... Shave-Head's your boyfriend, is he?'

'Who?'

'Cameron.'

'No way! He's just someone I hang out with. He's a bit of a numpty to be honest.' She looked at Zach. 'How did you make him *do* that? He just wet himself. Like a baby.'

'What makes you think *I* had anything to do with it?'

'Well... he's never done it before.'

'As far as you *know*, he hasn't. Maybe the thought of having to fight me made him do it.' He grinned at the idea. 'Maybe he was just terrified of me.'

Pepper laughed. 'Yeah, you do look kind of scary, now you mention it.' She saw a stone lying on the

85

road and kicked it, sending it rattling along the tarmac ahead of them. 'Are you rich and all that?'

'What makes you think I'm rich?'

'That big wad of money in your back pocket, for starters. I noticed it when you was talking to Beefy.'

'Ah, Beefy. Charming lad. Not the brightest though.'

'Did you see his face? He was bricking it that you won that money. See, he's got to answer to Tazer… that's the guy that owns the arcade and believe me, you do *not* want to mess with him.'

Zach thought for a moment. 'He the skinny one with glasses?'

'No, that's Ian. He's pretty harmless. Tazer is bad news, though. He lives in the flat above the arcade. He's got tattoos all over the place. Walks around with a pit bull on a lead to back him up. He won't be happy you won that money.'

Zach chuckled. 'See, I'm not getting this,' he said. 'That's what Beefy said. "People aren't supposed to win." But, it's an arcade right, so sometimes people *must* win, mustn't they?'

'Oh sure, a fiver or a tenner. But let me ask you something. How much have *you* won over the past few days?'

Zach did a quick mental calculation. 'Couple of hundred, I guess.'

'There you go. Tazer isn't going to be happy about that.'

Zach shrugged. 'I don't care,' he said.

She studied him, intrigued. 'You *don't*, do you?'

She seemed both amazed and delighted by this information. 'When Cameron was calling you out, you didn't break a sweat, not for a minute. And I've seen him hurt people. I mean, *really* hurt them. Were you always like that?'

Zach shook his head. 'No. Only since recently. Something weird happened to me and... well, now I feel like I can do anything I want.'

'Oh yeah?' She seemed impressed. 'What happened, exactly?'

He looked at her. He didn't know why but for the first time ever, he felt compelled to share his good fortune. 'You really wanna know?'

'Sure.'

'OK.' He took a breath. 'I found this magic stone under the ground and since then, everything I want, I get.'

She laughed, raised her eyebrows. 'Oh right, I *thought* it would be something like that.'

'Did you?'

'Yeah, you looked the sort. Soon as I saw you, I thought to myself, 'I bet he found a magic stone.'

Zach chuckled. 'I had that look about me, I suppose?'

'You sure did. And you get everything you want?'

'That's right.'

'*Everything*?'

'Pretty much. Like those fruit machines? I just kind of picture the fruits I need... you know, like in my head? And I... get them.'

She laughed at that. 'I don't believe you,' she said.

'You don't have to.'

'Does it only work with fruit machines?'

'No, it works with lots of things. I'm still finding out what it can do.' They'd just caught up with the stone that Pepper had kicked earlier. He stooped, picked it up. 'See this?' he said, holding it out in front of her.

'Er… yeah. Oh, wait, don't tell me. That's a magic stone, too, right?'

'Not exactly.' He looked around, trying to locate something suitably difficult. 'See that tree over there?' He pointed across a low stone wall to a solitary oak on the far side of a very wide field. 'Reckon I could hit that tree with this stone?' he asked her

She looked, judged the distance 'From here? No way.'

'You sure?'

'Pretty much. Unless you've got a catapult or something?'

He shook his head. 'No catapult,' he said. 'Just throwing. Think I could hit it from here?'

She shook her head. 'No,' she said.

'Would you like to bet?'

She made a face. 'Nothing to bet with,' she said, forlornly.

'Oh well, never mind. Watch and learn.' He pictured the outcome he wanted in his mind's eye, then pulled his arm back and without really trying, he threw the stone. It went arcing high over the wall, whizzed across the intervening space and hit the oak, right in the centre of its trunk, with a distant clunk. A bunch of crows went flapping up from the limbs of the tree, squawking in outrage. 'Does that prove it?' Zach asked Pepper; and as he did so, he wondered why he was being so open with this girl he didn't even know, when he'd been so adamant about keeping his discovery a complete secret from his father.

Pepper looked unimpressed. 'It proves you're a good shot,' she said. 'Not much else.'

Zach laughed at this. 'Oh come on, I bet *you* couldn't have done it,' he said.

'True, but then I'm a lousy shot. What else can you do?'

They walked on for a while in silence. Then Zach said, 'I bet I could make you kiss me.'

She looked at him challengingly. 'I'd like to see you try.'

He thought about it for a moment, but for some reason he wasn't sure of, he decided against it. He really didn't want to make Pepper do anything she didn't actually want to do.

'Well?' she prompted him. 'I'm waiting.'

He shook his head. 'It doesn't seem right,' he said.

'Why don't you just ask me?' she suggested. 'Maybe I'd kiss you anyway?'

There was a long uncomfortable silence. He started walking again and then, as if perfectly timed to save his face, the roof of Granddad's cottage came into view. 'Here's where I live,' he announced, trying not to sound relieved.

They strolled to the gate. Zach opened it, and led Pepper inside. He went to the front door, took out his keys and unlocked it. He pushed the door open and stepped inside, but she didn't make a move to follow him. 'Aren't you coming in?' he asked her.

She looked unsure. 'I'm not being funny,' she said. 'But we only just met. And my Mum always says not to accept invitations from strange men.'

'What's strange about me?' asked Zach.

'Where would I start?' she countered, giving him that crooked smile that he was already beginning to like far too much. 'Let's see now. You can win on the fruit machines because you found a magic stone under the ground…'

'Point taken,' he said. 'OK, go around the back and wait for me there.' He went inside, closing the door after him, then hurried around to the kitchen and opened up the french windows. She was standing on the patio, looking appreciatively around the big garden.

'My mum would love this,' she said. 'She likes gardening and all that stuff, but she only has a few old pots in the back yard.' She pointed to the patch of freshly dug earth where the pond had been. 'What's that?' she asked.

'We're supposed to be putting vegetables there,' said Zach.

'Isn't it a bit late in the year for that?'

He shrugged his shoulders. 'I'm not much of a gardener,' he said. 'I'm leaving all that to my dad.' He indicated the cast iron tables and chair on the patio. 'Have a seat,' he suggested. 'Fancy a coke?'

'Sure.' She sat and watched as he hurried back into the kitchen and opened the fridge. He grabbed a couple of cans and came out again. He slid one across the table to her and they both popped their ring pulls and took a drink. She turned to look up the garden and he noticed how she had to shield her eyes with the flat of one hand from the glare of the sun. 'Hold on a sec,' he said and ran inside again. He hurried up to his room, rooted around in the back of his wardrobe and returned carrying three pairs of *Ray Bans*. He set them down on the table and then took the chair opposite her. 'Choose a pair,' he suggested.

She looked down at them. 'I can't do that,' she said.

'Why not?'

'Well, they're… expensive and…'

'They didn't cost me anything,' he assured her. He thought for a moment. 'A pound,' he said. 'That's what I put in the machine. So, give me a pound if you really want to.'

'What will I tell my mum and dad? About how I got them?'

'Say you won them on the grabber.'

'Yeah, like they'd believe that! Nobody ever…' She broke off, remembering. 'Well, nobody who doesn't have a magic stone, anyway.'

'OK, tell them you bought them off a guy with a suitcase. Tell them they're fakes. They won't know.'

She sat there, looking doubtfully at the *Ray Bans* for

91

a moment. Then she seemed to come to a decision. She reached out and took a pair of aviator-style glasses. She tried them on and struck a rock star pose.

'How do I look?' she asked him.

'You look cool,' he told her.

'And you're sure it's OK?'

'Yeah, no worries.'

'Thanks.' She frowned. 'I'll have to owe you the pound though,' she said. 'My dad doesn't really let me have any money.'

Zach gave her a look. 'How come?' he asked.

She shrugged. 'It's complicated,' she said.

They sat looking at each other in silence. Then Zach's mobile shrilled, making them both start. Zach took the phone from his pocket and glanced at the display. Dad was calling him. He glanced apologetically at Pepper. 'Need to take this,' he said and she smiled, nodded, turned in her seat to look at the garden again.

Zach clicked 'Accept.'

'Hey, Sport, you OK? What you up to?'

'Nothing much.' Zach knew that Dad only ever called him 'Sport' when he was feeling guilty.

'Listen, mate, it's going to be another late one. Gerry's asked me to go over some paperwork for the meeting tomorrow…'

Zach frowned. Dad had been working at the agency for three days now and this was the third night in a row that 'Gerry' had asked him to work past his official hours. 'When are you supposed to relax?' asked Zach.

'Oh, I'm OK. And it won't be like this forever,

just until I get a bit more settled… actually, I've only got myself to blame, I suggested a few things and…' Dad broke off for a moment and Zach could hear somebody firing off a string of urgent questions and Dad answering them politely, 'Yes, Gerry. No, Gerry. Of course, Gerry, leave it to me…' Then Dad came back on. 'Sorry about that. I need to sort something out for another client, sharpish. Erm, anyway… are you OK? Not too bored, I hope?'

Zach looked across the table at Pepper who had stood up now and was strolling down the garden in the direction of the shed.

'No, I'm… not bored at all. Just, you know, chilling.'

'Well, I'll make it up to you, Sport. And don't worry about dinner, by the way, I'll pick up a Chinese on the way home. You want your usual?'

'Er… yeah, sure, that'd be great. Dad?'

'Yes?'

'Don't let him take advantage of you.'

'Who?'

'Gerry. It sounds like he's dumping everything on you.'

An unconvincing laugh. 'Well, that's the role, Zach, I *am* his assistant.'

'Even so. Don't let him take credit for your ideas.'

'Er… no. No, of course not. Good point.'

Pepper had reached the top of the garden now. Zach watched as she opened the door of the shed and peeped cautiously inside.

'Well, Zach, I'd er… better get on. The sooner I'm finished here, the sooner I can come home. Crackers?'

'Huh?'

'You want prawn crackers? With the meal?'

Hmm? Oh, yeah… yes, please.'

'Right, catch you later. Be good!' Dad hung up. Zach slid the phone back into his pocket. He sat for a moment, watching the shed, expecting Pepper to emerge, but she didn't. Time passed and he started to feel vaguely worried, so he stood up and hurried down the garden to the shed. The door was ajar and he went inside. She was standing by the cobweb-festooned worktop, tracing the words scratched into the ancient wood with the tip of one finger. He came and stood beside her.

'What does it mean?' she asked him. "We bury love?" She had pushed the *Ray Bans* back onto the top of her head and her face wore a serious expression. The afternoon light, coming in through the dusty window, seemed to frame her with a golden halo.

'I don't know,' he murmured. 'It's just something my Granddad…' His breath seemed to catch and his voice trailed away. She was looking directly at him now and her eyes were the deepest blue he had ever seen. Impulsively, he leaned forward and touched his lips to hers. Time seemed to stand still. The world stopped moving. He was aware only of a deep, sweet silence. Then they broke apart again.

She smiled. 'Hey,' she said. 'Better late than never.'

TEN

MOUTH ALMIGHTY

Pepper went home around six o clock, telling Zach that her parents would be expecting her back for tea and would get funny with her if she didn't turn up. Zach felt a sense of regret as he leaned on the gate, watching her stroll back down the lane. He already liked Pepper more than any other girl he'd ever spent time with. She had a way about her that made him feel relaxed and confident. She was funny and talkative and they'd spent the afternoon chatting about all kinds of nonsense. And kissing. She was a terrific kisser. The two of them had exchanged mobile numbers before she left and both promised that they would be in touch soon.

Back in the cottage, Zach switched on the TV, but thumbing through channel after channel, he couldn't find anything he wanted to watch. He was also starting to feel decidedly hungry, so it was a relief when around eight o clock, car headlights played across the front window, signalling that Dad was finally back from work.

Zach got to his feet and went to the front door. As he opened it, the Volkswagen was just pulling up on the drive. It was twilight time, somewhere between day and darkness. The car door opened and Dad got out, holding a huge bag of food. He looked a bit harassed, Zach thought. He slammed the car door and walked quickly towards his son.

'Hey, Zach. Listen, Sport, I'm sorry about this but we're going to have some company…'

Zach lifted his head at the muffled sound of approaching rock music and another car came in through the gate, a sleek yellow sports car. A Porsche, Zach thought, though he was no expert. The car door opened and the music swelled, the sound of a heavy metal band in full flow, then stopped as the ignition was turned off. Gerry got out of the car. Zach knew that was who it was without being introduced, because he looked exactly as he had when Zach had 'seen' him at Dad's interview – the same crumpled linen suit, the same cheesy hairstyle, the same smarmy grin. He stood for a moment, looking around and then strode forward, talking far louder than seemed necessary.

'Hey, Charlie-boy, this is a nice wee pad you've got here, you dark horse! So this is where you bring the ladies, is it?' He saw Zach standing in the front door and advanced towards him, one hand outstretched to shake. 'And this must be the sprog you told me so much about! What did you say his name was, Zane or something?'

'It's Zach,' said Zach, calmly. He allowed Gerry to

take his hand and felt his fingers crushed beneath a needlessly firm grip, but made a point of not wincing.

'Of course it is! I'm Gerry Little, but you can call me… Mr Little!' He laughed uproariously at his own poor joke. 'I hope you don't mind, Zane, but I heard your dad saying he was going to grab a takeaway and I thought to myself, "you know what, I'm just in the mood for the same thing," so I kind of invited myself along.'

'No worries.' Zach took the bag from Dad and led the way inside. 'I'll get some plates and cutlery sorted out,' he announced.

'Whoah, you've got him well trained!' bellowed Gerry. He followed Dad inside and did an exaggerated double take. 'Hey, what is this, the freaking Tardis? I swear it's bigger inside. Cos you know, from the garden it looks *tiny*.'

'It does the two of us fine,' said Dad. He seemed really uncomfortable and Zach could tell he'd only gone through with this on sufferance. 'Er… would you like a beer with your meal?'

'Thought you'd never ask!' said Gerry. 'I've got a gob like the Sahara Desert!' Dad moved to the fridge, while Zach dumped the takeaway bag on a worktop and started unpacking the plastic containers. 'I got extra of everything,' Dad told him, 'so there should be plenty to go round.'

He took a couple of cans of lager from the fridge and brought one over to Gerry. Gerry popped the ring-pull and took a generous swallow of the contents. He winked. 'First today,' he said. 'First of many, I hope. Keep 'em coming, Davy-boy.'

Dad frowned. 'I er… don't actually have much in,' he said, apologetically. 'I wasn't really expecting company, so…'

But Gerry was striding around the cottage, peering at the framed pictures on the wall, acting as though he was thinking of buying the place.

'Funny old dump this,' he observed, sniffing as though he detected a bad smell. 'Your Dad's old haunt, didn't you say?'

'Er… yes, he…'

'My old man has a beach house outside of Cullen. Lovely place. Valued at two million, just the other day. I said to him, "Dennis, I'll have a place bigger than this by the time I'm thirty-five!" He just laughed. "I bet you will," he said. 'He knows I'm a chip off the old block.'

Zach carried a tray full of cartons, plates and cutlery over to the dining table. He wondered where the money had come from for this little lot and had the distinct impression that Gerry wouldn't have put a hand into his own pocket. 'Must be quite useful, your dad owning the agency?' he observed as he set the tray down. Gerry gave him a sharp look.

'Well, yeah, but don't go thinking that cuts me any slack,' he said. 'The old man said to me, "Gerry, the fact that you're my son doesn't butter any parsnips with me. You've got to get in there and prove yourself, pretty damned quick." And by golly, I think I have.'

'Please, come and sit down,' said Dad, clearly not liking the direction the conversation had taken. 'Help yourself.'

Gerry took him at his word. He sat down and started heaping his plate with a generous selection from every container. 'Where did you go for this, Charlie-boy? The Pearl? Fabulous takeaway, that one.' He spooned food into his mouth and spoke through a churning mass of fried rice and foo yung. 'There's a young filly works behind the counter in there, I tell you what, I wouldn't mind a quick canter round *her* paddock, if you catch my drift.'

Dad looked dismayed. 'But... she can't be more than sixteen,' he said.

'Huh. Don't let that put you off! They start young over in the Orient.' Gerry looked at Zach, who was spooning a more modest portion onto his own plate. 'What about you, Zane...?'

'It's Zach!'

'Yeah, whatever. You got yourself a wee girlfriend yet? You must be what, fourteen, fifteen?'

'I'm sixteen, actually.'

'Ah hah, the golden age! Oh, I remember when *I* was sixteen, I tell you what, I didn't go short, know what I mean? What about it? You got somebody on the line, have you? Somebody... tucked away?'

Zach looked across the table at him. 'Might have,' he said and Dad glanced at him in surprise.

'I didn't think you knew anyone here,' he said.

Zach shrugged. 'Well, I can't sit around at home

99

all day watching the telly,' he said. 'There's a bunch of kids that hang out in the village.'

Gerry laughed. 'Aye, that's right, Zane, you play your cards close to your chest. Don't go giving away more than you have to.' He took a swig of lager and belched loudly. 'You know, when I was your age, I got up to all kinds of stuff my parents didn't have the first idea about. Best years of your life, childhood. It's all downhill from there, eh Davy-boy?' He chuckled. 'You look at your old man here,' he told Zach. 'I did a bit of research on him before I decided to take him on. Did you know he was the Managing Director of the biggest ad agency in London at the age of thirty seven?'

'Yes I did,' said Zach, flatly.

'Must have been riding pretty high, eh, Davy-boy? The world at your feet. But the truth is, you never know what's waiting for you just around the corner, do you? And now here you are, making my coffee, doing my paperwork, making *me* shine. Makes you think, doesn't it?'

Zach gazed across the table at Gerry and thought wistfully about burying his fork in the back of the man's hand, but told himself that wouldn't be the best help for Dad's career. So he simply said, 'You were very lucky to get him.'

'Aww,' said Gerry and he tapped a hand on his chest. 'Such loyalty. Kind of gets you right here, doesn't it?' He paused for effect. 'How much did you have to pay him to say that?' he added and sniggered. He drained the last of his lager, crumpled the can in his hand and threw it carelessly over his shoulder. 'I'll take another one of those, Davy-boy,' he said.

'Umm… are you sure that's wise?' Dad asked him.

'Oh come on, don't be tight with your booze. You want to stay in my good books, don't ye?'

'It's not that. It's just that you've got that big presentation tomorrow. And you're planning to drive home, so…'

'Don't you worry about me, sunshine! I'm untouchable round here.' He leaned closer as if to confide a secret. 'I play golf with the Police Commissioner every Saturday,' he said, in an exaggerated whisper. 'We always play for fifty quid a hole and I *always* beat him. He wouldn't dare let anybody nick me. He owes me a small fortune!' He laughed uproariously and Dad got up from the table and went to the fridge.

'So, what's this old dump worth, d'you reckon?' asked Gerry, looking around the room.

Dad came back with the lager and handed it over. 'Oh, not much, I imagine. It's in pretty poor nick.'

Gerry popped the ring-pull and took another swig of lager.

'I know a chap who could work wonders on this wee place. Modernise it completely, maybe extend out into that big garden you're not even using. You'd have to spend big to do it but you'd quadruple the value of this old shack, overnight.'

'Well, maybe that's something I could consider in

101

the future,' said Dad. 'For the moment, I'm a bit…'

'Where's the wee boy's room?' interrupted Gerry. 'Got a sudden urge to siphon the python.' He got up from the table.

'Up the stairs,' said Dad. 'First on the left.'

'Excellent.' Gerry strode out of the room and they heard his footsteps thudding heavily up the staircase. It seemed suddenly very quiet without him. Dad looked at Zach apologetically. 'I'm sorry, mate,' he murmured. 'I didn't want this, he just kind of invited himself along.'

Zach chewed a mouthful of food before saying, 'He's a jerk, Dad.'

'Think I don't know that? But he's got the power of life and death over me at the moment. He's my boss and I have to butter him up.'

'Hmm. I bet he didn't pay you anything towards this meal, right?'

Dad looked embarrassed. 'He… didn't offer. But, I can't really challenge him on it, can I?'

'I suppose not.'

'Why did you bring that up about his dad owning the company? I told you that in confidence.'

'It's true, isn't it?'

'Yes, but he hates to be reminded of it. Makes it look like that's the reason he got the job.'

'Oh right. When anyone can see he actually got it for his charm and wit.'

They looked at each other for a moment and then both of them burst out laughing. Dad took a gulp of his beer. 'What was that you were saying about a girlfriend?' he asked. 'Just making that up, were you?'

'Oh no, there is someone. Just a girl I got talking with in the village. She was... nice.'

Dad looked genuinely delighted. 'That's great news,' he said. 'You... planning to see her again?'

Zach nodded. 'Yeah, I think so...'

'Terrific. I'm really pleased for you. Look, you'll have to bring her over some time, I'd love to...'

Footsteps on the stairs warned them that Gerry was coming back. He resumed his seat and picked up his spoon. 'Did I miss anything?' he asked.

Zach looked him straight in the eyes and concentrated. 'Not really,' he said. 'We were just saying how nice this food is. Weren't we Dad?'

Gerry gazed back at him, his expression completely blank. Then he dropped his spoon, reached into his jacket and took out his wallet. 'You must let me make a contribution,' he said expressionlessly.

'Oh no, there's no need...' Dad broke off as Gerry pulled out a handful of notes and slapped them onto the table in front of him. Dad stared down at them in astonishment. 'But that's far too...'

He stopped as Zach aimed a well-directed kick against his shins. Dad muffled a grunt of pain and managed to turn it into a smile of gratitude. 'Well, that's very... kind of you, Gerry. I really appreciate it.' Dad took the notes and slid them into his pocket.

Gerry was staring down at his plate of food, as though momentarily confused. But after a few moments, he picked up his spoon and started to eat again. He looked up. 'What were you saying?' he muttered.

Zach smiled. He couldn't resist. 'We were just saying how nice the food was, weren't we Dad?'

Gerry dropped his spoon a second time, reached into his jacket and pulled out his wallet. 'You must let me make a contribution,' he said, again and before Dad could stop him, he'd pulled out another handful of notes and slapped them down on the table.

'But…' Dad looked at Zach, mystified and Zach shrugged. They watched as Gerry put the wallet away and went on with his food. 'Are you… Gerry, are you feeling OK?'

'I'm fine!' Gerry lifted his head and seemed to be back to his former self. 'Just loving this grub. By the way, did you ever notice that pretty wee thing that works behind the counter in The Pearl? Tell you what, she can batter my King Prawns any time she feels like it!'

At around eleven o'clock, Zach finally got fed up with listening to Garry's annoying prattle and announced that he was going to bed. Dad looked exhausted and pretty miserable, but Gerry was showing no signs of leaving and having finished up the last of the lager, had started in on Dad's sacred bottle of fifteen-year-old Scotch, the one he'd been saving for Christmas. Zach went to his room and got himself ready for sleep. Downstairs, he could hear the muffled sounds of Gerry alternately talking and bellowing with laughter.

Just before getting into bed, Zach rooted in the

back of the wardrobe and unwrapped the stone, which continued to emit its eerie, pulsing light. He cradled it in his arms for a moment, absorbing its energy and feeling it flow through his body like electricity. It occurred to him in that instant, that he was being dumb. He had the power to make Gerry leave. It was as simple as anything. He concentrated for a moment and visualised what he wanted to happen. The noise downstairs came to an abrupt end. He heard the front door being unlatched, the sound of feet on gravel and he heard Dad tell Gerry to for God's sake drive carefully. Then there was the roar of the Porsche's engine and headlights played across the windows.

Zach wrapped the stone back up, placed it in its accustomed spot and dived into bed, as he heard Dad's footsteps on the stairs. A moment later, his door opened and Dad peered in.

'You asleep?' he whispered.

'Not quite,' murmured Zach.

'Gerry insisted on driving home. Just stood up in the middle of a conversation and said he had to go. I told him he should sleep on our sofa, but he wasn't having any of it. Christ, he must be way over the limit.'

'I wouldn't worry, Dad. I'd say he's well used to driving like that.'

'But he must be bladdered! Mind you, he was acting weird before he got drunk. Did you see how he paid me twice for the takeaway? Gave me two hundred quid and the meal only cost forty!'

'I guess he can afford it.'

'I suppose. And I won't pretend it won't come in useful. But… wow, he was strange tonight. And the presentation we're doing tomorrow is so important. It'll be worth thousands to the agency if we can get the account.'

'*You* should be doing it,' said Zach sleepily. 'You'd make a much better job of it than him.'

Dad sighed, shook his head. 'I won't disagree with you,' he said. 'But Gerry's the MD, so it's his gig. Anyway… good night Zach. And… I'm sorry you had to suffer that buffoon.'

'That's all right, Dad. Night…'

Zach barely registered the soft sounds of Dad using the bathroom. Within minutes, he was drifting down into sleep. And that was where the dream was waiting for him.

ELEVEN

RIDE ON

He was in the passenger seat of a sports car, staring through the windscreen as headlights illuminated the straight run of tarmac ahead. The vehicle was racing along a remote stretch of road at a reckless speed. There was a full moon, riding on a sea of turbulent, stormy cloud, lighting the hills all around. Fierce winds blew, shaking the car as it drove.

Zach turned his head to one side to see Gerry, hunched over the wheel, staring at the way ahead. He had a mirthless grin on his face. It occurred to Zach that he should tell him to slow down. He opened his mouth to do exactly that, but instead what came out was a question. 'Is this as fast as this thing can go?'

Gerry didn't even seem to register that Zach was *there*, he kept his gaze on the way ahead, but his grin deepened and he pushed his foot down on the accelerator. The car lurched forward like a mad beast, eager to run. Zach could feel his spine pushing back against the leather seat. The taillights of another car came into view and Gerry swerved recklessly around it, his tyres shrieking on tarmac, leaving it behind him. A horn blared in annoyance and was lost in the night. Gerry sniggered. 'Yeah, yeah,' he said. 'Eat dust, sucker.'

Zach glanced nervously at the speedometer, which was creeping up past one hundred miles an hour. He didn't much like being here and wondered how he might escape, but the dream had him trapped and he could do nothing but grit his teeth and hope it ended soon.

The Porsche swung around a long right hand bend in the road and crash barriers blurred past Zach's window in a dazzling white line. Then, as the car accelerated into the straight, Zach saw something in the road ahead of them, a large, black glistening shape about the size of a small dog, that seemed to hug the ground as it moved forward in a series of grotesque hops. He opened his mouth to shout a warning but Gerry must have seen it too, because he wrenched the steering wheel hard to the left. The car lifted onto its two nearside wheels and went skidding towards the crash barriers. Zach's ears filled with a strange sound, a long, idiotic shriek of protest that seemed to resonate inside his skull. The barriers lurched towards them and Gerry threw up a hand to shield his face. The front bumper of the car connected with white metal and tore right through it, as though it had no more substance than a line of paper. The car pushed through and hung for a moment on the edge of a steep incline. Zach was left looking calmly down into a valley, some thirty feet below him, where a narrow stream meandered between jagged grey rocks, the restless water glittering in the moonlight. Beside him, he distinctly heard Gerry say two words. 'Oh shit.'

Then the bonnet of the car tipped forward and it plunged, straight down, the ground rushing up to meet it in a deadly embrace. Zach wanted to close his eyes then, but somehow couldn't. He sat there, watching in silence as the rocks came blurring up to meet him and he steeled himself for the impact…

It never came.

Zach opened his eyes. He was lying in bed and once again, he was out of breath and soaked with sweat, but he felt calmer this time, because he knew that it had only been a dream, a dream brought on by what had happened the previous night. A sound had woken him, the trilling of Dad's mobile, coming from his room. It rang and rang, but Zach knew Dad was a heavy sleeper and it would take time to register with him.

Zach let out a sigh and groped for his watch on the bedside cabinet. It was a little after four am. Who could be ringing at this time of the morning? Gerry, most likely. He'd be calling with some last-minute instructions for Dad, something about the presentation at the agency, later today. Now Zach became aware of the sound of blustery wind from outside and it occurred to him that a storm had been raging in his dream. It seemed odd because it had been as calm as anything when he went to bed.

Dad's phone finally stopped ringing as he answered the call. Zach lay there listening, hearing Dad's groggy voice saying 'Hello? Who is this?' Then a silence, quite a long one. Zach listened intently. He quite clearly heard Dad say, 'Oh Jesus.' Another silence and then, 'Oh my God.' A pause and then: 'Yes, yes, I'm still here. Go on...'

Now there was a *really* long silence and Zach imagined Dad, listening to the person on the other end of the line. He began to get a bad feeling about this. It had only been a dream he'd had, right? Nothing more than that. How could it be anything else? He was here, wasn't he, in his bed? And dreams were just dreams, they could scare you but they couldn't harm you...

The landing light came on, a strip of white under Zach's door, and he heard the soft padding of Dad's bare feet on the floorboards. He was probably heading for the bathroom, hoping Zach hadn't heard anything.

Zach sat up. 'Dad?' he called. 'Dad, what's going on?'

A silence. Then Dad's footsteps approached the door. It cracked open and he stood there, looking pale and anxious. The awful thing was, Zach knew exactly what he was going to say before he opened his mouth. 'That was the police,' he croaked. 'Gerry had an accident in his car last night. A bad one. He must have gone off the road on his way back home.' Dad shook his head. 'I begged him not to drive in that state, but would he listen? And... I warned him not to drink any more, you heard me say that, didn't you? He *insisted* on going.'

110

Zach swallowed. 'But he… he's OK, right?'

Dad's face was grim. 'They want me to go in and identify him. His parents are out of the country. They found my number on his mobile…'

'*Identify* him?' The truth hit Zach like a punch to the chest. 'You mean… oh Dad, you don't mean…?'

'Try and get some sleep,' Dad advised him. 'It's four o clock in the morning. I'll have to head up to the hospital in Aberdeen and then get back to the studio for the presentation at ten o clock. It's too late to call it off. We've got people coming from all over the country. I… hope the weather calms down a bit.'

Zach reached out to the curtained window and pulled it back to look out at the garden. The trees up at the top were swaying in the wind. 'When did this start?' he muttered.

'Just after I came up to bed. Took me ages to drift off. Didn't you hear it?

Zach shook his head.

'I can't believe the timing,' muttered Dad. 'I suppose I'll have to do it.'

'Do what?'

'The presentation. Well, I wrote it, I suppose, so…'

'Dad, Gerry can't be *dead*. He just… can't be.'

Dad looked at him, his expression blank. 'I know it's hard to take in,' he said. 'I'm still struggling with the idea, myself. Try and get back to sleep.' He closed the door. His footsteps moved away in the direction of the bathroom. Zach lay there, his mind turning his thoughts over and over. It had been a dream, nothing more. He couldn't be held responsible for a *dream*, for

111

goodness sake! And Gerry had been an idiot last night, drinking all that booze and insisting on driving. For a moment, Zach was back in the passenger seat of the Porsche as it raced along the highway...

And then his mind recalled a detail, something that had temporarily slipped his mind. There had been some kind of creature moving across the road in the moonlight, something dark and slippery-looking, something about the size of a small dog. And he recalled what Dad had said to him that time, something that Granddad Alistair had once told him.

'Used to tell me he'd seen things creeping around the garden at night. What did he call them once? Oh, yes. The Slithers.'

Zach's stomach turned. How else would you describe the thing he'd seen in the road, something that was neither toad, nor slug, nor squid, but somehow all three of them? And he knew, right then and there, that he wouldn't be getting any more sleep that morning.

By the time he came down to the kitchen, the storm had abated. He prepared himself a bowl of cereal and ate it dutifully, though it seemed to have no more flavour than wet sawdust. Dad appeared, washed and shaved, but still bleary-eyed. He grabbed a slice of toast and a quick cup of coffee, then unlocked the french windows and headed for his car, telling Zach to try not to worry too much, he'd be back as soon as he could get away.

Zach continued eating his cereal, listening as Dad's

car drove out onto the lane. He swallowed a last mouthful, dumped the bowl in the kitchen sink and headed upstairs. He found the hooked pole, opened the hatch to the attic and pulled down the loft ladder. He switched on the light and climbed up there. Everything looked just the same as he had left it. He took the key for the bureau out of his pocket and unlocked it, then slid back the wooden cover.

He picked up the scrapbook and thumbed through the pages until he came to those weird night photographs, the ones dated October 85 and January 86. He studied them, turning the book this way and that, trying to make out exactly what he was looking at. It seemed to him now that in the second photo, he could discern some kind of shape in the bottom right hand corner, an indistinct blob, but a shaft of moonlight was playing across something and he thought the surface of whatever it was looked oily and wet. He thought now about how the thing on the road had glistened in the car's headlights as it turned the corner.

'The Slithers,' he murmured. He closed the scrapbook and then his gaze fell on the other book, the one he'd discarded on his first visit up here. He picked it up and read the title again.

The Myths and Legends of Scotland by Professor Angus McVeigh. Once again, he felt like throwing it aside. The dust jacket had no illustration, just the words printed in an old-fashioned font and when he opened the book to a random page, he noted that the text was tiny and difficult to read. But then he noticed something that he had missed before. A strip of card had been placed in the middle of the book, presumably to mark a page, so he opened it there and saw the entry that had so interested Granddad Alistair, the heading highlighted in luminous yellow marker pen.

Nuckelavee – the Devil of the Sea

The **nuckelavee** (pronunciation: /nʌklɑːˈviː/) or **nuckalavee** is a horse-like demon from Orcadian mythology, the most pernicious and destructive of all the demons of Scottish tradition. It origins are in Norse mythology, and it is particularly associated with the Orkney Islands, though sightings have been reported throughout the north of Scotland. The *nuck* component of the name may be associated with the name *Nick,* as in Old Nick, (the Devil of Christian tradition). It was said that the breath of the Nuckelavee had the power to wither crops and spread a terrible contagion amongst livestock, (this phenomenon was known as the Mortasheen). The creature was also blamed for droughts and epidemics that occurred on land, despite the fact that it was predominantly a sea-dwelling creature. One early account made it clear how strong the belief in the Mortasheen was.

"If crops were blighted by sea-gust or mildew, if livestock fell over high rocks that skirt the shores, if an epidemic raged among men, or among the lower animals, Nuckelavee was the cause of all. His breath

was venom, falling like blight on vegetables, and with deadly disease on animal life."

Some accounts speak of the hideous 'minions' that accompanied the Nuckelavee, that were often seen as a portent of its imminent arrival. Descriptions of these creatures vary in size and shape, but they are often described as 'hopping along like great toads whilst issuing a ghostly high-pitched wail.' The presence of the Nuckelavee is also associated with bad weather. Storms and gales were thought to be a sign of its approach.

In appearance, the Nuckalevee was said to resemble a hideous fusion of horse and rider. It had transparent skin, through which all its internal organs could be seen. It was also said to have one huge red eye, manlike arms that hung to the ground and a huge wide mouth said to be able to swallow a man whole…

Zach sat back in his seat and thought about what he'd just read. So many things seemed to resonate with his dream. 'Hopping along like great toads!' Isn't that exactly what he'd glimpsed in the glare of Gerry's headlights? And it had been stormy too, the clouds racing in the sky, blasted by the wind. One other thing. As the car skidded towards the crash barriers, there'd been that sound, a long resonating shriek, that he'd put down to the sound of rubber skidding on tarmac. But now he thought about it, didn't the description in the book sound exactly right? A high-pitched wail?

He sat there, staring at the words on the page and

then his mobile pinged loudly, making him start. He pulled it from his pocket and looked at the screen, expecting it to be from Dad, but it was Pepper, just a short text message.

HEY. WANT 2 MEET UP?

He didn't need to think about it for very long. He texted straight back.

YEAH. NEED 2 TALK. MY PLACE?

Back came the answer.

K. SEE U IN 15. X

Zach locked up the bureau and went down the ladder to get ready.

TWELVE

PEPPER'S LAW

Back in the kitchen, Zach felt at a loose end, so he broke the habits of a lifetime by washing the breakfast things and putting them away. Then he walked to the french windows and looked out across the garden. The weather had settled completely now, the sky an unbroken slab of blue. But then he noticed something odd about the garden. There were two large piles of earth on the lawn, one some distance to the left of the pond site, the other up near the top of the garden, a few steps from the shed. Frowning, Zach went out through the french windows and walked to the nearest of them. He drew in a sharp breath, when he saw it in more detail.

Next to the mound of earth there was a hole, about the size of a tennis ball, from which the dirt had clearly been pushed. It looked more than anything else like a worm cast, the piles of curly mud deposited by worms burrowing in the garden, but these were surely way too big to be worms and Zach thought he detected a vaguely fishy odour coming from the soil. The sides of the hole glistened and when he reached down a finger to prod at them, it came away trailing a strand of thick slime. He grimaced, wiped his finger on his jeans then kneeled down, took out his mobile and switched on the torch app. He beamed the light into the hole, noting the way the shaft went straight down into the earth, going further than the feeble light could possibly penetrate. He moved his face closer, peering into the depths, trying to see if he could spot anything moving down there...

Something grabbed his shoulder and he leapt up with a yell of terror. He spun around, only to see Pepper standing there, laughing at his evident panic.

'Sorry,' she said. 'Did I startle you?'

He remembered to breathe. 'You scared the life out of me,' he protested. 'Jesus.' He turned back to the hole and brushed the earth back into it with the side of his shoe, then tamped it down hard with his heel.

'Moles?' asked Pepper.

Zach shook his head. 'Something else,' he said. 'Not sure what.'

'Something pretty big, judging by the hole,' she observed.

The two of them stood looking uncertainly at each other for a while, so Pepper took the initiative. 'Let's get past the awkward bit, shall we?' she suggested. She pulled him to her and kissed him, but when he proved unresponsive, she let go and took a step back. 'Well, *you* know how to make a girl feel welcome,' she observed briskly.

'Sorry. Got a lot on my mind, right now.' She must

have sensed that something was wrong and seemed to relax a little.

'What's up?' she asked.

He took her hand and led her over to the chairs and table on the patio. They sat down and he told her what had happened the previous night – about Gerry visiting the house and getting drunk, before driving away. He also told her about the accident and about the phone call that morning.

'OMG,' she whispered. 'And this guy is like… really dead?'

Zach nodded. 'Dad's had to go up there to sort it all out. I mean, it's Gerry's own fault, he drank loads and Dad told him he should stay the night, but…'

'That sucks. No wonder you needed to talk.'

'There's more,' said Zach, licking his lips. Now he had come to it, he was worried he would sound like a complete lunatic.

'Go on.'

'Well, I had this dream last night…'

'OK…'

'And, well *in* the dream, I was like… in the car with Gerry? We were driving along, you know and it was stormy and I… well, I'm kind of worried that maybe *I* made the car crash.'

'In the dream?' Pepper looked puzzled 'But this was after you got the phone call, right?'

'No, before… or maybe, even at the same time it was happening? I was thinking… well, what if I made the car… *really* crash.'

119

Pepper looked at him. 'See, now you're being 'weird Zach' again,' she said.

'What's weird about it? I'm worried, that's all.'

'Zach, you just said yourself, it was a dream, right? And everyone knows what happens in dreams is just… stuff. At least, everyone except 'weird Zach.'

'I'm not weird,' he protested.

'Oh not much! Weird, "I can win on the fruit machines," Zach Hamilton.' She smiled. 'Weird, "I found a glowing stone under the ground," Zach Hamilton.'

'You don't believe me about the stone, do you?' he said, testily.

'Well, I think maybe you just exaggerated,' she said. 'You know, like you found a pebble that in a certain light, looks a bit…'

'Right,' he said. He stood up. 'Come with me.'

'Come with you where?'

'Up to my bedroom.'

She fluttered her eyelashes. 'As chat-up lines go, I have to say that's not the best I've ever heard.'

'I'm being serious,' Zach told her. 'You have to trust me on this, OK? You *do* trust me, don't you?'

She sighed, shrugged. 'I suppose,' she said. 'I mean, I think you're crazy as a bed bug, but for some reason I can't quite explain, I *do* trust you.' She paused as though expecting a response, but when she didn't get one, she said, 'OK, lead on McDuff.'

They went in through the french windows, across the kitchen and up the stairs. At his bedroom door,

Zach turned and gave her a stern look. 'You have to promise,' he said, 'before you come in here. You have to promise that you'll never ever tell anybody else what I'm going to show you right now.'

She sniggered. 'It'd better be good after this build-up,' she said.

'Promise me!'

'OK, OK, you have my word.' She held up one hand and placed the other on her chest, as though taking an oath. 'Cross my heart and hope to die.'

Zach felt reassured. He opened the door and led the way inside, then hesitated at the sight of his clothes and belongings strewn all over the bedroom. 'Maybe I should have cleaned up a bit first,' he said.

'You're not kidding,' said Pepper. She went over to the window and opened it. 'Whew! It stinks of fresh boy in here,' she complained.

He ignored her and went to the wardrobe. He leaned in and started to root around at the back of it. He found the wrapped stone and pulled it out, then turned to face her, cradling it in his arms. 'This is it,' he said.

'I was expecting something a bit smaller,' she murmured. 'Are you going to take that stuff off it or do I just have to use my imagination?'

'Of course I'm going to… look, take this a bit more seriously, will you?'

'OK, sorry. It's because I'm nervous. I have no idea why I *should* be nervous, but I kind of am.'

She watched as he pulled the denim jacket and then the T-shirt away from the stone, allowing its green glow to radiate around the room. She took a deep breath.

'Christ on a bike,' she said quietly. 'As glowing stones go, that's a beauty.'

'You ever seen anything like this before?' he asked her.

She shook her head. 'Not outside of a fantasy movie.' She seemed entranced by the thing. 'Isn't it… heavy?'

'Not at all. Here, you want to hold it?' He moved closer to her.

'I'm not sure I should,' she said. 'What if it's… dangerous? Like, radioactive or something?'

'I don't think it is,' he assured her. 'I've held it lots of times. I *like* holding it. It feels… kind of warm and… buzzy, you know? Here, try it.'

He pushed it into her arms and she stood there, looking uncertain. Then her eyes widened. 'Oh, wow,' she murmured.

'Yeah. You feel it?'

She nodded, eagerly. 'It's like… it's kind of like a… tingling. You can feel it in every part of you.' She thought for a moment. 'Hey, does this mean I'll be able to do it too?'

'Do what?'

'Win on the fruit machines and stuff?'

He shrugged. 'I don't know,' he said. 'Maybe. Shall I put it back now?'

'No. Let me hold it a bit longer. It feels good. I mean, *really* good. It makes me feel strong, you know? Like

I could do anything.' She stared at him. 'Zach, what *is* this thing I'm holding?'

'I don't know,' he admitted. 'Like I told you, I found it under the ground.'

'Can you show me where?'

'No. See, it was under my Granddad's pond.'

'What? How did you breathe?'

'No, no, I drained it first. I pulled back the liner and... well, there was this big hole, going right down into the ground.'

'You knew it was there?'

'No. No, my dad asked me to dig out the pond and... there it was. My Granddad must have known about it, though, because he'd put in these metal handholds, to make it easier to climb in and out. Anyway, I went down and the stone was just... lying there in this kind of... big cave. So I took it.'

Pepper turned to look out of the bedroom window as something occurred to her. 'That's where the pond was,' she said. 'All that newly dug ground. You filled it in, didn't you?'

'Yeah. Well, that's what Dad wanted me to do, anyway.' Zach stepped forward and took the stone from her, started wrapping it up again.

'So... who do you think it belongs to?' Pepper asked him.

He paused, looked up at her. 'Why would it belong to anyone?' he asked her. 'It's a stone. It was just lying around down there.'

She sat on the edge of his bed. 'To be fair, Zach,

it's not "just a stone", is it? It's a very special stone. I mean, you know that better than anyone. And something that good, well it must belong to *somebody*. It's like…' She thought for a moment. 'It's like Jack and the Beanstalk.'

'Is it?' Zach lifted the stone and put it back into its regular place.

'Sure. You know the story. Jack climbs up the beanstalk and he finds this goose. But it's not just any old goose, is it? This one lays golden eggs. So he takes it home to his mum, but the goose belongs to a giant. He notices it's missing and he comes after Jack…' She paused and smiled goofily.

'What?' he asked her.

'Zach and the Beanstalk,' she said.

But he didn't feel like laughing. He went and sat beside her on the bed. 'Are you saying… that somebody is going to come after the stone?' asked Zach, nervously.

'Well, they'll have a job, won't they? 'Cos you've filled in the pond.'

Zach thought about that for a moment. Then he thought about the two fresh holes he'd seen in the garden this morning.

'Pepper, have you ever heard of the *Nuckelavee*?' he asked.

'The what?'

'The Nuckelavee. I suppose that's how you pronounce it. It's a Scottish thing. A… what do you call it? A myth. It's sort of like of a…' He struggled

124

to say what he wanted to without it sounding stupid. 'Sort of like an evil thing that lives in the sea. Only sometimes it comes out of the water and it has this weird breath that kills everything...'

She shook her head. 'We're back to weird Zach again,' she warned him. She looked around. 'Look, why don't we go out?' she suggested. 'This is doing my head in and...'

'And what?'

'Well, I want to see if any luck has rubbed off on me.' She gazed at her hands. 'I'm already feeling like *something* has changed.'

'Where do you want to go?' he asked her, though he thought he already knew what she was going to say.

She smiled. 'The amusement arcade?' she suggested.

He looked doubtful. 'I don't know,' he said. 'They told me I can't go back in there.'

'True,' said Pepper. 'But they haven't told *me*, have they?'

THIRTEEN

GAME ON

They walked downhill towards the esplanade and came to a halt outside the arcade, which looked as seedy as ever. There was no sign of Pepper's crowd hanging around outside. She looked at Zach.

'So tell me again, how I do it?'

'You just… picture the fruits you want to come up,' he told her. 'You sort of see them in your head. Like a photograph.'

'Sounds easy enough. OK, let's give it a go. You'll need to lend me a pound though.'

'No worries.' He reached into his pocket and found a spare coin which he handed to her. They walked into the dimly lit interior of the arcade. It was busier today, some eight or nine people standing at various machines, feeding in coins. Dials whirred and clicked, electric lights flashed on and off, but nobody appeared to be winning any money today. From his seat in the booth, Beefy saw them come in and walked out to intercept them, one massive hand held in front of him.

'You,' he said, pointing at Zach. I thought I told you to stay out of here. You're barred.'

'Relax,' Zach assured him. 'I'm not playing today, just watching.'

Beefy looked doubtful. 'I got a rocket off my boss last time you came in,' he complained. 'I'm warning you, if you go anywhere near a machine...'

'I won't,' Zach promised him. 'But you don't mind if *she* has a go, do you?'

Beefy frowned. 'I suppose not,' he said.

Pepper wandered the aisles for a moment, looking at the various machines. Zach trailed after her, with Beefy walking alongside, glaring at him.

'I'll try this one,' said Pepper after a while. She had stopped in front of an electronic machine called *Treasure Island*. It offered a top prize of £500 but to get that, you needed three consecutive scores, each featuring three 'treasure chests.' The odds were next to impossible, Zach thought.

Pepper stood for quite a while, studying the machine. Then she dropped her coin into the slot and hit the 'spin' button. The cylinders whirled around and clicked to a halt, one by one. Three treasure chests. A hundred pound symbol lit up on the display, advising her that she could cash in now if she wanted to.

Beside him, Zach heard Beefy take a sharp intake of breath. A couple of players at a neighbouring machine had noticed what had happened and their exclamations enticed other players to leave their own games and came over to watch.

'I think I'll spin again,' said Pepper calmly and she hit the button a second time. The cylinders spun, then stopped, one, two, three treasure chests. She had £250 pounds. There were gasps of delight from the people watching and now the remaining players left their machines to come and view the action.

'No way,' whispered Beefy. He looked nervously around at the crowd, realising that they were all witnesses to this. 'This can't be happening…'

'All or nothing,' said Pepper. She hit the spin button for a third time and watched as the cylinders blurred around. The first one clicked to a halt. One Treasure chest. The second one stopped. Two treasure chests. The third cylinder seemed to spin for an eternity and then finally came to a halt. One parrot. She'd lost the lot. There was a soft groan from the onlookers. She'd been so close.

'Hah!' exclaimed Beefy, relieved.

Pepper didn't react. She stood there staring intently at the machine and after a long pause, the final cylinder clicked over one more place. A third treasure chest!

The crowd reacted with whoops of delight, while Beefy gave a low moan, no doubt imagining the rocket he was going to get from Tazer. Pepper grinned. She hit the collect button and two-pound coins began to shower noisily into the metal tray. Zach ran to the booth to grab some polystyrene cups, while Beefy stood there, looking like he was about to have a heart attack.

Zach returned with the cups and handed them to

Pepper, who began to cram her winnings into them. Beefy looked at Zach, his face white.

'How did you do it?' he whimpered.

'I didn't do anything,' Zach assured him. 'You saw me, I didn't go near her.'

'But…'

Pepper turned away from the machine, proffering two large cups stuffed to the brim with coins. 'I'll take it in twenties,' she said.

'You ain't getting nothing until I talk to Tazer,' Beefy assured her. He hurried to the booth and grabbed his mobile phone, a different model to the one he'd been using last time Zach saw him.

'But I won fair and square!' protested Pepper. 'You *have* to pay me.'

'Hear, hear!' said somebody in the crowd.

'Pay the girl!' demanded a heavy-set man with a red complexion.

'Just a minute!' Beefy dialled a number and waited, his expression anxious. When the call was answered he said, 'Tazer, we've got a problem down here. Some kid just walked in off the street and won five hundred quid.'

There was a brief silence and then Zach heard the sound of bellowing on the other end of the line. Beefy flinched and attempted to get the odd word in without much success.

'No, not the same… a girl… well, she won it! I don't… no, but… but I… OK.'

Beefy ended the call and took a deep breath. 'Tazer's

coming down,' he said. He managed to make it sound like the end of all things. 'He'll talk to you… *outside*, away from the other customers.' He reached out and took the polystyrene cups from Pepper. 'I'll look after these,' he said.

Pepper glanced at Zach, her expression doubtful. 'Maybe we should just go,' she suggested.

'Without your winnings?' Zach shook his head. 'No, we'll talk to this Tazer,' he said. 'I'll explain.' They went out onto the street and waited. Beefy came and stood in the open doorway, holding the cups of coins, his bulk preventing the customers inside from seeing what was happening. After a few minutes, they saw Tazer come out onto a metal staircase to the right of the building. He came down, walking quickly, a white pit bull terrier on a lead trotting just in front of him. Zach appraised him as he came closer. Tazer looked like very bad news indeed, his head shaved, his bare arms covered with a multitude of tattoos. He was dressed like a teenager in a black muscle vest with a skull and crossbones logo on the chest, a pair of baggy camouflage pants and high top Doc Martens. Zach judged him to be in his late fifties, maybe older. He came to a halt in front of Zach and Pepper and appraised them with his pale blue eyes.

'You the kid who keeps winning in my arcade?' he asked Zach. He had a broad Glaswegian accent and spoke in a low, gravelly voice that was little more than a whisper.

'That's me,' said Zach, proudly. 'But not today.

Today, *she* won.' He indicated Pepper. 'Five hundred pounds,' he added, just to be clear.

Tazer laughed unpleasantly. 'Nobody wins that,' he snarled. 'Not in my arcade.'

'Well that's odd,' said Zach, 'because she just did.'

Tazer sneered. He reached into the back pocket of his trousers and pulled out a ten pound note, which he offered to Pepper. 'Here, take this and get lost,' he suggested. 'Sharpish.'

Pepper actually reached out a hand to take the money but Zach restrained her.

'No, hold on a minute,' he said. 'Perhaps I didn't explain properly. She won five hundred.' He held up his hand with the fingers splayed and spoke slowly, as if talking to an idiot. 'F-i-v-e. H-u-n-d-r-e-d. P-o-u-n-d-s.' He indicated Beefy, who was standing in the doorway, holding the cups. 'It's all there in those cups, it just needs changing up.'

Tazer actually gasped at Zach's cheek. He studied him, as he might study some dirt under his fingernails. 'Listen, pal,' he said. 'I don't know how you're doing it, but let me tell you something. Nobody talks to me like that, d'ya understand? Not the toughest geezer in the country, let alone some wee punk like you.' He spat on the ground to emphasise his point. 'Now, I'm going to say something and you'd better listen up good.' He pointed to the pit bull standing beside him. 'This is Lucifer,' he said. 'He's an attack dog. If I was to say one single word to him, he'd have you by the throat and he wouldn't let go until I gave him the signal. You got that? Now, I suggest that you and your… skinny-assed wee girlfriend here, move yourselves off my property and stop wasting my time.'

Zach considered Tazer's threat and decided he didn't much like the tone of it. 'Number one,' he said. 'That place of yours is an amusement arcade. The machine she played offered a top prize of five hundred quid and she won it, fair and square. Number two, I'm not wasting your time, I'm telling you that you owe her that money and we're not leaving until we get it. Number three, I don't *care* about your dog with the stupid name.'

There was a long silence then, before Tazer gave a low, throaty chuckle. 'You're going to be a riot down at the hospital,' he said. He looked down at the dog. 'Lucifer,' he said. 'Sic 'im!'

The pit bull reacted as though it had been jabbed with an electric prod. It snapped upright and emitted a low growl. Tazer slipped the lead and the dog sprang towards Zach, its teeth bared, its eyes wild.

There was a moment where Zach nearly lost it. He almost turned on his heels and ran. But somehow he forced himself to stay right where he was and his confidence came back, pure and strong. He looked directly into Lucifer's eyes and said, 'Who's a good boy, then? Who wants his tummy rubbed?'

Lucifer's demeanour changed in an instant. His stumpy tail began to wag and he flopped down on the ground and rolled onto his back, his legs splayed. Zach kneeled beside him and started to rub his stomach.

Pepper, seeing that the dog wasn't going to harm anyone, went to join in.

Tazer stood there, his mouth open, his eyes bulging. He clearly couldn't believe what he was seeing. 'Lucifer!' he bellowed. 'Lucifer, sic 'im, I said! Attack! Attack, you useless pile of...' Exasperated, he lifted the leather lead he was holding and brought it down across the dog's chest with a loud slap, obliging Zach and Pepper to leap aside. Lucifer whimpered, rolled over and cowered as Tazer rained down another blow onto his back and then another and then another...

Pepper pointed to Tazer and said, 'Hey, you!'

Tazer stopped in mid swing as though he'd been frozen in place. He looked at Pepper in mute astonishment. 'Big man hitting a defenceless wee dog,' she said. 'Why don't you try hitting yourself for a change?' Tazer's expression was blank, but the next moment, he obeyed, swinging the heavy lead across his left shoulder, the thick leather making a thwacking sound against his back. His eyes widened with the shock of the pain, but he did it again and again, the sound making Zach flinch.

Beefy came out of the doorway, looking bewildered. 'Boss, what you doing?' he cried.

'Stop me!' Tazer ordered him. 'Agghh! Stop me!'

Beefy didn't know what to do. He stood there indecisively for a moment and then handed the two cups to Zach. He went to try and restrain Tazer and got the lead across his face for his trouble. He howled and cowered away as Tazer continued to beat himself mercilessly, crying out at every blow. Baffled passers-by paused to see what was going on.

'I tell you what,' said Zach. 'Shall I just go inside and change up the money for you?'

'Do it!' screamed Tazer. 'Do it!' A particularly vicious blow dropped him to his knees.

Zach wandered inside, approached the booth and opened the cash register. The other players had gone back to their fruitless games. He took out ten fifty-pound notes and tipped the coins into an empty drawer, before sliding it shut and heading back outside. When he emerged into the sunlight, Beefy was hanging desperately on to one end of the lead, while Tazer madly tried to pull it free so he could continue with the grim task of whipping himself. Several astonished holidaymakers were standing in a cluster watching the proceedings as though it was some kind of bizarre street theatre. Some people were filming it on their phones. 'How are you doing this?' bellowed Tazer. 'Are you witches?'

Pepper glanced at Zach. 'Not a very nice thing to say, is it?' she murmured. 'You got my winnings?'

'Yeah.' Zach fanned out the notes and waved them. 'You're in the money.'

Pepper grinned. 'I've been thinking,' she said, her words punctuated by a series of grunts and moans from Beefy and Tazer. By now, some of the cheekier members of the crowd were urging Tazer on, telling him to try a bit harder. Pepper nodded towards the arcade. 'Maybe we could spread the joy around a bit? What do you think?'

He understood what she was driving at. 'I suppose if we both work together?' he suggested.

She smiled, nodded. They turned and concentrated their joint attention on the front of the arcade. Tazer finally stopped punishing himself and slumped exhausted onto the pavement with a moan of relief. Beefy stood beside him, holding the leash, looking like he didn't have the first idea what was happening. And Lucifer was wandering off along the street, wagging his stumpy tail.

Zach imagined the interior of the arcade. He imagined the poor, pale-faced people in there, feeding their coins endlessly into the slots. Then he tried to imagine every machine paying out its top prize. Weirdly, he could feel Pepper alongside him, doing exactly the same. There was a low vibration in his skull as their two minds mingled and then a sensation of incredible power rippled through his entire body. Suddenly, from within the arcade came a startling sound – the sound of a multitude of coins, clattering into several trays, all at the same time. An instant later, there were whoops of astonishment from the other customers, who must have waited a very long time to see something like this.

Tazer and Beefy exchanged baffled looks. 'Oh no!' whimpered Tazer. He scrambled to his feet and he and Beefy raced madly inside, as yet more coins began to fall. The crowd of onlookers, lured by the sound of money, followed them in. After a moment, Zach could hear Tazer bellowing at the other players to step away from their machines, but judging by the continuing clatter of coins, nobody was taking any notice of him.

Zach laughed. 'Think we've done enough now?' he asked Pepper.

She nodded, turned away and took his hand. 'Come on,' she said. 'I'll treat you to an ice-cream.'

And they walked away, leaving pandemonium behind them.

FOURTEEN

CHILLI CON CARNE

It was late afternoon, the heat slowly going out of the day. The two of them sat up in Zach's room, taking turns to hold the stone, cradling it on their laps as though it was some kind of baby. Every time he held it, Zach was aware of its strange, exhilarating power washing through him and he could tell from Pepper's awed expression, that she felt exactly the same.

'I wish I knew what this thing *was*,' said Pepper. 'I mean, we call it a stone, but we don't even know if that's right. You said something before about your Granddad finding it?' She was holding the stone as she spoke, the palms of her hands resting on its smooth surface, the colours shifting and swirling restlessly beneath her palms.

'Yeah. It was back in the 1980s. He left a scrapbook with photographs in it. They showed him finding the hole in the ground and everything.'

'So... I don't really understand how it ended up back underground?'

'Well, I'm not sure exactly why, but he must have

decided to put it back down there. He'd already built the pond over the hole, I suppose so nobody else would know it existed. So he had to completely drain the pond and everything, before he could get back down there. When he was done, he filled the pond up again, replanted the flowers and made it look like it had before.'

Pepper frowned. 'Why would he *do* that? I mean, this stone, it's fantastic. And he must have known that, so…'

'It was after my Grandma disappeared,' said Zach. He felt awkward mentioning it, but knew that he had to.

'Do you think he thought there was some kind of connection?'

Zach sighed, shook his head. 'In the scrapbook, he just wrote, "I gave it back." That's all. He doesn't say why.'

'I can't imagine why anyone would give up something like this,' said Pepper. 'It's like… the most amazing thing in the world, *ever*. You know, the more I think about it, the more I believe that we could do so much more with it.'

He looked at her suspiciously. 'What do you mean?' he asked.

'Well, what we've done so far… winning stuff on the fruit machines and all. It's kind of selfish, isn't it? I mean, great for us, obviously, but kind of… shallow. Don't you think?'

'I hadn't really thought about it too much,' said

Zach. 'I was just having so much fun doing it.'

'Yeah, but that last thing we did… helping all those people at the arcade get some of their money back. Well, that felt much more worthwhile. I kind of enjoyed that more than winning the five hundred quid.'

Zach shrugged. 'I suppose,' he said.

'So imagine what else we could do for other people… raising money for charity, say, or… or helping people who are ill to get better. I don't know, there must be all kinds of things we could do if we put our minds to it.'

'True. But… then we'd have to explain *how* we were doing it, wouldn't we? And… I don't know, I kind of feel we need to keep this a secret between us.' He thought for a moment. 'What about people like Tazer?' he said. 'What if they found out about the stone? They'd want to take it from us, wouldn't they? And people like that, they don't care who gets hurt. Things might get nasty, so…'

'But we wouldn't have to *tell* people about the stone. We could just do things secretly and they'd never know it was us. I think it would be really cool. We'd be like… super heroes, only secret ones.'

'It's something to think about,' admitted Zach. 'But not just yet, eh? Let's just enjoy having it for a while and finding out what else we can do.'

The sound of a car engine came from the garden below and Zach instinctively grabbed the stone from Pepper's lap and carried it to the wardrobe.

'It's my dad,' he said, draping the protective layers over the stone. 'He doesn't know about the stone.'

'How come?'

'I never told him about it. The weird thing is, Pepper, his luck's improved lately and I think the stone is kind of... helping him.'

'See, that's what I'm talking about. Helping other people.' Pepper got up from the bed. She looked suddenly rather anxious. 'Perhaps I should go,' she said.

'Don't be daft,' he told her. 'Come down and meet him.'

'He might not like me being here,' she said.

Zach smiled at her nervousness. 'He's all right, my dad,' he assured her. 'He'll *want* to meet you.' He placed the stone reverently into a corner of the wardrobe and slid the door shut. 'Come on,' he said. 'What's up with you? You look really worried.'

'I'm not great meeting people for the first time.'

'It didn't seem to bother you much the first time *we* met.'

'That was different. You put a spell on me.'

'No I didn't!'

'Well, you made me feel different, OK?'

They went down the stairs and through the kitchen to the french

windows. Dad was standing by the open boot of the Volkswagen holding what looked like a big cardboard box full of provisions. He started towards the house and smiled when he saw Zach step into the garden. The smile deepened when he saw Pepper, trailing shyly after him.

'Hello,' he said. 'Who's this?'

'This is Pepper,' said Zach. 'The girl I told you about?'

'Ah, yes. Pleased to meet you. I'd shake hands but…'

Zach stepped forward and took the box from him, so Dad could do exactly that. Pepper took the proffered hand, but her eyes were fixed to her feet. 'Pepper. What an unusual name,' said Dad. 'But somehow, really cool.'

'Thanks,' muttered Pepper, her face flushed.

So, you're from Portknockie, is that right?'

'Yeah.' Pepper still seemed to be finding it difficult to look Dad in the eye and that surprised Zach, because she had always struck him as a confident girl. 'Nice to meet you, Mr Hamilton. Zach's told me all about you.'

Dad gave Zach a surprised look. 'Nothing bad, I hope.'

'Oh no, not at all!' Now she looked genuinely flustered. Zach wondered what the problem was.

There was an uncomfortable silence. Zach looked into the box, which was stuffed with food and drink, fancier than the kind of groceries that they usually bought. 'Someone's been lashing out,' he observed.

'There's two more boxes in the boot,' announced Dad. 'Well, we were running low on provisions and… it's been quite a day.'

Zach and Pepper helped him get all the boxes into the

kitchen and they started to unpack the contents as Dad told them how his day had gone. Clearly the stone's powers extended further than Zach had realised.

'Obviously, I started at the hospital, early this morning,' said Dad. 'The morgue.' He grimaced. 'That was not a pleasant start to the day.' He looked apologetically at Pepper. 'Sorry, Pepper, did Zach tell you what happened to my boss?' he asked her.

'Yes,' she said. 'He told me about the car crash.'

Dad nodded. 'I'm not going to go into any detail, but it was pretty horrible. He was in a bit of a state, you know? Came off the road at over a hundred miles an hour, they reckon. Anyway, after that, I had to get back to the studio for the big meeting. On the way there I was panicking, to tell you the truth. The people I was presenting to were from Staintons... you know, the dairy people?'

'We always get their butter,' said Pepper. 'And they do fantastic yoghurt and ice cream.'

'Yeah, that's them. Big Scottish company. The traffic into work was dreadful, so I got there just as the clients were arriving and to tell you the truth, I was completely flustered. But Cheryl got them all seated...'

'Cheryl?' repeated Zach.

'Oh, she's the company's dogsbody. Bit of a godsend, really. Very organised. Don't know how I'd manage without her...' Zach noticed a strange kind of smile on Dad's face when he spoke about Cheryl.

'Anyway, there they were, the MD of the company

and his creative team and in I came, like some blow-in… and, I don't know how, but as I stepped into the conference room, I suddenly felt… really powerful, as though I could achieve anything I set my mind to. The same feeling I had at the interview with Gerry.'

Zach and Pepper exchanged glances at this.

'I'd prepared the pitch of course… the one that Gerry was supposed to present, but for some reason, I just abandoned it. I went off-script and started in with this completely different idea. Haven't a clue where it came from, but I was on fire! We were going to completely tear up the book and start over, I told them. We were going to create the most dynamic campaign ever seen in the industry. I came up with half a dozen straplines off the top of my head. And after a few minutes, I sensed that I had them…' He reached out a hand and stared at it, as though visualising a tiny group of people sitting there. 'I had them in the palm of my hand and I knew… I knew right then and there, they'd sign with us. And sure enough, they did. Didn't even want to go away and discuss it.' He looked at Zach. 'That's a five hundred thousand pound deal, right up front, with plenty more to come. Our agency will create their look, their adverts, their press, the works.'

Zach grinned. 'Wow! That's great news, Dad.'

Dad opened the fridge and started putting salads and vegetables into the drawers. 'It gets better,' he said. 'After they'd gone and I'd briefed our creative team, I went into Gerry's office to go through his

143

emails and, you know, try and sort out any loose ends he'd left. Anyway, his phone rang and I answered it. It was Dennis Little… or *Sir* Dennis, to give him his full title. Gerry's father.'

Zach winced. 'Whoah! That must have been tricky.'

'Well, of course it was! The man was distraught. He's in Spain at the moment and he and his wife will have to fly over for the funeral. So of course, he wanted to know all about the last time I'd seen Gerry. I had to tell him that he'd been drink-driving, but he wasn't surprised, he knew that's how Gerry rolled. So, as I say, he was grieving but at the same time, he was clear-headed. At the end of the day, he's a businessman above all else. He asked me if everything was OK at the agency and I told him there was no need to worry, I was taking care of everything. And I happened to mention that I'd just signed Staintons for the biggest advance in the agency's history and he… well, to cut a long story short, he asked me to take on Gerry's role, with immediate effect. Zach, I'm MD of the bloody company! Obviously, I hate to get it this way, but… well, I'm not going to turn it down, am I? It's everything I've ever dreamed of.'

'That's great, Dad, I'm really pleased for you.'

'No, it's better than that! Don't you see, Zach, we're off the hook? I was beginning to think I was on a one-way train to nowhere and now, in the space of a few days, everything has turned around. I'm back in charge of an agency, something I'm really good at and the future looks… brilliant. It's like… like I'm charmed or something. Like I'm the luckiest man in the world.'

He paused, made a little self-conscious by his own exuberance.

'Anyway, that's enough about my day. What about you two? Get up to anything interesting?'

'Oh, we just hung around Portknockie,' Zach told him. 'Called in at the amusement arcade.'

Dad looked unimpressed. 'Hmm. I don't much care for those places,' he said. 'Ripping off people who can't afford to lose money.'

Pepper smiled. 'That one seemed to be giving quite a bit back today,' she said and she and Zach shared a knowing smile.

Dad was intrigued. 'Am I missing something?' he asked.

'No,' Zach assured him. 'No, there's a guy who works in there. Tazer, he calls himself. He makes us laugh, that's all.'

Dad closed the fridge door. 'Well,' he said, 'as we're celebrating again, I thought I might make my famous chilli con carne. Pepper, can I persuade you to stay and sample it? With a name like yours, you probably enjoy spicy food.'

Pepper shook her head. 'No, I... I think I'd better head back for tea,' she said. 'They like me to be home for that.'

'Can't you phone them?' asked Zach, disappointed. 'Seriously, he *does* make a great chilli.'

'No, I'd better get back. They're a bit funny about me staying out late.'

145

'But it's not that late, surely?' Dad glanced at his watch. 'If I start cooking now, and we run you back afterwards, we could have you home for... seven o' clock?'

'No really, they can be a bit funny.'

'I'd be happy to talk to them, if you like,' offered Dad. 'Assure them of our good intentions and...'

'No! No, really.' Pepper made a big show of looking at her watch. 'You know, I should be on my way.' She nodded to Dad. 'Nice to meet you, Mr Hamilton. And... congratulations on your new job. It sounds great.'

'Thanks, Pepper. Sorry, I'm aware I've been rabbiting away about myself ever since I got back and you've barely been able to get a word in edgeways. I hope I'll see you again, soon. It's good that Zach has found a friend.'

Pepper stood there looking awkward.

'I'll walk you to the gate,' offered Zach and they strolled out of the kitchen together. The sun was low on the horizon now, painting the clouds in lurid shades of red. For some reason, Pepper's reaction to the dinner invitation had made Zach feel uneasy. 'You OK?' he asked, as they walked towards the gate.

'Sure, I'm fine.'

'I don't get why you can't stay for tea,' he said.

'My dad likes me to be there when he gets home from work,' said Pepper.

'But surely...'

She paused for a moment and glared at him. 'Look,

Zach, not all dads are like yours, OK?' Then she softened and moved closer to kiss him on the lips. She held it there for a moment, before stepping back. 'I'll text you,' she said, and went out of the gate and down the lane. Zach watched her walk away, her hands in the back pockets of her jeans. He thought about how she'd been when Dad first arrived, shy, nervous, not really able to look him in the eye. He wondered what things were like between Pepper and her father. For the first time, it began to dawn on him, that maybe the two of them didn't get on too well.

Pepper turned at the bottom of the lane and waved to him. He waved back and then she turned the corner out of sight. Zach strolled back to the house and into the kitchen, where Dad had the chopping board out and was slicing onions, their sharp aroma on the air.

'She's nice,' said Dad. He looked slightly odd because his eyes were watering from the onions.

'Yeah, she's OK.'

'How old is she?'

'Just a year younger than me.'

'Well, you two look great together. Like you *belong,* you know?' Dad wiped his eyes with the back of his wrist. 'It's a shame she couldn't stay to eat. Still, another time, eh?' Dad opened a paper bag and took out several big red chillies. 'What do you think, Zach?' he murmured. 'Will we go "hot," "very hot" or "nuclear meltdown?"'

Zach laughed. 'Well, like you say, it's a celebration. Let's go for it!'

FIFTEEN

A VISITOR

Zach went to bed that night, his stomach pleasantly full of chilli con carne, and quickly fell into a deep, dreamless sleep. But he woke suddenly in the early hours of the morning with the distinct feeling that something was wrong. For a start, the bedroom felt icy cold, as if it had been plunged into the depths of winter. As he struggled upright in bed he was aware of his own breath clouding in front of his face. He was just about to reach out to switch on the lamp when he saw, in a shaft of moonlight that had found its way through a gap in the curtains, that somebody was sitting on the end of his bed.

'Dad?' he whispered, but even as he said it, he could see that though the figure was turned away, he was nothing like Dad. This man was skinny, dressed in a ragged pair of overalls and the wild hair that stuck up from his head in random tufts was snow white. He was gazing towards the curtained window as though waiting for something.

Zach took a deep breath. He felt very scared but

148

was determined not to lose control. 'Who are you?' he gasped, but he somehow knew the answer to that, even before the man turned to look over his shoulder. Zach really only knew the long, thin face from old photographs, though Granddad Alistair looked worse than he ever had in any of his pictures. His features were unnaturally pale, the skin grey and papery, his cheeks sunken, and there were dark, saggy rings beneath his colourless eyes. When he spoke, his voice was a guttural croak that made the hairs on Zach's neck stand up straight.

'You've got to give it back,' he said.

Zach instinctively pulled the duvet up to his chin.

'You're not real,' he said. 'I'm dreaming this.'

Granddad smiled, a sad smile. 'If only,' he said. Then he leaned closer, close enough for Zach's nostrils to register the foul stink emanating from him. 'Trust me, boy, you're wide awake.'

He sat back, then stood up from the bed and turned so that Zach could see him properly. He was no more than a collection of skin and bone. His bare wrists, where they emerged from a filthy, mildewed shirt were shockingly thin and when he drew back his lips to give what was probably intended as a reassuring grin, Zach saw that the old man's teeth were a collection of rotting stumps.

I'm dreaming this, Zach told himself again and, slipping one hand under the covers, he pinched himself hard on the thigh in a desperate attempt to wake himself up. 'Oww!' he exclaimed. The pain certainly felt real enough, but the old man stayed right where he was, looking down at his grandson, as if waiting for him to say something.

'What do you want?' asked Zach, miserably.

'I want to show you something,' croaked Granddad.

'I don't want to see it,' said Zach.

'But you don't know what it is yet.'

'I don't *want* to know.'

'Don't be silly, boy. I'm trying to help you. Come with me.'

Zach shook his head. 'I'd rather stay here,' he insisted.

'I'm sure you would,' said Granddad. But he reached out a hand, took a firm hold of Zach's duvet and pulled it from the bed. Now Zach could really feel how cold it was in the room – like an icebox. He realised that he had a stark choice. He could either lie here shivering or get out of bed. Eventually, he chose the latter.

'Good,' said Granddad Alistair. He turned and began to walk towards the closed bedroom door.

'Where are we going?' asked Zach.

Granddad Alistair turned to look at him and raised an index finger to his own shrivelled lips. 'Shush,' he said. 'We don't want to wake Davie.'

It was this little detail that finally convinced Zach this wasn't a dream. The old man hadn't said, 'We don't want to wake your father,' or 'your dad,' but had used not his son's Christian name, but his nickname. Zach was fairly sure that his own mind wouldn't have created a little detail like that. He watched as the old man extended a hand to grip the door handle, then turned it gently and swung the door wide. In a dream, wouldn't he have just floated *through* the door? And Zach was aware of every tiny detail, the soft touch of the carpet under his bare feet, the faint wash of moonlight coming through the window on the landing and, worst of all, the awful gut-wrenching stench emanating from the old man's body. This was happening, it was actually happening and Zach seemed to have little option but to go along with it! He glanced towards the door of Dad's room but Granddad Alistair seemed to guess at his intent. 'Don't involve him,' he whispered. 'This is your mess, you need to be the one to sort it out.'

'What *mess*?' hissed Zach, but Granddad Alistair had started down the stairs now and Zach had no option but to follow him. The ancient stairs creaked under Zach's weight, another detail that made this seem horribly real.

In a few moments, they were downstairs and walking through the open doorway of the kitchen. Zach reached out a hand to switch on the lights but Granddad Alistair grabbed his wrist before he could do so. Zach flinched, his skin crawling. The flesh that encircled his wrist was a cold as a fall of December snow. 'You'll see much better in the moonlight,' Granddad Alistair told him.

'I'm not going outside,' Zach warned him. 'Not for anything.'

'There's no need,' said Granddad Alistair. He

released Zach's arm and walked over to the french windows. He stood, staring out across the garden for a moment, then turned and gestured for Zach to come closer. Zach hesitated for a moment, reluctant to be any closer to that smell, but finally complied, rubbing the cold band of flesh on his wrist with his other hand as he did so. He stopped beside Granddad Alistair.

'Look,' said the old man, pointing to the glass. 'Tell me what you see.'

Zach did as he was told. The garden lay stretched out before him, the lawn pale blue in the moonlight. Everything was exactly as it had been before, Zach thought, except… he noticed something new. A couple more piles of earth like the ones he had seen the other day. 'Moles,' he said, dismissively, though he knew deep down inside, that wasn't the right answer.

The old man made a weird sound – a kind of rasping, throaty wheeze. His narrow shoulders began to move up and down and Zach realised that he was laughing. Coming from him, it was a most unpleasant sound.

'Moles!' he hissed. 'You know, I used to have a mole in my garden, back in the day. Damned thing kept digging up my flowerbeds. But I had my revenge on him. Do you know what I did?'

Zach shook his head and Granddad Alistair grinned his rotten grin. 'I buried him alive,' he said; and then did that hideous wheezy laugh again.

Zach didn't know what to do now. What was the usual etiquette when a dead man told you a joke? Were you supposed to laugh along with him or should you just stand there looking uncomfortable? He chose the latter.

Eventually, Granddad Alistair stopped sniggering. 'Look again,' he suggested. 'Look *properly*.'

Zach gazed out across the lawn. This time, his heart jolted as he saw something move. He gasped, took a step closer to the glass. A *thing* was hopping across the lawn. He didn't know what else to call it. At first, he took it to be a large frog or a toad, but when he focused on it, he saw that it was nothing of the kind. It was a wet, slug-like thing, with rubbery, transparent skin and it had four splayed limbs, which hugged the ground and ended in webbed claws. Zach remembered the creature he'd seen crossing the road in front of Gerry's car and thought that this looked like a smaller version of that. He was horribly aware of a pair of large reptilian eyes, mounted up on the top of the creature's head. As he watched, the wide jaw flipped open and a long forked tongue flicked momentarily out.

Now Zach's appalled gaze detected more movement, further up the garden and he saw another of the things, heading towards the shed, then a third, over by the hedge to the left side of the garden. They were all moving in a series of ungainly hops and Zach could see, shimmering in the moonlight, the glittering, viscous trails they were leaving behind them.

He turned to glare at Granddad Alistair. 'What *are* they?' he asked.

Granddad Alistair looked at him and shook his head despairingly, a movement that made his neck creak softly. 'You *know* what they are,' he said. 'You've seen the books in the attic. You've read what's there.'

'Are they… *the Nuckelavee*?' asked Zach.

The old man shook his head. 'These are just minions,' he said. 'Small fry.'

'Well, why… why are they…?'

The old man gestured him to silence. 'Stop it, boy, he said. 'You know what they are and you know what they *want*.' He pointed a skinny finger towards the creatures on the lawn 'These are just for starters,' he assured Zach. 'The advance guard. Soon, they'll start to home in on the stone and when they know exactly where it is… then the Slithers will come.'

'The… Slithers?' Zach swallowed. 'But I thought *they* were…?'

'No boy. There are others,' Granddad Alistair told him. 'Just when you think you've got the measure of them, along come the next ones. And in time they will summon *the Nuckelavee*.'

'But… why?' gasped Zach. 'What does he want with the stone?'

'The same as you want. It's the source of life for him. It's his power. And they will take it back at any cost. You must return it to him before you learn, the hard way, exactly what that cost is. Please boy, don't make the mistake I made. Don't hesitate. Do it tomorrow, at first light.'

'But…'

'Listen to me! I was where you are now. Think I don't know how seductive it is? Think I don't

154

understand the allure? I couldn't make myself give up the stone, not until it was too late.'

'I only want to…'

The light snapped on, momentarily dazzling Zach. Blinking, he turned to see Dad standing in the open doorway of the kitchen, his hand still on the light switch. 'Zach,' he said. 'What's the hell's going on?'

Zach turned to look at Granddad Alistair, except that he wasn't there anymore. Zach also noticed that the kitchen light was reflecting his own image and that of the interior of the kitchen back at him from the glass of the french window, making it difficult to see out into the garden, something that Zach was oddly grateful for. He turned his attention back to Dad.

'I… I just came down to get a drink,' he said.

'Then why are you standing by the window?'

'I was just… looking out,' said Zach. 'At the garden.'

Dad walked into the kitchen and Zach went to block his way, not wanting him to look outside. 'I'll just grab a coke and go back to bed,' he said. 'I'm sorry if I woke you up.'

But Dad clearly wasn't satisfied with that answer. 'Who were you talking to?' he asked

'What? Er… nobody!'

'Zach, I quite clearly heard you talking. That's why I came downstairs. And I…' He glanced around the deserted kitchen. 'As I was coming down, I… I thought I heard another voice, talking back to you.'

Zach forced a dismissive laugh.

'Yeah, like that would happen,' he said. 'I think somebody had too many beers with his dinner last night.'

Dad frowned. 'I could have sworn,' he said. 'I heard two voices. And one of them sounded like...'

Zach spread his hands wide. 'Feel free to search the place,' he suggested. He went to the fridge and opened the door. He took out a can of coke, snapped the ring pull and took a swig, turning as he did so back towards the french windows. He nearly choked. He had just glimpsed Granddad Alistair's pale features staring in at him from the other side of the glass and the shock sent a spray of coke across the tiled floor.

'Watch it!' snapped Dad.

'Sorry,' spluttered Zach. 'Went down the wrong way.' He grabbed a piece of kitchen roll and dropped to his knees to mop up the spillage.

Now Dad was sniffing the air. 'There's a bad smell in here,' he said.

'Is there?' Zach did an elaborate pantomime, sniffing the air ostentatiously. 'I can't smell anything,' he said.

Dad shook his head. 'It might be the drains,' he said. 'Maybe I should get them checked.'

'Maybe.' Zach went on mopping up the spilled coke.

'Well, I have to get up in the morning, even if you don't,' said Dad. 'Turn off the light when you come up.' He went out of the kitchen and headed back up the stairs.

'Yeah, I'll be right there,' Zach called after him. He

waited until he was sure Dad was back in his room. Then he stood up, dropped the tissue into the bin and snapped off the kitchen light. Granddad Alistair was still standing on the other side of the glass, staring mournfully in at him. As Zach stared back, the old man raised a finger and waved it admonishingly. Then he turned and strolled off down the garden, ignoring the creatures that hopped around his feet. When he got to the top of the lawn, he opened the door of the shed and went inside.

'Great,' murmured Zach.

He stood for a few moments, watching the ugly wet creatures flopping around in the grass, their ugly heads twisting this way and that, as though searching for something.

Then he turned and went up to his room, knowing that once again, any hope of a decent night's sleep had just gone right out of the window.

SIXTEEN

HOLES

Zach found an old bag of ready-mix cement in Granddad Alistair's shed. He mixed some of it up in a plastic bucket, following the instructions printed on the side of the bag and then wandered out into the garden, filling in the holes to the best of his ability. Because the shafts dropped straight down, he lost quite a bit of the mixture, but after a bit of experimentation, he found that if he pressed the cement hard into the sides of the hole, it stayed in place. It was a grey, overcast sort of morning, strangely muggy and looking like it might rain at any moment. The weather seemed to match Zach's mood.

He was just filling in the last of the holes when Pepper ambled in through the gateway. 'Hey,' she said. 'What are you doing?'

'What does it look like?' he muttered sourly.

'It looks like your mole problem is getting a bit out of hand,' she said.

'What if I told you it isn't moles?' he asked her and she gave him a puzzled look. 'There were things in the garden last night,' he added.

'Things? What things?'

He sighed, dropped the trowel back into the empty bucket and wiped his hands on his jeans. 'How come you didn't text me?' he asked her, getting to his feet. 'You usually do.'

She looked dismayed. 'Sorry, I didn't realise I had to,' she said. 'I thought I'd just… surprise you.'

'Yeah, well I've had enough surprises lately, thanks.'

She gave him a wary look. 'Whoah! I think somebody got out of bed on the wrong side this morning.'

'I had a bad night,' he told her; but he went over to her and gave her a kiss. 'We need to talk,' he said.

'OK.' She smiled. 'Shall we go up and hold the stone while we do it?' she asked eagerly.

'Is that all you can think about?' he snapped. 'The stone.'

'What's wrong with you?' she asked him. 'You're being really weird.'

He led her over to the table and chairs and they sat down. 'What if I told you I had a visit from my Granddad last night?' he asked her.

'I'd be surprised,' she admitted. 'I thought you said he was dead.'

'Yeah, that's just the problem. He is. But it didn't stop him from turning up in my bedroom in the middle of the night.'

She started to laugh, but caught herself when she saw his serious expression. 'You mean… you had another bad dream?'

'I don't think it *was* a dream. It felt too real.'

'But that's… crazy,' she said.

'Is it? Like finding a magic stone is crazy? Like being able to make things happen is crazy? He was here, Pepper and trust me, he did *not* look pleasant. He didn't smell like *Lynx for Men* either.'

'Well, what did he want?'

'He wanted to warn me. About the stone. He was telling me I needed to give it back if I didn't want to end up like him.'

'Like him? You mean… *dead*?'

'No, not exactly. But… listen, you remember what I asked you about before? The *Nuckelevee*?'

'Oh yeah. I asked my mum about that. She'd heard of it. Some old wives' tale from the Orkney Islands. That's hundreds of miles away from here, across the sea.'

Zach shook his head. 'Oh right, so this thing can't travel then?'

'Travel? What do you mean?'

'It's like you're saying if a thing comes from a certain place, it has to stay there. But this creature can move, surely?'

Pepper looked baffled. 'I don't understand,' she said.

'Look, come with me, I need to show you something.'

He led her inside and they went up the stairs to the landing. He got the hooked pole and let down the loft ladder, then switched on the light up there. 'It's up here,' he told her, aware as he said it that her gaze was straying to the doorway of his bedroom. He knew that she wanted to be in there, holding the stone and soaking up its power, but he needed to show her Granddad's stuff first. 'Follow me,' he said, and started up the ladder.

Pepper pushed aside Granddad Alistair's scrapbook and leaned back in her chair. Zach was standing behind her, looking over her shoulder.

'It's really weird,' she said. She indicated the scatter of books and press cuttings on the bureau. 'All of it. But, no offence, Zach, your Granddad was supposed to have had a few screws loose, right?'

Zach frowned. 'Well, that's what people thought. But what if he wasn't crazy? What if he was just... telling the truth?'

'What, that there were fairies in his garden?'

'Will you stop using the F-word? I told you, the things I saw looked more like... like big toads.'

'Maybe that's exactly what they were!'

He glared at her. 'I think I know a toad when I see one.'

'No, think about it,' she told him. 'It was dark, right?'

'Yes, and...'

'There used to be a pond, didn't there? Which you filled in.'

'Yes...'

'And everyone knows that frogs and toads come back to the same pond, year after year, to lay their eggs and stuff...'

'You wouldn't be saying that if you'd seen them!

161

They were like… weird. Toads but… *not* toads. All slimy and slithery.'

'But that could have been part of the dream!'

'No, Pepper, believe me, it wasn't a dream. That's about the only thing I'm sure of. If you'd seen Granddad… if you'd *smelled* him…' He shook his head. 'Even Dad could smell it.'

'Your dad saw him too?'

'Well no, he didn't actually *see* anything… but he could smell where Granddad had been.'

'What about the toad-things? He saw those, did he?'

'No, he didn't.' Zach glared at Pepper. 'I know what you're trying to say, but I didn't imagine any of it.'

'All right, calm down.' She thought for a moment. 'They don't sound like they're dangerous…'

'Granddad Alistair said they were just the beginning. He said that other things would come. The Slithers, he called them.'

'So, what are you saying? That we should put the stone back where you found it? Under the ground?'

'Well…'

'The stone? Really? The most amazing thing in our lives, like, *ever*? The thing that gives us power and makes us feel confident? That lets us win money and change things we don't like? You're saying we should just… give that up?'

Zach had to admit that, put that way, it didn't sound like the best idea he'd ever had. 'I don't like it any more than you do,' he admitted. 'But… I'm beginning to feel scared. What if… what if somebody gets hurt?

My dad or… or you? How would I live with myself?'

'It isn't going to come to that,' Pepper reassured him. 'It's not. The stone makes us strong, Zach. And it belongs to us now. We can fight off anything that comes after us. I know that now. We can make things the way we want them. It's like what happened with my dad…'

'Your *dad*?'

'Yeah. I fixed him, last night.'

'You fixed him?' Zach didn't like the sound of that one bit. 'What's that supposed to mean?'

Pepper sighed. 'I was a bit late back last night and he started in on me.'

Zach sat down cross-legged beside her chair. He gazed up at her. 'Pepper, he doesn't… you know…?'

'Oh God no, nothing like that! And it's not like he hits me, either. Well, maybe a slap if I'm really cheeky. But he's a bully, Zach, he always has been. He shouts at me and he shouts at Mum, whenever she tries to defend me. So I came in last night and he started, didn't he?' She adopted a gruff voice. '"Where've you been, girl? I've told you before, I want you in when I get back from work, I'm not having you traipsing all over the town, getting up to mischief…"' Pepper smiled. 'And I just thought to myself how good it would be if he lost his voice for a while…'

'Pepper, you *didn't*!'

'I did. Right in the middle of his bellowing, he stopped all of a sudden and made this weird croaking sound. You should have seen the look on his face! It was mint. He couldn't say a single word! He was trying to and his face was all red and sweat was coming out of his forehead…' She grinned. 'He looked like he was about to have a heart attack. And I just turned to my mum, calm as anything and asked her what was for tea!'

Zach stared at her. 'You've put him right, though?'

She shook her head. 'Not yet.' She saw his appalled expression and reacted. 'Oh come on, I've got to have a bit of fun with it! I'll let him sweat it out for a few days. He's gone to the doctors this morning, to see if they can do anything, but they won't be able to.' She grinned. 'I'll let him speak again when I feel good and ready. And the next time he starts on me, you know what? The same thing is going to happen. Until he learns.'

Zach frowned. 'You don't think that's going a bit far?' he asked her. 'I mean, it's one thing messing up a piece of scum like Tazer, but this is your *dad*!'

'No. I tell you what. It was lovely and peaceful last night. Mum's pretending that she's all concerned, but I can see, deep down, she's loving it. It must be the first time she's got her own way in years. Last night, she was able to watch the TV programmes *she* wanted and he couldn't say anything about it!' She looked down at Zach. 'By the way, talking of Tazer? I came past the arcade on the way here and it's all shut up. There's a big sign that says, "Closed for refurbishment!"' She laughed delightedly. 'We've put that scumbag out of business, Zach. He's been leeching off the people of this town for years and now he's gone bust! Come on, you've got to love that!'

Zach smiled but somehow felt guilty. Pepper was right, Tazer was a lowlife, but Zach hadn't realised that their little stunt would bankrupt him.

'Anyway, what do you say?' asked Pepper. 'Let's go to your room and soak up some more vibes from the stone.'

Zach shrugged. 'OK,' he said.

'And don't worry about this *Nuckle-whatever* nonsense,' she assured him. 'We'll figure something out. We get more powerful every time we touch that stone. Pretty soon we're going to be unbeatable.' She got up from her chair and went over to the hatch. Zach stood up and locked up the bureau. He turned and looked at Pepper, half-in, half-out of the attic.

'If things get bad,' he told her. 'I mean, if it ever gets so we can't handle it... we might have to think again about what we should do.'

'Of course,' she assured him, and then her head and shoulders disappeared and he followed her down. By the time he'd secured the hatch and walked to his bedroom, she already had the stone unwrapped and was sitting on the bed, cradling the glowing oval shape in her arms. The look on her face was one of complete ecstasy. 'Oh Zach,' she murmured, as he wandered in. 'It feels *so* good today. Like it's alive.'

It's turning us into a pair of junkies, he thought, but that didn't stop him from sitting on the bed beside Pepper and waiting eagerly for his turn.

SEVENTEEN

CHERYL

'Watch this,' said Pepper. She and Zach were stretched out on his bed, the stone resting on the duvet between them, its warmth flowing through both of them. Pepper concentrated for a moment, staring at the wooden shelf on the wall above the foot of Zach's bed. As Zach watched, astonished, a book slid smoothly out from between its companions and drifted slowly down into Zach's outstretched hand. He caught it, looked at the title. *Magic For Beginners*. But he knew that nothing in there would be a patch on what he'd just witnessed.

'Wow,' he said. 'I've gotta try that.' He stared up at the same shelf and tried to focus his thoughts. Several books began to shudder then jerked suddenly upwards and came tumbling down in a litter of pages. 'Rats,' he muttered. 'I haven't quite got it.'

'You're trying too hard,' Pepper assured him. 'You've got to… focus more.' Now she pointed to a chalkboard affixed to the wall on the other side of the room. 'Look and learn,' she murmured. As Zach watched, amazed, a length of chalk lying on a shelf at the bottom of the board rose slowly into the air and began to scrape words on the black surface. It was barely legible but Zach could just about read it.

Zach & Pepper 4 Ever

'Hey, you're too good at this,' he observed. 'Let me have a go!'

'OK.' Pepper concentrated and the chalk moved smoothly back to its resting place. 'All yours,' she said.

'Right.' Zach made an effort to marshal his thoughts, directing his energy into that slender length of chalk. Gently, gently, it lifted into the air and positioned itself with one end resting against the board. The tip of Zach's tongue slid out, as he attempted to make it form letters.

I l…u…v…

The unexpected sound of a car pulling into the drive interrupted his thoughts and the chalk dropped unceremoniously to the carpet. Zach scrambled up off the bed, lifting the stone and pulling the usual garments around it.

'What's Dad doing home at lunchtime?' he wondered aloud.

Pepper got up off the bed and watched as Zach stowed their shared treasure safely out of sight. Then the two of them went down the stairs and out to the garden. Dad was standing by the Volkswagen, talking to a tall dark-haired woman in a black and white check dress and a pair of high-heeled shoes. As Zach and Pepper approached she turned to look at them and Zach disliked her on sight, though he wasn't sure exactly why. She was pretty, he supposed, in that older woman kind of way, her straight black hair meticulously arranged in a perfect bob, her mouth painted a glossy dark red. She appraised Zach coolly, her green eyes fringed with thick black lashes.

'You must be Zach,' she said, extending a hand, the fingers of which were adorned with long, blood-red nails. 'Charles's told me so much about you.' Her accent was local, Zach thought, but adapted to sound more like Edinburgh. Now her gaze moved to Pepper. 'And who's this?' She glanced sideways to Dad in mock outrage. 'A girlfriend already?' she exclaimed. 'You Hamiltons obviously like to start young.'

Dad smiled, looked awkward. 'Zach, this is Cheryl,' he announced. 'Cheryl, my son Zach and his er… friend, Pepper.'

'Pepper! Ooh, I bet you're a spicy one!' Cheryl tilted back her head and made a strange kind of braying sound, which Zach assumed was probably intended as laughter. 'You probably hear that a lot,' she said, once she'd finished.

'All the time,' said Pepper, but she smiled politely as she said it.

Now Cheryl did an exaggerated double take and

gazed around at the garden and the front of the cottage. 'Charles, you never told me how pretty this place is! It's like something from a fairy tale.'

Dad simpered. 'It's really only temporary, Cheryl, until we find something more… suitable.'

'We're moving?' asked Zach. It was the first he'd heard about it.

'Well Zach, the MD of a major agency has to have the right kind of pad,' said Dad, sounding quite unlike himself. 'But I'm sure this place will do until I've had a chance to look properly. Come on, Cheryl, I'll give you the guided tour,' he added, leading her across the patio.

'Stay out of my room,' Zach warned him.

'Oh don't worry,' said Dad, 'we're not going in there.' He winked at Cheryl. 'Not without our malaria shots.' This remark caused another braying burst of laughter.

'Oh Charles, you should be on the stage!'

'Fair enough. What time does it leave?'

They disappeared inside and Cheryl's raucous laughter echoed around the tiny kitchen.

Pepper looked at Zach. 'Who's *she*?' she murmured.

'The receptionist from work,' said Zach quietly. 'Never met her before.'

'Hmm. Lucky you.' She smiled. 'I reckon you've just met your future step mum,' she said.

'No way!'

'Way! Didn't you see the looks your dad was giving her? Like she was pulling gold coins out of her backside. And to be fair, she's not bad looking… for her age. I reckon she's spent some hours down the gym keeping that figure.'

'But she's… nothing like my mum,' protested Zach.

'There's no law that says she *has* to be.'

'Oh, but come on, did you hear her *laugh*? She sounds like a hyena.'

Dad leaned out from an upstairs window. 'Do me a favour, Zach, and put the kettle on. We had a meeting in Cullen and I thought we might as well call in here for lunch. You guys hungry?'

Zach shrugged. 'I guess,' he said.

'Good. We'll be down in a minute. There's fresh bagels in the breadbin.' Dad went back inside and Zach and Pepper followed. Zach filled the kettle and switched it on. Pepper found the bagels and started rooting in the fridge for something to fill them with. From upstairs they could hear Dad providing a running commentary interspersed with shrieks of laughter from Cheryl.

'That laugh could get annoying,' murmured Pepper, slicing bagels and feeding them into the toaster.

Zach was getting the decent mugs out of a cupboard, remembering as he did so, the way that Dad had smiled when he'd mentioned Cheryl's name the other day. Surely he couldn't be thinking of…

Dad and Cheryl appeared in the doorway. 'Ooh, you've got them well-trained,' observed Cheryl. 'That's what I like to see.'

'Zach's not normally this helpful,' said Dad. He

smiled at Pepper. 'Must be your influence,' he said.

Pepper smiled brightly. 'What would you like on the bagels, Mr Hamilton?' she asked.

Dad came over to the worktop. 'There should be some smoked salmon in the fridge,' he said. 'And cream cheese.' He looked at Cheryl. 'Sound OK?'

'Sounds like absolute heaven,' said Cheryl. She gave Pepper a sharp look. 'Easy on the cream cheese though, I need to watch my figure.'

'Oh, I can always do that for you,' offered Dad and was rewarded with the donkey impersonation again.

'Ooh, you are naughty!' said Cheryl.

'I do my best. Please, go and have a seat,' suggested Dad, motioning her over to the table. Cheryl started across the room, her high heels clicking on the tiles and Zach suddenly felt a powerful rush of mischief overtake him. He glanced briefly at her feet and concentrated. There was a sharp cracking sound and Cheryl pitched headlong onto the floor. She came down hard, skidded a short distance on her front and then rolled into a sitting position, looking dazed. There was a shocked silence, during which Pepper shot Zach a questioning look, but he ignored it.

'Oh my God!' Dad was over to Cheryl in an instant, looking horrified. 'Cheryl, are you all right?' He kneeled beside her. 'What happened?'

'I broke a heel,' she said. She held up a shoe, displaying how one needle thin heel had simply snapped across the middle. 'Jimmy Choos, they are, cost me a blumming fortune!'

'I'm so sorry.' Dad helped her upright and got her over to a chair. 'Are you injured at all?'

'Only my pride.' She reached up to pat her hair into shape. She took off the other shoe and set it carefully down beside the broken one.

'There's a heel bar in Cullen,' said Dad, trying to be helpful. 'We'll stop off there on the way back to work, if you like.'

'A heel bar?' Cheryl gave him an outraged look. 'I hardly think so. They're Jimmy Choos,' she added, as if this explained everything. 'I've got some sandals at work,' she added. 'I'll wear those this afternoon.'

'Probably be more comfortable,' said Dad and then realising he probably hadn't said the right thing, went back to the counter to supervise the making of lunch. Within a few minutes everything was ready and the four of them were seated at the table with bagels and cups of coffee. They started to eat.

'So Zach, how are you occupying your time?' asked Cheryl.

He looked at her blankly. 'How do you mean?'

'Well, you can't just sit around watching telly all day, can you? Haven't you got yourself a wee summer job?'

'No he hasn't,' said Dad. 'I know where you're coming from, Cheryl. I've suggested a few things, but Zach seems to enjoy living a life of leisure.'

Cheryl made a face. 'I *always* had a job during the school holidays,' she announced. 'It's good to get that work ethic established. You know what they say, Zach. The devil makes work for idle hands.' She glanced pointedly at Pepper. 'What about you, love, you making yourself useful somewhere?'

'Not really,' said Pepper, staring intently at Cheryl's bagel as she picked it up from her plate.

'Well, it wouldn't harm to put your CV around a few places,' said Cheryl. 'I could give you a few suggestions, if you like.' She took a generous bite of her bagel and then made a funny choking sound. She leaned forwards and spat a mouthful of food onto her plate. Sitting on top of it was a bright red fingernail.

Dad stared down at it in astonishment.

'Bloody hell!' spat Cheryl. 'I only had them done yesterday!' She held up a hand from which a nail was conspicuously absent. As she stared at it another one detached itself from her index finger and fell with a sharp clack onto the table.

'I... didn't realise they were false,' said Dad.

'Of course they are!' snapped Cheryl, her accent sounding considerably closer to a local one, now. 'Who has real nails *this* perfect?' She scowled. 'I'll go round to that salon and give them a piece of my mind. Thirty quid I paid for this little lot.'

Zach glanced at Pepper and smothered a laugh by cramming his bagel into his mouth.

'Not your lucky day,' said Dad, sounding distraught. 'I'm so sorry.'

'It's hardly your fault, Charles, and at the end of the day, it's only money.' Cheryl tried to laugh it off, but she didn't look particularly amused. She went to pick up her bagel again and seemed to think better of it. She chose her coffee cup instead and lifted it to her lips.

Zach knew he shouldn't do it, but he felt he had to outdo Pepper. He concentrated on Cheryl's cup, using just enough power. A trickle of coffee spurted from the bottom of it and spilled down the front of her dress, making a dark stain. Dad noticed before Cheryl did. 'Oh my God,' he said. 'Cheryl, you…'

Then she registered the feel of the hot liquid on her chest and gave a kind of squawk. She slammed the cup down into its saucer and pulled the wet fabric away from her flesh. 'Aggh!' she groaned. 'I don't believe it!'

'Primark?' inquired Pepper, politely and Cheryl flashed her an angry look.

'Yves St Laurent, if you must know!' she snarled. 'And it's absolutely ruined.' She got up from the table, brushing at her chest with a paper napkin. 'Where's the bathroom?' she cried.

'Upstairs,' said Dad, miserably. 'First left. I'm so sorry…'

Cheryl ran barefoot out of the kitchen and they heard her pounding up the stairs. Dad was examining the coffee mug, mystified. There was no sign of a leak anywhere. 'What the hell's going on?' he asked the room at large.

Zach and Pepper could only shrug their shoulders.

'It's almost as if…'

'As if what?' asked Zach, through a mouthful of food.

Dad shook his head, dismissing whatever impossible

thought he'd had. 'She's nice, Cheryl, don't you think? Been a great help to me.'

'Bit accident prone,' observed Zach.

'She isn't normally,' said Dad.

Zach took a slurp of coffee. 'What was that about us moving out of here?' he asked.

'Well…' Dad stared into his own coffee cup. 'We don't want to stay here forever, do we? I thought we could find a nice apartment in Aberdeen and go back to renting this place out. Could be a nice little earner.'

'But I like it here,' Zach told him.

'I wasn't talking about moving out tomorrow,' Dad assured him. 'I'm just looking to the future.'

'OK,' said Zach. 'It's just nice to be told stuff before somebody else hears about it,' he said. He turned and looked at Pepper, saw that her eyes were closed in concentration. He wondered what she was planning, but didn't have to wait long to find out. In the bathroom above them, the toilet flushed, making much more noise than it normally did. An instant later, an ear-splitting scream filled the house.

Dad looked towards the ceiling aghast. 'Cheryl?' he called.

Then they heard a new noise. A pounding sound. Cheryl's muffled voice was yelling down to them. 'I'm soaked to the skin and the door won't open! Charles? CHARLES!!!'

Dad jumped up from the table and raced madly up the stairs. Zach looked at Pepper. 'All right,' he said. 'That's probably enough now.'

She smiled back at him and seemed to relax. Above them, there was the sound of the door suddenly crashing open, followed by Cheryl's distraught sobbing and Dad's desperate entreaties. They both distinctly heard Cheryl wail, 'I'm covered in it!'

'I hope you didn't go too far,' said Zach.

'I did it for you,' said Pepper. She leaned forward and kissed him.

And they went on with their meal.

EIGHTEEN

GUILT TRIP

'We went too far,' said Zach.

He and Pepper were in the bathroom, cleaning up the mess left by Cheryl's 'accident'. Pepper was mopping the floor and Zach was on his knees, his hands encased in a pair of yellow rubber gloves, wiping the splashes off the walls and the side of the bath. Dad had just driven Cheryl back to her place for a change of clothes. She'd been crying her eyes out when she got in Dad's car, dressed in his towelling bathrobe, thick mascara running down her face. Her expensive dress was quite beyond saving. Soaked through and smeared with unmentionable stains, it had been placed in a black plastic bag and thrown straight in the bin. It had all seemed hilarious at the time, but now it was over, Zach couldn't help feeling horribly guilty.

'Oh, come on,' said Pepper. 'It was just a laugh. And *you* started it.'

'I know I did. But I don't feel good about it. Dad likes her…'

'God knows why. She's so *fake*.'

'Maybe, but that's no reason to do what we did to her. I mean, snapping her heel like that. What was I thinking? What if she'd been injured? She could have broken her neck. Wouldn't have been so funny then, would it?'

Pepper wrung out the mop into the plastic bucket. 'Well, she's fine. She just looked stupid. It's not the end of the world, is it?'

'Yeah, but try to put yourself in her place. It was the first time she'd met us. She must have been mortified.'

Pepper frowned. 'I suppose,' she said. 'It's your fault for egging me on.'

'I didn't,' he protested.

'Well, it *felt* like you did. I just wanted to go one better.' Pepper stood back and surveyed the bathroom. I think that's about the best we can do with this,' she said. Zach got to his feet.

'I still don't really understand how you *did* it,' said Zach.

'Well, I knew she was up here, using the sink. So I just pictured all the water coming up from the loo, like a fountain and soaking her…'

'Water is one thing,' muttered Zach. 'It's what else came up along with it that was the problem.'

'Yeah, well, I didn't plan that bit, did I? How was I to know that half the sewer would come up as well?'

'See, that's what I mean. It's too much. We've got to try and rein things in.'

'Says the boy who made Cameron pee himself!'

178

'Well, yeah, now you mention it that was pretty horrible too. Have you seen him since?'

'*Nobody's* seen him. He's too embarrassed to go out these days. Sits at home, playing computer games.'

'There, see, now I feel guilty about that.'

Pepper chuckled. 'You're a hopeless case,' she said. 'Cameron would have broken your nose and thought nothing of it. He's a nasty piece of work, Zach. You needn't go feeling sorry for him.'

'Even so. He didn't deserve to have all his mates laughing at him.'

Zach stripped off the rubber gloves and dropped them in the litterbin. He washed his hands in the sink and dried them on a towel. Pepper picked up the bucket and the two of them went out of the bathroom and down the stairs to the kitchen.

'We need to agree on something,' said Zach, as she turned back to face him. 'From now on, no more nasty stuff, OK? I mean, we've got these powers and it's brilliant, of course it is, but… we have to agree that we don't do anything to harm people.'

Pepper scowled. 'What? So, if something bad is about to happen to you, I can't step in and help?'

'That's different. That would be… self-defence. But… I'm worried that the stone is making us mean.' He looked at her. 'It was just nasty, what we did to Cheryl. Really nasty. And I… I keep thinking about Gerry…'

'The guy who died? Well, that was nothing to do with you.'

'I'm not so sure. I didn't like him, Pepper. I didn't like the way he talked to Dad. And when he was here, I had bad thoughts about him. Then I had that dream and it all seemed so... so real.'

'Yes, but that's all it was, Zach, a dream. You can't blame yourself for what you dream. Nobody can control that.'

Zach sighed. 'Maybe,' he said. 'But what if it was me that caused his car to go off the road? That would make me a murderer.'

'Hey.' She moved closer and put her hands on his shoulders. 'You can't think like that. You'll mess yourself up if you do. It was an accident, pure and simple. Things like that happen every day.'

Zach thought about if for a moment and told himself that she was probably right. But he couldn't rid himself of a nagging doubt. He remembered what he'd said in the dream. "Is this as fast as this thing will go?" He made an effort to push that thought out of his mind.

'Anyway, I mean what I say, Pepper, we have to agree that we're not going to misuse the powers anymore. Agreed?'

She shrugged. 'Yeah, whatever.'

'No, Pepper. I want you to promise.'

Pepper looked at him. For a moment, defiance flared in her pretty eyes, but then she seemed to soften. 'All right,' she said. She stood up straight and placed a hand on her chest, as though taking an oath. 'I promise not to misuse my powers,' she said. She thought for a moment. 'Does that mean we can't win money on the slot machines any more?' she asked him.

'The arcade's closed,' he reminded her.

'But there *are* other ones we could go to.'

Zach thought about it. 'I suppose that's different,' he admitted. 'It's not really harming anyone. And the people that run those places are mostly scumbags. But we should put a limit on it. Say… no more than a hundred quid a time in any arcade. We don't want to put anyone else out of business.'

'Oh no, we don't want to do that,' said Pepper, rolling her eyes.

'I mean it, Pepper. No making people look stupid. And… your dad.'

'What about him?'

'I want you to give him his voice back.'

'Ah, Zach, come on. He asked for it!'

'Pepper…'

'All right, all right, you win. I'll sort it tonight.'

'Promise?'

'Yes, I promise.' She glanced at her watch. 'I need to go,' she said.

'Got something on?'

'Yeah, I said I'd go into Aberdeen with my mum this afternoon. She wants to go shopping, you know, the two girls together sort of thing. I thought maybe I'd talk her into going into one of the big amusement arcades on the prom. And I thought…'

'Yeah?'

'Maybe I could arrange for her to win some money. It's just… Zach, I'd like to see her win for once, you know? I don't think she's ever won anything in her entire life. Not one penny. She'd be thrilled. That would be OK, wouldn't it?'

Zach smiled. 'Sure. That's a nice thing to do,' he said. He took her hands in his. 'Pepper, all I'm saying is, we've got to do things properly. What's the line from *Spiderman*? "With great power comes great responsibility." Well from now on, that's going to be our motto.'

Pepper smiled. 'You're dead serious about this, aren't you?' she said. 'All right, we've got a deal. But I really do have to go.' She kissed him, then turned and headed for the french windows. 'I'll see you tomorrow,' she told him. 'And don't worry, I'll text you first.'

'Oh, you don't have to do that. I was just being ratty.'

She smiled and stepped out into the sunshine. Zach walked to the french windows and watched as she strolled to the gate. She waved once and then headed off along the lane.

A powerful feeling of apprehension overtook him. For the first time, it hit him how he'd feel if he didn't have Pepper in his world. They were a team now. He thought about Granddad Alistair and how he must have felt when Grandma Mary went missing. It must have been awful for him, stuck out here, all alone. For a moment, Zach felt like running after Pepper and telling her to be careful out there. But it was a bright summer's day, the sun streaming down like honey and the garden looked the most tranquil place on earth. He turned and walked back to the house, wondering how he was going to pass the hours till Dad got home.

The Volkswagen pulled into the drive a little after six o clock. Zach had been watching a nature documentary. It was about dolphins, but something about the great wallowing shapes drifting silently about in the water was making him feel uneasy, so he was glad of the interruption. He switched off the TV and walked to the french windows. It was still sunny out in the garden.

Dad got out of the car and trudged towards the house, carrying the leather briefcase. He looked tired, Zach thought and a little rumpled. No wonder, after the day he'd had.

Zach concentrated and the microwave pinged into life. The lasagne he'd put together earlier just needed a few minutes. He'd taken a lot of trouble with it, using one of mum's old recipe books to guide him through the process. It probably wouldn't be the nicest lasagne ever made, but he thought it looked OK.

'Hey, Sport,' said Dad. 'You all right?'

'I'm good,' Zach told him. 'You sit down and relax, dinner will be ready in a few minutes.'

Dad stared at him open-mouthed for a moment, then turned his head to look at the microwave. 'Seriously?' he murmured.

'Don't worry,' Zach told him. 'It's a proper meal. I

didn't know exactly when you'd be home, so I'm just warming it up a bit.'

Dad grinned. 'Be careful, I could get used to this,' he said. He took off his jacket and hung it over the back of a chair. 'What are we having?'

'Lasagne. The same recipe Mum used to make. You want a beer?'

'I'd love one.' Dad looked around. 'No Pepper?' he asked.

'It's on the table, with the salt,' joked Zach, then added: 'She went shopping with her mum.' He got a can of lager from the fridge and brought it to the table. Dad sat down, popped the ring pull and took a long swig.

'That's just what the doctor ordered,' he said.

'How's Cheryl?' asked Zach, trying not to look guilty.

'I gave her the afternoon off,' said Dad. 'I offered to pay for a new dress, but she said there was no need. I've ordered a bunch of flowers to be sent. It felt like the least I could do.' He shook his head. 'Christ, Zach, what a disaster! Everything that could go wrong, went wrong. I tell you what, I don't think she'll be in a great hurry to visit our place again.'

Zach sat opposite Dad. 'I'm really sorry,' he said.

Dad looked puzzled. 'Don't be,' he said. 'It's hardly your fault, is it?'

'No,' said Zach, a little too quickly. 'Of course not.'

Dad thought for a moment. 'The bathroom?' he asked.

'Me and Pepper cleaned it up. I think it's OK now.'

'Thanks, Zach. I really appreciate that. Couldn't have been a pleasant job mopping up in there. God knows what happened, it looked like the aftermath of the Titanic. I'll need to get somebody out to have a look at that system, I've never heard of a toilet doing anything like that. Poor Cheryl, she came out of there looking like a drowned rat. Her dress…' Dad's face contorted and for a shocking moment, Zach thought he was going to burst into tears. But then it dawned on him. Dad was actually trying not to laugh. 'Oh God, Zach, poor Cheryl! She's always so fastidious… and she was… she was covered in…' Now he couldn't hold it any longer. He burst out laughing. 'What a series of disasters!' he chortled. 'First the heel of her fancy shoe…'

'Dad, it's not funny.'

'Then that business with the fingernail! I thought it couldn't get any worse, but the coffee…' He waved a finger at his own shirt as if to indicate a stain on it.

'Dad, stop!"

'And finally… finally…' That was it. Dad threw back his head and roared. 'Did you *ever* see anything so embarrassing in your life?'

Zach was dismayed. 'But Dad, you fancy her and…'

Dad stopped laughing suddenly. He stared at Zach.

'What?' he cried.

'Pepper was saying how she'd probably be my stepmum and you brought her round here and now she won't ever want to come here again and it's probably ruined everything.'

Dad's eyes widened. 'Oh Zach, you didn't really think... Me and Cheryl?'

'Well, yeah, I...'

'Son, you couldn't be further off the mark. Cheryl is just someone from the office. I mean we're friendly and everything, but... she's got a serious boyfriend. They're engaged to be married.'

'Oh.' Zach felt rather stupid. 'Oh, I thought...'

Dad was shaking his head. 'Trust me, there was never any thought of...' He laughed again. 'Me and *Cheryl*?' He looked suddenly very serious. 'Zach, there was only ever one woman for me and believe me, she was a very tough act to follow. I mean, I'm not saying there won't *ever* be somebody else, who knows what's around the corner? But right now, I'd rather be on my own.' He looked awkward. 'Well, not on my own, obviously. The two of us. That suits me fine.'

They sat there looking at each other in silence for a moment. Then the microwave pinged, making Zach jump. He got up from his chair and went over to it. He grabbed the oven gloves, opened the door and took out the serving dish. The lasagne was bubbling enticingly and actually looked edible. He carried it over and set it down on a tablemat.

'Wow,' said Dad. 'This looks great. We'll have you on *Masterchef* yet.'

Zach went back to the cupboards and brought plates, cutlery and a serving spoon to the table. He set a plate down in front of Dad.

'I feel like an idiot,' he said.

'Don't,' Dad assured him. 'It's funny, that's all. The main reason I brought Cheryl back here, was… well, I know it sounds corny, but I wanted her to meet you. I wanted her to see what a great son I have. It just didn't quite go according to plan.'

Zach sat down again. 'Help yourself,' he suggested.

'I will, thanks.' Dad picked up the serving spoon and heaped a generous portion onto his plate. 'Just the way your mum used to make it,' he observed. 'You've got hidden talents.'

'What do you mean?' asked Zach, suspiciously.

'I mean you've obviously been hiding your light under a bushel. This is Jamie Oliver stuff.'

'It's only lasagne,' said Zach, but he couldn't deny that he felt proud of what he'd done. He filled his own plate and they began to eat.

'It's delicious,' Dad told him.

'Yeah, not too bad, eh?'

'Actually, Zach, I need to have a talk with you about something.'

'Oh yeah?'

'Yes. I have to go away this weekend.'

'Away?'

'Yes. There's this big conference in Glasgow. All the major agencies will be there and it's a great opportunity to pick up more business. Oh, by the way, they're giving me a new motor. A company car, a BMW.'

'Wow!'

'I know. I'm picking it up tomorrow. Well, it's important to make the right impression, I suppose. It's just as well, because I'm not entirely sure the Volkswagen would have made it as far as Glasgow.' He chuckled. 'It's been a decent car and everything, but I think it's had its day.'

'Will you trade it in?' asked Zach.

Dad shook his head. 'I'll sell it for scrap,' he said. 'That's all it's good for now.' He frowned. 'Look, Zach, if there was somebody else I could send on this trip, I would, but… well, Gerry was booked to go and obviously, now I'm the MD of the company, it really should be me. I've been trying to decide what to do for the best regarding you. I suppose you could come with me, but that way you'll be sitting around in a hotel all day, bored out of your mind. At least here, you've got your computer games and whatever… and I think you're responsible enough now to look after things.'

Zach nodded. 'Yeah, no problem,' he said.

'What I thought I'd do is leave you Cheryl's number.'

Zach looked at him doubtfully. 'Cheryl?' he said.

'Yeah, don't worry, I've OK'd it with her. If there's any problem, anything at all, you'd just need to ring her and she could be here in ten minutes. She only lives down the road.' He thought for a moment and smiled. 'She'll probably turn up wearing a waterproof suit, mind, but she said she'd be perfectly happy to come if you need her.'

'There won't be a problem,' Zach assured him. 'I'll be fine.'

'And if you want Pepper to come over and keep you company... provided she can square it with her parents, I'd trust you to... you know, be sensible. Not take any risks.'

Zach felt his face colouring. 'Dad,' he said. 'Leave it out.'

"Well, the offer's there. Have a think about it. We've a couple of days before I go. The point is, Zach, you've had to do a lot of growing up over the past year and I know it hasn't been easy for you. So, I suppose what I'm saying is, I'm proud of how you've handled things and I trust you to act sensibly.'

'Thanks,' said Zach, feeling guiltier than ever.

'Oh, and one other thing.'

'Yeah?'

'You know you've done it now, don't you?'

'Done what?'

'Well, now I know you can make food *this* good,' He pointed at his plate. 'then I'm afraid I'm going to have to put you on permanent cooking duty.'

'Yeah, in your dreams,' laughed Zach.

But he had to agree, it *was* pretty good lasagne.

NINETEEN

HOP TOAD

Zach woke once again in the small hours of the morning. He sighed. This was getting to be a habit. He lay there for a moment, blinking himself fully awake, then sat up in bed and looked cautiously around, dreading the thought that Granddad Alistair might be paying him another nocturnal visit. He was relieved to see that there was nobody sitting on the end of his bed. But something had woken him. What?

A sound.

He listened for a moment and there it was again – a soft squelching noise, coming from over by the door. And all at once the feeling of relief evaporated. He turned his head to look. A soft wash of moonlight was coming in through a gap in the door, which hadn't been closed properly. Something was moving through the gap, something small and wet, moving in a series of jerky hops. Terror flooded through Zach's veins and for a moment he was frozen in place, unable to move a muscle. The thing kept coming, advancing into the room, moving as if with a sense of purpose and Zach was finally galvanised into motion.

He flung out an arm, meaning to switch on his bedside light but fear had made him clumsy and, in his haste, he managed to knock the lamp off the edge of the cabinet onto the carpeted floor. He cringed, imagining Dad being woken by the sound, coming to investigate, but there was no time to worry about that. After a moment's hesitation Zach grabbed his mobile instead, activated the torch app and sent a beam of white light straight onto the creature. It paused for an instant, blinking, its wide mouth opened in a kind of grimace. Close up, it did resemble a toad, its permanently wet skin covered with a myriad warty lumps. Its translucent body was dark on top, graduating to a smooth white swollen belly, flecked with darker spots. The limbs looked somehow floppy and useless, as though they had never properly developed. The creature's snakelike eyes stared back into the glare of the torch for a moment, then swivelled aside, fixing their gaze on the wardrobe, as though the creature could sense what was hidden in there.

Now it turned sideways and began to hop towards the wardrobe doors, which Zach noticed, had been left slightly open, emitting the faintest trace of a green glow. Zach cursed himself for being careless and wondered how the creature had got into the house in the first place. He remembered that he and Dad has sat up chatting till well after dark and that the french windows had been wide open the whole time. Zach wondered if this was the only creature that had found its way inside. He really hoped so.

Well, he told himself, this was bad and he needed to sort it out, as quickly and as quietly as possible. He marshalled his energy and concentrated on the creature, imagining it simply rolling over and dying.

Nothing happened. The creature kept moving, intent on its goal.

Puzzled, Zach tried again. This time, he extended a hand toward the creature and pictured it lifting into the air and smacking hard against the nearest wall, but again, the thought had no effect whatsoever. He stifled a curse. Did this mean the creatures were immune to his powers? But why? He thought for a moment. Was it because they derived their power from the same source as he did? The stone?

Now the creature had reached the wardrobe and was scrabbling frantically at the open entrance, trying to squeeze its bloated body through the narrow gap, clearly desperate to get to the stone. Zach took a deep breath. He threw back the covers and jumped out of bed, looking wildly around the room for some kind of weapon. His gaze came to rest on an ancient hockey stick, standing in one corner. Zach had played the game at school for a year or so, had been considered quite good at it before other interests took over, but he'd never quite got around to getting rid of the stick. He crossed the room in a few steps, grabbed the weapon and turned back, just in time to see the toad-thing push its rubbery body through the gap in the door and disappear inside the wardrobe.

'Oh great,' muttered Zach. He walked to the wardrobe,

keeping as far away from it as possible and extended the hockey stick to slide the door fully open. He couldn't see anything in there, so he moved back to the bed and grabbed the mobile, the torch still switched on. He moved cautiously back to the wardrobe and directed the light into its interior, the harsh glare revealing a jumble of clothing, bags, books and other bits and pieces. Then he found what he was looking for in one corner.

He stared, open-mouthed. The creature had located the cloth-wrapped stone and was pushed up against it, its body flattened out, its stumpy legs extended as though it was trying to cover as much of the stone as possible. And it was changing. As Zach watched, horrified, the creature was swelling up like some obscene balloon, its lumpy flesh expanding, doubling in size in just a few moments. Desperate to stop the transformation, Zach leaned into the wardrobe and jabbed the thing's warty back hard with the end of the hockey stick.

The effect was dramatic. The creature's head twisted around, its open mouth issuing a kind of venomous hiss, its eyes bulging in anger. Zach took a step back in surprise and that was when the creature somehow launched itself off the stone like a slimy missile, zooming out of the wardrobe and straight at Zach's chest. It hit him hard, the impact making him gasp and almost knocking him off his feet. He dropped the mobile, lifted his left hand to try and claw the thing away from him, feeling its viscous, undulating form under his fingers. He managed to slide them under its belly and with an effort, ripped the creature from his pyjama top, aware of its horrible wetness as he pushed it away. It fell to the carpet and flopped off into shadow. Zach looked frantically this way and that, but for the moment, he'd had lost sight of his quarry. He saw the mobile lying on the floor a short distance away, its light uselessly illuminating the area at the foot of the bed. He hurried over and stooped to pick up the torch...

And it came at him again, shooting out from the darkness under the bed, lunging this time for his unprotected face. He had a brief vision of its open mouth and its wild staring eyes and then its repulsive body thwacked against his right cheek. Again, he dropped the torch and, with a grunt of revulsion, tried to claw the thing free with his left hand, but instinct had made him hang on to the hockey stick and as he pushed the creature away and it fell for a second time, he lashed out wildly with the stick. More by chance than design the head of the stick connected with its body, making a dull squelching sound. It dropped to the carpet, rolled over a couple of times, then frantically twisted around onto its legs and started scrambling back towards the wardrobe. Zach realised that it wanted to replenish itself by touching the stone again, but when he found the torch and shone the beam onto the creature, he could see that it was badly injured, its back legs dragging uselessly behind it in a long trail of slime.

Zach steeled himself. He angled the torch on the carpet so it would illuminate the creature, then stepped quickly towards it and, lifting the hockey stick with both hands, he brought it down with all his force. The

194

creature burst open like a watermelon, spilling its guts all over the carpet. Its front legs gave a last convulsive quiver and then it lay still.

Zach tried not to heave. He turned away and stood for a moment, breathing heavily, listening for any movement from Dad's room, but there was nothing. He went and sat on his bed, staring at the splattered remains on the carpet and tried to make some sense of what had just happened.

OK, so he couldn't affect these things with his mind, like he could with just about anything else he wanted to and that was puzzling, but he had at least proved that they could be vanquished with good old-fashioned brute force. Nevertheless, it was worrying. One of them had got into the house. From now on, he was going to have to be much more careful about those french windows.

When he felt calm enough, he went about the gruesome task of disposing of the creature's broken body. This necessitated a trip down to the kitchen. Realising that he couldn't help but make a lot of noise doing this, he concentrated and imagined Dad sleeping too soundly to be woken. Then he went downstairs, switched on the light and got the mop and bucket which he filled at the sink with hot water and disinfectant. He put on some rubber gloves and pulled a roll of bin bags from under the sink, then headed back upstairs to his room. Kneeling beside the creature's splattered remains, he eased them gingerly into a bin bag with his gloved hands, his nostrils twitching as the fishy smell they exuded. He tied the top of the bag in a tight knot, just in case the thing had the power to regenerate and then, to make doubly sure, he put the first bag into a second one and secured that too.

Now he immersed the mop in the hot water, squeezed it out and scrubbed frantically at the stained carpet until it was as clean as he could get it. He also wiped the end of the hockey stick free of blood before putting it back in its usual place. As a final measure, he lifted the table lamp and set it back on his bedside cabinet.

He looked around. Everything appeared normal again. He lifted the mop and bucket and the black bin bag and went out of the room and back down the stairs. He emptied the bucket and put it back in its place, then deposited the bag that held the creature's body at the very bottom of the litterbin, even going as far as rearranging other items of rubbish on top of it. Finally, he stripped off the rubber gloves and dropped them into the trash too. He looked quickly around and decided that he had done as much as he possibly could. He went to the door and switched off the light.

He was about to go back up to his room, but something stopped him. Sounds. Soft squelching sounds from over by the french windows. He walked slowly back to them, staring in mute disbelief. Switching the light off had revealed the lawn, covered with the creatures, hopping frantically around in the moonlight. There was a thick fringe of them pressed against the bottom of the glass, their white speckled stomachs inflating and deflating as they clambered over each other in their frantic haste to get inside the house.

And he finally understood why Granddad Alistair had installed the metal shutters. Zach actually considered going out there and pulling them down, but decided against it. By the time he'd got them closed, there'd be dozens of them in the kitchen, all intent on one thing. Getting to the stone. No, he would simply have to go back to his room and hope against hope that they wouldn't be able to break through the glass…

Not surprisingly he didn't get any sleep that night. It wasn't until the dawn was up, when the rising sun had driven the creatures back to their holes, that he finally managed to drift away…

TWENTY

WAKE UP CALL

Zach opened his eyes to the sound of his mobile buzzing urgently on the bedside cabinet. He found himself stretched, fully clothed on his bed. Sunlight was coming through the gaps in the curtains. He groaned, reached for the phone and answered it.

'Yeah?' he grunted.

'Hey, where are you?' It was Pepper's voice, sounding impatient.

'Uh… I'm in my room. Where are *you*?'

'I'm at the front door! I've been ringing the bell for the last, like, ten minutes. OMG, were you *asleep*?'

'Yeah. I had a rough night. Hang on, I'll come down and let you in. Go around the back…' He swung himself off the bed and paused for a moment to examine the carpet that he'd cleaned last night. Apart from a damp patch and the faint smell of pine disinfectant, there was no sign that anything untoward had happened here, which he told himself, was something to be grateful for. He headed for the door, went out onto the landing and then stopped in

198

his tracks, realising that something didn't feel quite right.

He looked down the landing and saw that Dad's bedroom door was closed, which was odd because he usually left it open when he went to work...

Now Zach experienced a sudden rush of panic. He remembered how, last night, when he'd wanted to clean up the kitchen, he'd pictured Dad fast asleep, so there'd be no danger of waking him up. The trouble was, Zach had forgotten all about him after that. Surely Dad wasn't still...? He walked to Dad's door and tapped on it, but got no response.

'Dad?' He pushed the door open and stepped into the room. His worst fears were instantly confirmed. Dad lay fast asleep in bed, his head on the pillow, his eyes shut, his mouth slightly open as he snored contentedly. Beside him, on the bedside cabinet, the digital alarm clock revealed that it was eleven fifteen. Zach winced, knowing how Dad always liked to be at work before everyone else.

He walked over to the bed and pictured Dad waking up. Dad stirred but didn't open his eyes, so Zach reached out and shook him gently. He sighed, opened his eyes, smiled up at Zach. 'Hey,' he said, calmly. 'Everything OK?'

'Erm... I think... maybe you might want to get to work?' Zach told him.

'Work?' Dad turned his head sideways to look at the clock. He gazed at it for a few moments, as though trying to figure it out. Then, with an oath, he was kicking the duvet aside and scrambling up in a total panic. 'Zach, for Christ's sake, why didn't you wake me? I must have slept through the alarm!'

'Sorry, Dad, I only just woke up myself…'

'It's eleven fifteen! I was supposed to be taking a meeting at nine o clock!'

'Er… I didn't sleep much last night, so…'

Dad didn't wait to listen to any more explanations. He headed straight to the bathroom, slamming the door behind him. 'I'll make some coffee,' Zach shouted after him, but got no reply. He went out onto the landing and down the stairs. Walking into the kitchen, he saw Pepper standing on the patio, staring puzzled at a thick band of slime that covered the bottom foot of the glass doors. Zach unlatched the bolts and slid the door open.

'What's all this gook?' asked Pepper, pointing.

'We had visitors last night,' Zach told her. He went to the sink, opened the cupboard beneath it and pulled out a spray bottle of Flash and a cloth. He went back outside to Pepper and slid the glass door shut again.

'And good morning to you,' said Pepper.

He ignored her. He dropped to his knees, sprayed the affected area and started scrubbing the glass clean, before Dad could get a look at it.

Pepper watched him in silence for a moment. 'The toad-things?' she asked, after a while.

Zach nodded. 'They came out last night,' he said, jerking a thumb over his shoulder at the garden. 'Big time.'

Pepper turned to look and then took a sharp intake of breath. 'OMG,' she murmured.

Zach stopped scrubbing and turned his own head to look. He cursed softly. He hadn't realised the extent of the damage.

The lawn was covered with heaps of soil. Zach started counting but gave up when he got to twenty. 'I had no idea,' he murmured. He finished wiping the glass and got to his feet. 'One of them got inside,' he told Pepper in a hushed voice, afraid that Dad might somehow overhear.

'What do you mean?' she asked.

'What do you *think* I mean? It was in my bedroom.'

Pepper grimaced. 'How did it get up there?' she gasped.

'I don't know how it got there. Perhaps it came up on an escalator! All I know is it was *there*. I had to kill it.'

She nodded, seemingly unperturbed. 'Did it give you much trouble?' she asked, calmly.

He stared at her for a moment. 'Yes, it gave me some trouble,' he said. 'Pepper, I have to tell you something and I want you to listen carefully. Our powers don't work on those things. You got that? Not at all. I tried, but it just… had no effect. I had to go old school on that thing.'

'Meaning?'

'I whacked it with a hockey stick. Made a horrible mess…'

Pepper pulled a face. 'That doesn't sound pleasant,' she observed.

He grabbed her wrist. 'It wasn't. But, the thing is Pepper, the toad-thing had got to the stone. It was kind of hugging it and… and then it started to grow.'

'The stone?'

'No, not the bloody stone! The toad-thing!'

'It grew?'

'Yeah, it swelled up. Really quickly. Doubled in size. Like a… like a balloon or something.'

'Whoah! Well, we'd better keep them away from the stone, then.'

He glared at her. 'Is that all you've got to say?' he asked her. She looked back at him in silence for a moment, her expression blank and he made a tutting sound and went back inside. 'I need to make Dad some coffee,' he said.

'Your *dad*?' Pepper followed him into the kitchen. 'How come he's still here? Shouldn't he be at work?'

'He overslept.' Zach dumped the bottle of spray on the worktop and switched on the kettle. He didn't feel inclined to explain any more than that. He wanted Pepper to advise him what to do about the toad-things and she wasn't being much use in that department. He pulled mugs out of the cabinet. 'You want coffee?' he asked her.

'I'll have a cup of tea,' she said. She watched as he busied himself making the drinks, noticing, no doubt, his unsteady hands. 'You seem a bit freaked out,' she observed.

'Oh, do you think so?' He laughed manically. 'Yeah, tell you the truth, I am a little bit shaky this morning.' He paused, lowered his voice. 'I had one of those things in my room, last night. I woke up and it was there, hopping around like a… like a…' He couldn't think of an apt description, so he abandoned the idea. 'It was horrible, Pepper. And then when the usual powers didn't work on it, I panicked. I had to really belt it with the stick.'

'That can't have been easy.'

'It wasn't. I'm… beginning to think I should tell Dad.'

'Tell me what?' asked Dad as he bustled into the room, after what must have been the fastest shower in history

Zach looked at him in dismay

'Er…. I need to tell you that…'

'That moles have been at the lawn in the night,' finished Pepper, pointing through the french windows.

Dad went over to them and stared out. 'Wow,' he said. 'It wasn't like that yesterday!'

'No, the moles are terrible round here,' said Pepper, slipping into the lie easily. 'My mum and dad had the same problem.'

'Did they manage to sort it?' asked Dad, going back to the counter and grabbing one of the coffee mugs.

'Yeah,' said Zach, remembering something Granddad Alistair had told him. 'They got their own back on those moles. Buried them alive.'

Both Dad and Pepper stared at him blankly.

'Joke,' he muttered.

'Don't give up the day job,' Dad advised him. He

gulped hot coffee. 'I suppose I'd better phone around, see if I can get somebody over to sort it.'

'Don't worry about that, Mr Hamilton, my dad knows a man who does it for a living,' said Pepper. 'Everyone says he's the best. I'll get his phone number, if you like.'

'That would be really useful, thanks.'

Zach marvelled at Pepper's ease. Now he was unsure if she was making it all up or she actually *did* know somebody who could get rid of moles. 'You want some toast?' he asked.

Dad shook his head. 'It'll be lunch by the time I get to work,' he said. 'I don't understand why Cheryl didn't ring me, when I didn't turn up this morning.' He pulled his mobile from his pocket and checked the screen. 'Oh,' he said. 'She *did* ring me. Three times. And left two messages.'

'Must have been on silent,' suggested Pepper.

Dad shook his head. 'No, it wasn't. I *never* leave it on silent, too paranoid about missing calls. It's weird. I haven't slept through the alarm since I was a teenager.' He went and grabbed his jacket from the back of the dining chair where he'd left it the night before and slipped it on. 'I'll have to get going,' he said. 'Got to pick up the new motor this afternoon.' He glanced at Zach. 'Did you ask Pepper? About the weekend?'

'Dad, she only just got here,' protested Zach.

'What about the weekend?' asked Pepper.

'Dad's got to go off on this jolly to Glasgow…'

'It's not a *jolly*,' Dad corrected him. 'It's a conference. There's a difference.'

'Yeah, whatever. Anyway, he's going to be away all weekend and he thought that you might like to come over and keep me company?'

'Only if it's OK with your parents,' added Dad, collecting his briefcase.

'Oh, don't worry about *them*,' said Pepper dismissively.

Zach fixed her with a look. 'Pepper,' he murmured.

'I mean, I'm sure they won't mind,' said Pepper hastily. 'They're… quite open-minded, really.'

Zach raised his eyebrows. From what he'd heard, open-minded was the last thing they were. Particularly her father.

'Right, well, I'd better get going,' said Dad. 'Zach, if you want to say goodbye to the old car, here's your last chance.'

Zach shook his head. 'Nah,' he said. 'I'd rather say hello to the new one.'

'Suit yourself.' Dad went out of the french windows and across the drive to the Volkswagen. Then they heard him shout. 'Jesus! What's all this slime on my windscreen?'

Zach groaned. He grabbed the spray and a cloth and ran out to clean it off. Dad was standing there looking at the screen in dismay.

'What is it?' he asked, tracing an index finger through the congealing sludge.

'Birds, I expect,' said Zach. He directed a liberal spray of cleaning fluid onto the windscreen and started wiping furiously.

205

'What bird could make a mess like that?' asked Dad. He held up his glistening finger for inspection.

'Seagulls,' said Pepper, approaching the car, her expression calm. 'They eat all the leftover muck from the kebab house on the esplanade and it gives them the runs. My Dad's always getting that stuff on his car.' Dad regarded his finger with a grimace and Zach handed him the cloth, so he could wipe it clean.

'That's disgusting,' said Dad. He took one last look at the ruined lawn and shook his head. Then he handed the cloth to Zach, got into the car and drove away, sounding his horn as he went.

Zach and Pepper stood watching as the car motored up the lane beyond.

'God, you're a good liar,' observed Zach.

'Thanks,' said Pepper. 'I do my best.'

He turned to look at her. 'What are we going to do?' he asked her. 'Last night was just the start. It's only going to get worse.'

'You don't know that,' she told him.

'But I do. Granddad Alistair told me it would.'

'In a dream,' Pepper reminded him.

'I keep telling you, I don't think it *was* a dream! We might have to accept it, Pepper. Maybe we need to put the stone back where I found it.'

She sighed. 'Look, before you make your mind up about that, there's something I want you to see.'

'What's that?' murmured Zach, suspiciously.

'I want you to come home with me,' she said.

He studied her. Something didn't seem to make

sense here. 'Really?' he murmured.

She nodded. 'I want you to meet my mum and dad.'

TWENTY-ONE

MEET THE PARENTS

Pepper didn't want to go home straight away, so the two of them killed time playing computer games, soaking up some rays from the stone and generally wasting time, something they were both very good at. Finally, around four thirty, Pepper announced that it was time to go. They locked up the house and wandered down the hill to Portknockie. It was five thirty by the time they got to Pepper's place, a semi-detached house on a small estate that bordered the village. The exterior walls of the house had been pebble-dashed at some point back in time and might have looked nice when freshly painted, but now the original white exterior had faded to a drab, patchy grey and there were large areas where the pebbles had fallen out completely, giving the place an oddly mangy appearance. The paint-blistered black front door opened directly onto the pavement, but Pepper led Zach down a narrow ginnel at the side of the house and opened a gate onto a small yard. Clustered along the length of a brick wall were a line of stone pots, each one filled with brightly-coloured flowers and shrubs. Zach noticed that they were the only burst of colour in the yard; everything else was rendered in washed-out shades of grey.

'Mum's pride and joy,' said Pepper as she walked past the flowerpots. The back door stood open and a powerful smell of cabbage and potato spilled out onto the warm air. A woman was standing at the stove, stirring something in a pot, but she turned when she heard footsteps approaching. She was a small, thickset woman with a kindly, ruddy face and a thatch of tightly coiled brunette curls. The weird thing was, she kind of looked like Pepper but at the same time, Zach thought, nothing like her. Her pale blue eyes moved from Pepper to Zach and her smile wavered a little.

'Who's this then?' she asked, trying to appear friendly, but sounding decidedly nervous about something.

'This is Zach,' said Pepper. 'My friend.' She paused, looked pointedly at her mother and added, 'My *boy* friend.'

Mrs Murray sniffed. 'Pleased to meet you, I'm sure,' she said.

'Hello, Mrs Murray,' said Zach, trying to be jovial. 'How are you?' He held out a hand to shake and she took it, moved it half-heartedly up and down.

'You don't sound like a local boy,' she observed.

'He's not,' said Pepper, seeming to relish the fact. 'He's from that London, aren't you Zach?'

'Is he now?' Mrs Murray forced a polite smile. 'Can I offer you a cup of tea?' she asked.

'I'd rather have a coffee, if you don't mind.'

Mrs Murray's outraged expression suggested that he'd just asked for a glass of champagne. 'I'm afraid we don't keep coffee in the house,' she said, as though it was some kind of banned substance.

'Sure we do,' said Pepper, smiling. 'There's a jar in the drinks cupboard.'

'I don't think so, dear,' said Mrs Murray.

'Go and look,' suggested Pepper, quietly. Her mother shook her head but she turned obediently away and opened a cupboard. There, right at the front, was a brand new jar of Nescafe. She took it out, staring at it. 'I'm sure that wasn't there the last time I looked,' she said. She turned back to Zach. 'How do you take it?' she asked him.

'Milk, two sugars,' he said. 'Thanks.'

'Why don't you two go and sit in the lounge?' suggested Mrs Murray. 'I'll bring your drinks through on a tray.' She looked sharply at Pepper. 'Perhaps Zach shouldn't hang around too long,' she warned her. 'Your father will be home from work any minute.'

'I know,' said Pepper. 'I'd kind of like Zach to meet him.'

'Oh, would you, dear?' said Mrs Murray and she looked worried. 'Is that a good idea?'

Zach followed Pepper through an open doorway into a gloomy little sitting room and the two of them dropped onto a saggy, olive green sofa. 'What's going on?' whispered Zach.

'Nothing,' Pepper assured him. 'I just thought it was time you met my mum and dad. That's why I waited

210

till now. I wanted to be sure Dad would be back from work. You wouldn't get the full experience without him. That's OK, isn't it?'

'I suppose.' Zach looked around the room. It was dingy, papered in what looked like a faded chintz design and the small space was cluttered with various fripperies – little china figurines of animals wearing waistcoats and top hats, tiny fairy tale buildings made of resin. Over the fireplace hung a decorative plaque with a couplet printed on it.

I COMPLAINED BECAUSE I HAD NO SHOES
UNTIL I MET A MAN WHO HAD NO LEGS

There was a wooden mantelpiece above a two bar electric fire and it was littered with miniature picture frames containing images of grimacing babies and black and white photographs of elderly people at weddings.

'Who's that?' asked Zach, pointing to one of them, trying to make conversation.

Pepper shrugged. 'Who cares?' she replied.

He stared at her. 'What's wrong with you?' he whispered. 'You're being really weird.'

Mrs Murray came into the room, carrying a tray in front of her. For some reason Zach had been expecting a plate of biscuits, but there were just two mugs, one printed with the words HOME SWEET HOME, the other featuring a photograph of a kitten playing with a ball of wool. 'Thanks,' said Zach and took the coffee

211

from the tray. He sipped it and made an exaggerated display of finding it to his liking. 'Lovely,' he said.

Mrs Murray stood there for a moment, the empty tray tucked under one arm. She seemed to be waiting anxiously for something. 'Clive will be home soon,' she said and the way she spoke made it somehow sound like a threat. Now her evident nervousness was beginning to get to Zach.

'Where does... Mr Murray work?' he asked, trying to make conversation.

'At the harbour, dear. He's the harbour master. He's been there for fifteen years or more. Tells everyone what to do.'

'Just like at home,' muttered Pepper and Mrs Murray gave her a sharp look, as though warning her not to start anything. Zach tried to think of something else to say.

'So, er... how did you enjoy your shopping trip yesterday?' he asked, his voice sounding somehow too loud in the quiet room.

Mrs Murray looked startled by the comment and she looked accusingly at Pepper.

'I told him about it,' said Pepper.

'Oh. Well, it was er... very pleasant,' said Mrs Murray. 'Yes, it was... nice to spend some time together. Just me and Dorothy.'

Zach stared at her, puzzled. 'Dorothy?' he echoed.

'Yes. Oh, I know she likes to be called Pepper but, well... that's not a name, is it? That's something you sprinkle on your dinner.'

212

Zach couldn't help throwing an amused smirk at Pepper, and she responded with a look that warned him not to push it. 'Well, well,' he murmured. 'Dorothy. Who knew?'

'It's a lovely name, isn't it, Zach? A nice old-fashioned name. I've no idea why she hates it so much.' She seemed to consider for a moment. 'Is Zach short for something? Zachary? Or Zachariah, perhaps?'

'No. It's just Zach.'

'Is that what it says on your birth certificate?'

'Yeah... at least, I *think* so. I don't remember ever seeing it. Not even sure if I've *got* one.'

'Don't be daft. Everyone has a birth certificate. It's the law.'

'Mum won some money when we went shopping,' said Pepper, brightly, as though trying to change the subject. 'Didn't you, Mum?'

'Oh, well... we don't have to go telling *everyone*, dear,' said Mrs Murray, looking anxious again.

'Why not? What do you think Zach's going to do? Creep round here in the middle of the night and steal it?'

'No, of course not!'

'Then tell him how much you won.'

'Well, I'd rather...'

'Go on.' She looked at Zach. 'You won't tell anyone, will you, Zach?

Zach shook his head.

Mrs Murray seemed a little happier but she still looked from side-to-side as if assuring herself that there was nobody to overhear what she said next. 'I won three hundred pounds,' she whispered. 'I still can't quite believe it. First time I've ever had a go on those things.'

Zach glanced at Pepper and raised his eyebrows. '*Three* hundred?' he murmured.

'Got a bit carried away,' she admitted.

'Oh, well… that's great,' said Zach. 'What are you going to spend it on?'

'I haven't thought about that,' said Mrs Murray. 'A holiday would be nice, I suppose. We don't really go away much.'

'We n*ever* go away,' Pepper corrected her, flatly. She looked at Zach. 'Of course, she hasn't told Dad yet. About the money.'

'I *will* tell him, dear,' said Mrs Murray. 'I just have to think of a story to explain how I came by it.'

Now Zach was mystified. 'But you just said you…'

'Dad doesn't approve of amusement arcades,' explained Pepper. 'He never goes in them and he doesn't think we should, either.'

'I see.' Zach was beginning to feel more and more uncomfortable with this visit. 'Well, er… can't you say you won it on something else?'

'Clive doesn't approve of gambling in any form,' said Mrs Murray, in a tone that suggested she didn't want to discuss the matter any further. Zach took another gulp of his coffee. 'So… er, how long have you lived here?' he asked.

The question hung unanswered on the air as the

front door swung open and a man stepped into the room, a big, square-shouldered man in a white shirt, black trousers and polished black shoes. There were brightly-coloured epaulettes on the shirt and, despite the heat, he wore a black tie and a nautical-style peaked cap. He closed the door behind him and swung around to look at Zach and Pepper sitting on the sofa. He had a big, jowly face and a thick black moustache. When he took off the cap Zach saw that he'd lost most of the hair on the top of his head but the thick tufts around his ears were jet black. He looked at Zach and his expression suggested that he had just caught a bad smell.

'Who's this?' he grunted.

'This is Zach,' said Pepper and once again, Zach could see she was delighting in this moment, as though she'd been anticipating it. Mr Murray glared at Zach for several moments then nodded brusquely, but didn't say anything. He turned back to the door, removed his jacket and hung his cap on a peg. Then he went to an armchair, sat down and carefully unlaced his shoes, which he removed and placed on a shelf under the coffee table, swapping them for a pair of tartan slippers. While he was doing all this, Mrs Murray had scurried into the kitchen and by the time he had got himself comfortable, she was back carrying a huge mug of tea which she offered to him at arm's length. He took it and she stood there watching as her husband took a cautious sip of the contents. There was a long silence and when he nodded his approval, Zach saw her visibly relax.

'How long before dinner?' asked Mr Murray.

'Ten minutes,' she said and hurried back into the kitchen.

Mr Murray studied Zach again, the expression on his face a glum scowl. 'I'd invite you to stay for something to eat but there's only enough for three,' he said, as though he'd actually cooked the food himself and was able to assess the quantities available.

'Oh, that's OK,' said Zach. 'I need to get home to have dinner with my dad anyway.'

'Where's home?' asked Mr Murray gruffly. 'You don't sound like you're from round here.'

'No, no, I'm from London. But my dad's from here. We live in a cottage up on the hill. Maybe you know it? Cliff View.'

Mr Murray smiled. 'Rather you than me,' he said, and Zach almost laughed out loud at the rudeness of it. 'I wouldn't live there if you paid me a hundred thousand pounds.'

'Why's that?' asked Zach.

'That place used to be owned by a bloody lunatic.'

'That would be my granddad,' said Zach, expecting him to be embarrassed, but he only looked gleeful.

'You're a *Hamilton*?' he exclaimed. 'By God, yes, I can see the old man in you, now you mention it!' He took a slurp at his tea. 'Something about the eyes.'

'You knew him?'

'We *all* knew him,' said Mr Murray. 'Couldn't really miss him, what with all that hoo-hah in the papers. Didn't see him often in the flesh, mind. Liked to keep himself to himself, didn't he? Thought he was too good for the likes of us. But then, when the murder happened, you couldn't open a paper without seeing his miserable old face plastered all over it.'

'What *murder*?' protested Zach. 'My Grandma disappeared!'

'Huh. What does that prove? Only that the police never found a body. But they questioned him, I know that much. They must have had their suspicions, mustn't they? And I tell you what, you only needed to talk to him for five minutes to know he had a screw loose.'

Zach felt shocked that somebody would talk about one of his relatives so negatively. Clearly Mr Murray didn't care who he upset.

'Well, I… wouldn't be so sure,' said Zach.

'Did you spend any time with him?' asked Mr Murray.

'Not much. I was only little when he died.'

'So, your old man must be Alistair's son. What was he called? Christopher? Cameron?'

'Charles,' Zach corrected him.

'Ah yeah. He soon cleared off, didn't he? Probably knew his old man was a wrong 'un. Didn't want to stick around and get tarred with the same brush.'

'You can't go saying…'

'That old cottage of his. I bet that's worth a bob or two now, eh?'

Zach shrugged. 'I wouldn't know,' he said.

'It was used by blow-ins, for years…'

'Blow-ins?' echoed Zach.

'He means tourists,' said Pepper, by way of explanation.

'Comin' up here in their fancy cars, prancin' round the shops looking for probiotic yoghurt and wholemeal bread.' He snorted in disgust. 'What's your old man do for a living, then?'

'He works at an advertising agency.'

'Now why does that not surprise me?' Mr Murray made a face. 'I suppose it's what passes for work in this day and age.'

Zach felt his hackles start to rise. 'My dad's the managing director,' he protested.

'Is he now? That must be nice for him.' He transferred his attention to Pepper. 'So, this your boyfriend, is it?' he asked.

'What if he is?' asked Pepper, defiantly.

'Well, let me tell you something, missy, you're too young to be having thoughts about things like that. Come back when you're eighteen and we'll discuss it then.'

Pepper looked at Zach and then back at her father. 'Right,' she said, 'I think that's about enough.' She clicked her fingers and a weird thing happened. Mr Murray froze in his seat, his mouth open to say something else, one finger raised to emphasise a point, the other hand still clutching his mug of steaming tea. Mrs Murray appeared in the open doorway of the kitchen and started to speak. 'Dinner is…' Pepper clicked her fingers a second time and Mrs Murray stopped mid-sentence, her mouth slightly open, her expression blank. Zach looked from her to her husband and back again.

'What have you done to them?' he asked Pepper.

'I've shut them up for a minute,' she said. 'I just wanted you to see what they were like, so you'd understand.'

Zach frowned. 'Understand what?' he muttered.

Pepper looked him in the eyes. 'If we give the stone back, this is what I'll have to look forward to,' she said. She waved a hand to indicate her two frozen parents. 'This,' she repeated, as if to emphasise the point. 'I wanted you to see what it was like for me. How it *feels*.'

'I don't under…'

'No, you don't, do you? And why would you, living out there in that nice cottage with the great big garden? You've got it all, haven't you? A nice dad who likes you, listens to you, helps you out. A decent life. All I've got is this crap house, a dad who shoots his mouth off about anything that comes into his head and a mum who's afraid of her own shadow.' She took Zach's hands in his. 'When you showed me the stone and what it could do… it was like my "get out of jail free" card, my passport to something new, something different. And now you're talking about *giving it back*!'

'Because I'm starting to get a bit scared,' said Zach. 'Look, Pepper, I don't like the idea any more than you do. The stone is the most amazing thing that ever happened to me, but that *creature* that came into the

219

house last night.' He shook his head. 'You saw the state of the lawn, there must be hundreds of them out there and who knows what else? What if they come for us? What if something bad happened to you? I'd never forgive myself.'

'Something bad *is* going to happen to me if you give the stone back,' said Pepper. 'I'll be here with *them*.' She got up from the sofa and walked over to her father. She stood looking down at him in disgust for a moment, then leaned over and spat a big gobbet of saliva into his mug of tea.

'Pepper, don't!' said Zach.

She spun around to glare at him. 'Why not?' she asked him. 'Don't you think he deserves it? Didn't you feel like punching him when he was talking about your granddad like that?'

'Well…'

'I hate him, Zach. I hate him! Sometimes I feel like… like switching him off forever. Then at least my mum could have some kind of life.'

'You can't do that!' protested Zach. 'That would be murder.'

'Yes, but it might be worth it. It really might.'

Zach got up from the sofa and put his arms around her. As he did so, he was uncomfortably aware of Mr Murray's blank expression, only inches away from him. 'You can't think like that,' he told Pepper. 'It'll drive you crazy.'

'I don't care.' She looked pleadingly at him, her eyes filled with tears. 'Please, Zach, I don't want to give the stone back. Not yet, anyway. We've only had it a few days, we haven't really found out what it can *do* for us.'

Zach stood back from her and nodded. 'Look,' he said, 'Dad's going to Glasgow tomorrow. Come over for the weekend and we'll work out some kind of plan, the two of us. OK?'

She nodded, wiped her eyes on her sleeve. 'Sure,' she said.

'Think you'll be able to…?' Zach looked at her frozen parents and laughed. 'Yeah, of course you will,' he said. 'One way or another.' He glanced at his watch. 'I should be heading back,' he said. 'To my fancy cottage with the big garden.'

Pepper winced. 'You know what I mean,' she said. 'Zach?'

'Yeah?'

'I don't want you to think that I don't appreciate *you*.'

He grinned. 'I know, you're only after me for my stone,' he said.

'I'm not!' she insisted. 'It's you, mostly. If you didn't have the stone, you'd still be pretty cool.'

'I bet you say that to…' Zach broke off and wrinkled his nose. He'd just detected a burning smell. He looked at Pepper and then she registered it too. She grabbed his arm and pulled him back to sit on the sofa. Then she clicked her fingers.

'… just about ready,' said Mrs Murray. She paused for a moment and sniffed the air, then gave a squawk and scuttled back into the kitchen.

'I hope I've made myself clear,' said Mr Murray. He

took a big gulp of tea and Zach tried not to grimace.

'Perfectly, daddy dear,' said Pepper, in a posh girl's voice. 'Zach was just going anyway, weren't you, Zach?'

'Er… yes.' Zach got up from the sofa again. 'Nice to meet you, Mr Murray.' He turned his head towards the kitchen. 'Goodbye, Mrs Murray!' he shouted, but there was no reply. From the kitchen came a frantic clattering and scraping as Mrs Murray desperately tried to rescue whatever it was that had burned.

Pepper went to the front door and held it open. 'See you tomorrow,' she whispered. He was going to snatch a quick kiss but was too aware of Mr Murray, sitting there, staring daggers at him, so he contented himself with a nod.

Then he stepped out onto the pavement and started walking home.

TWENTY-TWO

LOOMINGS

Zach wandered slowly homewards in the lengthening shadows of late afternoon, thinking about everything that Pepper had said. He got it, he really did. The stone was this incredible thing that he'd chanced upon and the thought of losing it now was awful. But at the same time, he could only guess at the possible cost of *not* giving it back to the creatures it belonged to. What was it that Granddad Alistair had said?

'There are always others. Just when you think you've got the measure of them, along come the next ones. And they will not stop until they have what belongs to them.' And as if that wasn't ominous enough, Zach had to remind himself that these words had actually been spoken to him by a dead man. Any way you looked at it, it wasn't promising.

The growl of an engine approaching along the road behind him made him move automatically to the grass verge, but he didn't look up until a familiar voice spoke from right beside him, making him jump.

'All right, sport? Want a lift?'

Zach looked up in surprise to see Dad grinning at him from behind the wheel of his new BMW, a sleek, midnight blue convertible. The top was rolled back and Dad was grinning like the cat that got the cream. 'Well? What do you think?' he asked.

'Wow,' said Zach. 'It's fantastic!'

'Isn't it just? Makes the old Volkswagen look like a skip, eh?'

'God, Dad, it must have cost a fortune.'

'Yeah. Well, thankfully I wasn't the one paying for it. That's why they call it a company car. Are you getting in or what?'

Zach opened the passenger door and slipped into the soft brown leather seat. He sat there, looking at the flash walnut dashboard with its built-in Sat Nav system and once again, he reminded himself that it was the stone that had enabled all this. Before Zach had found it, Dad's luck had been at absolute rock bottom. Now he was soaring. If Zach gave the stone back, would it return Dad's career to the doldrums? There was so much at stake here.

'Are you going to belt up?' asked Dad impatiently.

'But I didn't say anyth… oh, right.' Zach slid the seatbelt across his shoulder and clipped it into the lock. Dad put the car into gear and put his foot on the accelerator. The car moved forward with a smooth growl of pent-up power.

'It's the Eco Pro model,' said Dad. 'Really good for the environment.'

'That's nice,' said Zach.

'I told 'em, I wasn't going to have a gas-guzzler. That's not who I am.'

'No,' said Zach, trying not to smile.

'What?' asked Dad, sensing his amusement.

'And you told them you wanted a convertible because… you needed to get plenty of fresh air, I suppose.'

Dad gave a guilty grin. 'I suppose you're right,' he said. 'I was all set to take a hatchback and then I saw this baby in the showroom and…' He shrugged. 'I guess I did push it a bit.' He made an unnecessary right turn. 'Let's go along the esplanade,' he suggested.

'What, so you can show off your new car?'

'Why not? Indulge me, Zach, it's been such a tough year and suddenly… suddenly I'm King Midas.'

'Who?'

'You know, the Greek king? Everything he touched turned to gold? When I think about what's happened in just a few days, well, it's almost too good to be true. It's like my wildest fantasies have been made real. Kind of makes me wonder if I had some help.'

Zach eyed him doubtfully. 'What do you mean?' he asked. 'Help?'

'It makes me think that maybe *Mum* had something to do with this.'

Zach shook his head. 'But you've always said, you don't believe in that stuff. Life after death and everything.'

'I never *used* to. Now, I'm beginning to wonder. What about you, Zach? You were asking me about it

225

the other day and I wasn't very forthcoming. Do you think there's any chance of it?'

Zach had a vivid flashback of Granddad Alistair's pale face, his hollow cheeks, the dark rings under his eyes. 'Maybe,' he said, uneasily. 'But whatever it is, I don't think it's very nice.'

They were entering the outskirts of the village now. They drove down the hill to the beachfront, the expensive car catching admiring glances from the holidaymakers wandering the pavements. Dad turned left to drive along the esplanade. There was the locked amusement arcade, still with the banner, CLOSED FOR REFURBISHMENT, hanging across the front of it. A small group of people were sitting on the low wall outside. Zach recognised the two girls that used to hang out with Pepper and then he saw Cameron, who must have finally worked up the courage to leave his room. Oddly, Beefy was standing with them, his hands in his pockets, a disgruntled expression on his bearded face. As the BMW cruised past, Beefy clocked Zach in the passenger seat and sent a disagreeable scowl in his direction. He said something and Cameron looked up too. Zach smiled and gave him a cheery wave but Cameron, clearly panicked, ducked his head and looked the other way, terrified no doubt that Zach might cause him once again to lose control of his bladder. But Zach wasn't even tempted. He was done with all that nonsense.

'Who was that?' asked Dad.

'Ah, just some kid who hangs around the amusement arcade,' said Zach.

226

Dad looked suddenly rather serious. 'You don't go in there, do you?' he asked. 'Only, I'd rather you didn't.'

'*Nobody* goes in it anymore,' said Zach. 'It's closed down.'

'Yes, but before that.'

Zach shrugged. 'Been in once or twice, you know, when I was bored.'

Dad nodded. 'I heard something at work today,' he said. 'Everyone was talking about it when I got there. The bloke that used to run that place? What did they call him, Gator or something?'

'Tazer,' ventured Zach.

'Yeah, that's the guy. He was found dead in the harbour yesterday.'

Zach felt like he'd been punched hard in the stomach. 'Dead?' he gasped.

'Yeah, apparently. What's up? You've gone white. You weren't a friend of his or anything?'

'Er… no! No, I just saw him at the arcade, one time. He was a bit of a jerk, to be honest. Do they know what happened to him? Was it suicide?'

Dad shook his head. 'Doesn't seem like it. The word on the street is he was connected to some very bad people. He borrowed money to set that place up and when the arcade went bust, he couldn't pay them back… so…' Dad drew his index finger across his throat. 'That's only gossip, you understand. The police are investigating. But Cheryl knows his cousin and she said that he told her that the people he was in debt to were a gang of real hard nuts who…'

Dad kept talking but Zach was no longer listening. He was once again feeling incredibly guilty. OK, so Tazer had been a nasty piece of work, a lowlife. That was indisputable. But it was Zach and Pepper who'd put him out of business. Was that why he was killed? Were they now responsible for his murder?

Dad stopped talking. 'Is something wrong?' he asked. 'You look like you've got the weight of the world resting on your shoulders.'

'Oh, no, I just...' Zach shrugged. He didn't know what to say. 'I'm just tired,' he muttered. It sounded lame, but he couldn't think of a better excuse.

'What were you doing on the lane, anyway?' Dad asked him.

'The lane?'

'Where I picked you up.'

'Oh, I'd just been to meet Pepper's mum and dad.'

Dad made a goofy face. 'Hey, it's clearly more serious than I thought!'

'No, don't be daft! She just wanted me to say hello to them.'

'Well, that's how it starts, Zach. Come home and meet the family. Next thing you know, you're *joining* the family!'

'Leave it out!' snapped Zach.

Dad looked crestfallen. 'Sorry,' he said. 'Only pulling your leg. Sheesh, you're on a hair trigger today!'

'Sorry,'

'So what are they like? Pepper's parents?'

Zach wondered how best to answer that question. What *were* they like exactly? They were messed up, that's what they were. Messed up and weird. The dad in particular was downright unpleasant. But he couldn't say any of that.

'They're OK,' he said. 'Her dad works at the harbour. And her mum,' he didn't really know what to say about Pepper's mum. 'She… doesn't like coffee.'

'That's hardly a crime,' said Dad. They were leaving the village now and heading uphill again. 'Were they all right with Pepper staying for the weekend?'

Zach nodded. 'Er, yeah, they're fine with that,' he said.

'Good. I'll be happier knowing you've got some company,' said Dad. 'I'm going to head off tomorrow around two. See how this baby performs on the motorway.' He patted the steering wheel fondly. 'Obviously, I'll leave you some cash, so you guys can get yourselves a couple of takeaways or whatever. And there are beers in the fridge, you're welcome to have a couple but don't overdo it, all right?'

'Sure, whatever.' Zach couldn't think straight. His head was filled with an image of Tazer, kneeling on the pavement in front of the Arcade and whipping himself frantically with a dog lead. Tazer, who was dead now, probably because of something that Zach and Pepper had done. Where would all this end? People dying, people going missing… Zach thought about Granddad Alistair, who had lost the most important thing in his entire life. Grandma. Was Zach supposed to believe that she'd just wandered off one night? Or had something come up from under the ground and *taken* her?

Dad turned the car onto the narrow lane that led up to the cottage. 'You're worrying me,' he said.

Zach tried not to look guilty. 'What do you mean?' he asked.

'There's something you're not telling me.'

'What makes you say that?'

'I can just tell. I *know* you, Zach. There's something on your mind. What is it? Talk to me. Tell me what's wrong.'

'It's just… it's just…' They drove through the open gateway and Zach could see the dirt-heaped garden ahead of him. He sighed. 'I forgot to ask Pepper for that phone number,' he said. 'You know, the one for the mole catcher?'

Dad laughed. He pulled the BMW to a halt. 'Is that all?' he asked.

'Yeah. But don't worry, I'll text her and ask her to bring it tomorrow.'

'It's too late to do anything before the weekend, anyway.' Dad looked at Zach excitedly and for a moment he was like a kid with a new toy. 'Hey, watch this,' he said. He pressed a button on the dash and the convertible top began to slide silently up into the closed position. It locked shut with a sharp click. 'How's about that?' said Dad. 'Is that cool or what?'

'It's really cool,' said Zach, but he felt unable to work up enthusiasm for anything. Dad got out of the car and

230

Zach followed. Dad tapped the electronic key and the doors locked with a satisfying clunk. Zach started walking towards the front door but Dad hesitated and instead, strolled out onto the lawn. He stopped by the nearest hole and prodded at it with one foot. 'Big,' he said.

Zach hesitated. 'What?' he murmured.

'I didn't realise that moles made such big holes. And what's all this slime around the entrance?' He lifted his toe away and a harp string of jelly clung to his shoe. 'It looks like the stuff that was on my windscreen this morning. But Pepper said that was seagulls.'

Zach shrugged. 'Go figure,' he said. 'Maybe we've got slimy moles.'

'Slimy *flying* moles,' said Dad.

'What are you talking about?'

'Well, I didn't think about it at the time, because I was in such a hurry to get to work... but if the same stuff that was on the windscreen is also around the holes... and whatever's making the holes is slimy... then how do they get high enough to deposit this stuff on a car windscreen? I mean, moles can't climb up the side of a car, can they?'

Zach thought about that and his blood ran cold within him. Dad was right. The toad-things couldn't possibly have hopped up onto the car. How would they have clung on to the shiny surfaces? They hadn't managed to get very far up the glass of the french window, had they? Which meant that something different had been on the car. Something bigger.

Now Dad was walking further up the lawn and Zach followed him, nervously. 'I'm getting kind of hungry,' he said, trying to distract him, but Dad waved him to silence. He was studying the ground up ahead of him.

'Jesus,' he said.

Zach saw it too. Another hole in the lawn, but this one was the size of a football. It was surrounded by a heaped circle of clods and turf. Dad went down on one knee to stare into the darkness.

'Now, I don't claim to be David Attenborough,' he said. 'But if a mole did *that*, then it's been on steroids.'

Zach just stood there. He didn't know what to say. 'I'll get Pepper to bring over the phone number,' was all he could come up with. 'And I'll ring the guy myself. Tomorrow. He'll sort it. He's supposed to be an expert.'

'Yeah, do that, would you?' said Dad. 'And maybe you'd better tell him to bring a bazooka with him when he comes.' He stood up again and turned back to the house. 'Well,' he said. 'There's no sense in worrying about it now. I don't know about you, but I fancy something simple for dinner. Beans on toast, maybe. With a fried egg on the top...'

They walked back to the house and Zach threw an anxious glance back towards the horizon, where the sun was gradually sinking out of sight. Soon it would be dark again and he didn't want to think about what might happen then.

TWENTY-THREE

LULL BEFORE THE STORM

Dad made the simple dinner he'd suggested and he and Zach sat down at the kitchen table to eat. Zach insisted on closing the french windows as soon as twilight fell, complaining that he didn't want the light to attract moths into the house.

'Since when have you been worried about moths?' Dad asked him.

'They've always creeped me out,' Zach told him.

'Yeah? That's news to me.'

Once the dishes were washed and put away, Dad went up to his room to pack a few things for the trip and Zach tried to settle down to watch TV, but he couldn't relax. At six thirty, the local news came on and right on cue, up came a scowling photo of Tazer, whose real name it turned out, was Maurice Renton. The newsreader said that the police were appealing for anyone who might have seen 'Maurice' the previous day to contact them, so they could be ruled out of the investigation. Maurice, it turned out, had previous convictions for armed robbery and fraud. Police were

233

looking into the possibility that the crime – and it was most definitely being treated as one – might be 'gang-related.'

The bulletin switched to another subject and Zach's mobile trilled. He glanced at the screen and wasn't surprised to see that it was Pepper. He answered it, keeping his voice low.

'Hello?'

'Did you see the local news?' asked Pepper.

'Yeah, I did. I already knew about it though. Dad said people were talking about it at work. What do you think, Pepper? About Tazer?'

'What do I *think*? I think he was a scumbag who probably deserved everything that was coming to him.'

'Pepper, you can't say that!'

'I just did.' A pause. 'Oh, come on, you heard what they said. He was a villain, Zach. Armed robbery!'

'And you don't feel in any way responsible for what happened to him?'

There was a long silence at the other end of the line before she spoke again. 'All I'm saying is, if he was a straight-up guy he wouldn't be owing money to bad people in the first place, would he? And we didn't do anything wrong. We just fixed it so that ordinary people – people who've been paying him through the nose for years – got some of their money back.'

'I know that, but… you must see, Pepper, that if we hadn't done what we did, he'd probably still be alive.'

'You don't know that!'

'Yeah, but that's what I *think*!'

Another long silence. Then Pepper said, 'I know what you're trying to do.'

'I'm not trying to *do* anything!'

'Yes you are. You're looking for reasons to give the stone back.'

'I'm not! But it must worry you, surely? It worries *me*. I can't get the thought out of my head. Tazer's face when all that money dropped – he was bricking it, Pepper. Terrified. He must have known what would happen to him!'

'You've got to get a handle on this,' Pepper urged him. 'We are not to blame for what happened to Tazer. Got that?'

'Sure. Whatever you say… *Dorothy.*'

'Hey, watch it! Only my mum and dad get to call me that.'

'How are they?' asked Zach.

'What do you mean? They're fine. They're just… resting.'

'Pepper, you didn't freeze them again?'

'Only while I'm on the phone. Didn't want them listening in, did I?'

'You'll put them right though?'

'Sure, relax. You're starting to be a real worry-guts, do you know that? How's everything there?'

'OK, I think.' Zach got up from the sofa and walked into the kitchen, without switching on the light. He walked to the french windows and gazed out onto the moonlit garden. Everything looked quiet enough, the full moon sailing in a serene, cloudless sky. 'I keep expecting them to come out again,' he whispered.

'Them?'

'The toad-things. And if they do, I'm not sure what happens. What would I tell Dad?'

'You don't have to tell him anything. Just act astonished. You can do that, can't you?'

'I suppose…

'Look, maybe they were a one-off, eh? Maybe that's all that will ever happen. And if they do come back, well, you can handle a few toads, can't you?'

'Pepper, we found holes in the garden that are bigger than any toad I've ever seen. I'll show you tomorrow…' Zach heard Dad coming down the stairs. 'Gotta go,' he said and rang off. He shoved the mobile back in his pocket and stood there, gazing through the french window.

'What are you doing standing in the dark?' asked Dad.

'Oh, I was just… looking at the garden,' said Zach. See if I can spot a mole.' He turned away. 'Nothing much happening out there,' he said and tried to keep the note of relief out of his voice. He followed Dad into the lounge and the two of them flopped down onto the sofa.

'Fancy watching the box?' asked Dad.

'There's not much on,' said Zach, dismissively.

'There must be *something*!'

'Nah. I looked at the guide. Programmes about baking and decorating.'

'We could play that X-box game, if you like. You

know, the one where you run through the caves and all those monsters jump out at you?'

Zach swallowed. 'I'd rather not,' he said.

'You used to love that game.'

'I'm just not in the mood tonight.' Zach looked at Dad. 'Maybe we could just… talk?'

'Talk?' Dad raised his eyebrows. 'Well, that would be a novelty, I suppose. Anything in particular you want to talk about?'

'Yeah. Granddad Alistair.'

'Him again?' Dad smiled. 'You seem to have a bit of a bee in the bonnet about your granddad. I think I've already told you pretty much all I know.'

'What about Grandma Mary?'

'What about her?'

'When she disappeared. You and your dad must have spoken about that.'

'Well, of course we did. I drove straight over here when the cops called me that night. Got there the following morning. Dad didn't have a phone, of course, so he'd had to run down the hill to the local police station to sound the alarm. He told me the whole story the next day, about how he woken up in the night and Mum wasn't in bed.'

'What did he do next?'

'He came down here and he saw that the window was open and the shutters raised and of course, he knew he'd locked them up when he went to bed. He always did. He was very particular about that. He said he went to the open window and shouted her name but he could hardly make himself heard over the storm…'

'The storm?'

'Yeah, there was a bad one that night. Which only made her wandering off like she did, even stranger. It was blowing a gale and pouring down with rain, yet she went out in her nightdress. Didn't even put on her slippers.'

'How come you didn't mention the storm before?'

Dad stared at him. 'I guess I forgot.' He thought for a moment. 'You know, now that you mention it, that *was* weird…'

'What was?'

'Well, like I said, I didn't get there until late the next morning, by which time the storm had blown itself out. It was as calm as anything but you could see it had caused real damage. There were branches blown off the trees, slates fallen of the roof, that kind of thing. But the cops told me that there wasn't any sign of a storm until they were maybe half a mile away from here. It had been as clear as anything all the way and then the rain came down like somebody had unzipped the sky, they said. And the *sounds*,'

'What… sounds?' asked Zach, nervously.

'Well, the cop I spoke to, he said it was like a howling noise. Just the wind, you understand, but he said he'd never heard anything like it in his life. Dad kept saying to him, "D'you hear that? They've taken my wife and now they're *singing* about it."' Dad rolled his eyes. 'No wonder the police thought he was barmy.'

Zach was thinking about the book of Scottish folklore

he'd looked at up in the attic, in particular something that he'd read in the section on the *Nuckelavee.*

The presence of the Nuckelavee is also associated with bad weather. Storms and gales were thought to be a sign of its approach…

'What else did Granddad Alistair tell you?' asked Zach.

'Oh, once the police left he started spouting all kinds of nonsense. Kept saying something about it all being his fault, that he should have "given it back" sooner, that he'd "hung on too long." Dad was thinking about it now, trying to recall exactly what had happened. 'He said… that he'd wanted to do it before but Mary had "talked him out of it." He was rambling, to be honest. The doctor had left some sedatives for him, so I dosed him up with those and put him to bed.'

'And the new pond. When did he do that?'

'What do you mean, the *new* pond? I know he made some changes to it, a few weeks after Mum disappeared, but…'

'He didn't, Dad. He took the whole thing up and replaced it.'

Dad looked baffled. 'How on earth would you know that?' he asked.

'Because I saw something up in the attic. A scrapbook that he made.'

'I thought you said you didn't find anything of interest up there?'

'Well, I forgot. There was this scrapbook… sort of like a project book, you know? And it had all about the pond in there. Photographs and stuff. And dates to show when things were done.'

'Hmm. I must have a look at that some time,' said Dad. 'Sounds like a lot of work. Does he say *why* he replaced it?'

Zach shook his head. 'No. Not really. Just that he did.'

'I suppose he was trying to keep himself occupied. Must have had a lot of time on his hands after Mum went. You know, it's kind of a shame that the pond isn't there any more. Oh, I know I asked you to get rid of it, but… there's a small part of me that kind of wishes it was still there. Dad was so proud of it.' He shook his head. 'It would be an immense job though.' He smiled. 'Who knows, now that things are looking so promising, we might think about redoing it one day. There's a big garden centre in Cullen, they have everything we'd need and they deliver. It could be a long-term project for the two of us. What do you think?'

'Like you said,' muttered Zach. 'It sounds like a lot of work.'

'But I thought you enjoyed doing the pond?' said Dad.

'Yeah, well… it was OK for a while, but I wouldn't be in a big hurry to do it all over again.'

Dad stared at him. 'You are a mystery to me,' he said.

Zach glared at him. 'What's that supposed to mean?'

'It means, I don't know what makes you tick. Sometimes I get the impression that there's things going on in your head… things that I can only begin to guess at.'

'There's nothing going on in my head,' Zach assured him. He leaned over, grabbed the remote control and switched on the TV. Dad glared at him.

'I thought you just said…'

'I'm thinking about learning to bake,' said Zach and left it at that.

Zach woke for just a moment in the small hours of the morning, dimly aware that out in the world something was different. Restless winds were sighing and whooshing as they began to gather strength. Perhaps the thought that a storm was coming flowered briefly in his slumbering mind, but it didn't register strongly enough to wake him.

He turned over and went back to sleep.

TWENTY-FOUR

STORM WARNING

By the following afternoon the wind had risen to a steady forty miles an hour and there were squally pockets of rain hidden within it. Dad sat at the dining table, drinking a last cup of coffee and staring doubtfully through the french windows at the trees at the top of the garden, their branches swaying in the wind. 'That's just great,' he muttered. 'The one day I have a long car journey to make and the weather decides to go bonkers.' He glanced at Zach who was sitting across from him, sipping at a glass of cola. Dad was supposed to have left at two and now it was a quarter past. 'I hate to leave you alone when it's like this,' he said. 'When's Pepper supposed to be getting here?'

Zach shrugged. 'Any time now,' he said. 'She phoned half an hour ago and said she was setting off. Look, don't worry about me. You get going. Just drive carefully.'

Dad frowned and glanced once again at his watch. 'You're right, I'm gonna have to go,' he announced.

'I'm supposed to be meeting up with some people for dinner.' He drained the last dregs from his cup, then got up from the table and collected his briefcase and overnight bag from the hallway. When he went to the french windows and slid the glass back, wind rushed into the kitchen like something alive. Zach could feel it stirring his hair. He followed Dad outside to the car and watched as he stored his bags in the boot.

'I don't think you'll be driving with the top down in this,' said Zach.

'Afraid not. Maybe I should have gone with the hatchback after all. At least the weather seems to have kept the moles away from the car.' As Dad slammed the boot, Pepper appeared at the gate, hunched over against the wind, her denim jacket pulled tight around her throat.

'Great timing!' shouted Dad. 'I thought I was going to have to leave Zach on his own.'

Pepper came into the garden and slipped an arm around Zach's waist. 'I'll look after him,' she told Dad. 'You want to be careful out there. That wind nearly blew me off my feet on the way over. That's why I'm so late.'

'I'll take it easy,' Dad assured her. He turned to look at Zach. 'OK, Sport, you know where everything is. There's cash in the cupboard, you've got my number and Cheryl's phone number is written on the chalkboard in the kitchen. If you've any worries at all, just give her a ring, OK?'

'Don't worry, Dad, we'll be fine.'

Dad smiled. 'Sure you will. Look after each other. I'll see you on Sunday.' He seemed about to hug Zach, but then thought better of it and shook his hand instead. He opened the door of the BMW and got behind the wheel. The car moved off through the gate and along the lane. Zach and Pepper watched until it was out of sight. Then Zach led her into the cottage and pulled the french window shut.

'This weather is freaky,' said Pepper, pushing her hair back into place.

'I know,' said Zach, grimly. 'I'm worried about it.'

Pepper grinned at him. 'Aw, don't be scared,' she said. 'I'll look after you.'

'You don't get it. There was a storm the night my grandma disappeared.'

She gave him a puzzled look. 'So?'

'And storms are mentioned in the book. The one up in the attic? It's supposed to be a sign that the *Nuckelavee* is coming.'

She laughed. 'I think you're putting two and two together and coming up with five,' she said. 'It's just some wind and rain. Happens all the time here.'

'I *hope* that's all it is,' he said.

'What else would it be? Look, Zach, I'm not being funny, but you're letting it all get to you. That business about Tazer… we're not responsible for what happened to him.'

'You don't think so?' He moved across to the kettle and switched it on, wanting to occupy himself with something, no matter how trivial. 'You have to admit,

Pepper, if we hadn't fixed it so those people won on all those machines, he wouldn't have ended up owing money to the bad guys and...'

'But you can't think like that! You know, there's an old saying, my mum uses. "What goes around, comes around." People like Tazer, they give out so much misery and they don't ever care what happens to other people. So, surprise, surprise, one day they get their come-uppance. If it hadn't happened to him now, it would have happened sooner or later.'

'Yeah, but that just lets us off the hook, doesn't it?' Zach opened a cupboard and took out a couple of mugs. He started preparing drinks. 'Do you ever think, Pepper, that the stone is changing us? Making us different?'

'Duh! Of course it is! Now we can make things happen.'

'That's not what I mean and you know it! What I'm asking is... is it making us... harder? Nastier?'

'Well, clearly not, if you're feeling bad about a piece of scum like Tazer. Jesus, even Ghandi would have given up on him.'

'But *you're* not feeling bad about him, are you?'

'No, and shall I tell you why? Because he's not worth it.' She watched as Zach poured boiling water into the two mugs. 'Well, is he?'

Zach shrugged. 'I suppose not,' he muttered.

'So there you go,' she said, 'Auntie Pepper sorts out another problem.' She paused, gave him a searching look. 'Listen, if you're feeling so bad about the stone...'

'Yes?'

245

'Well, I was thinking, maybe you should give it to me.'

'What?' He turned to look at her.

'Yeah, I mean it. I could take it back with me and store it at my place. Then you wouldn't have the stress of looking after it the whole time and it would be away from here, wouldn't it?' She gestured towards the garden. 'Those toad-things you told me about. Well, they'd never be able to find it down in the village, would they? Can you imagine them hopping all that way?'

Zach frowned. He wasn't entirely sure why, but this seemed to him to be a bad idea. 'I don't know,' he said. 'I'm not sure I could...' He broke off.

'Go on,' she urged him. 'Say what you're thinking.'

He frowned. 'I'm not sure I could trust you to use it properly,' he said.

She looked shocked by this statement. 'What's *that* supposed to mean?' she protested.

'It's just that... well, you're reckless, Pepper. That stuff with your mum and dad... what you *did* to them. That just didn't feel right to me. And now I think about it, it was *your* idea to make all those slot machines pay out at the same time.'

Anger flared in Pepper's eyes. 'Oh right, so what you're saying is, it's *my* fault that Tazer's dead?'

'No, no, of course not! We're both to blame. I mean, I could have said no, couldn't I? It's just that... if I let you take the stone away from here...'

'Yes?'

'I'd feel responsible if anything bad happened to you.'

'You don't have to worry about me,' she assured him. 'I can take care of myself. And let's face it, I…'

'What?'

'I'm better with the stone.'

'*Better* with it?'

'More suited to it. I mean, I can do stuff you can't do. Oh, come on, Zach, you have to admit that's true.'

'Maybe. But that's no reason to put you in charge of it!'

They stood there glaring at each other in silence for a moment. 'I could just take it,' said Pepper, slyly.

'What do you mean?' he asked her.

'I could fight you for it. The winner takes the stone.'

'I'm not going to fight you,' he protested. 'You're not serious, are you?'

She looked away. 'Course not,' she said, but he wasn't entirely convinced. 'And when I say, "fight," I don't mean like, punching each other. I meant like a contest. We'd both have to do something with our minds and whoever was best at it, they'd be the winner.'

'But you know you'd win that.'

'Maybe… maybe not.'

'Look,' he said. 'Let me think about it. About you taking it home and all.' He handed her a mug of tea and she stared into it for a moment, as though looking for an answer to a question.

'Let's go and charge ourselves up,' she said. 'Just in case those toad-things come back.'

247

'I've already told you. It won't make any difference. You can't deal with them that way. It doesn't have any effect on them. I'm not sure why.'

'Humour me,' she suggested. 'Besides, it's been ages since I held the stone. You can do it whenever you feel like it.'

'See, that's another reason why I think it's a bad idea, you taking the stone. Pepper, it's like you're addicted to it.'

'That's nonsense,' she said, but she was already heading towards the stairs as she said it. Zach sighed and followed her up to his room. Once there, she set down her mug of tea, went eagerly to the wardrobe and pulled out the stone; but when she'd removed the covers from it, there was a surprise in store. 'It's a different colour today,' she said. Zach saw that she was right. The stone was usually pale green and turned an orangey red at someone's touch, but this afternoon it was glowing a rich, deep purple and changed to a shimmering gold where Pepper's hand touched it. 'It *feels* kind of different too,' said Pepper.

'What do you mean?' asked Zach, anxiously.

'Try it for yourself,' she said and placed it into his hands. She was right, he decided. The feeling that emitted from the stone was not the usual electrical pulse of exhilaration, but a strange, vibrating shudder that seemed to make the very bones within him tingle. It wasn't a pleasant sensation at all. It felt to Zach as though the stone was *anticipating* something, though he couldn't exactly say why he thought that.

248

'Why is it so different?' he muttered.

His mobile trilled so he handed the stone back to Pepper and pulled the phone from his pocket. He looked at the screen and saw it was Dad. He hit the 'answer' icon and Dad's voice emerged through his hands-free receiver, sounding as clear and as close as if he was actually in the room. 'How's the weather there?' he asked, sounding puzzled.

'Rotten,' said Zach. 'Why do you ask?'

'Because I've driven a few miles down the road and I've suddenly come out of it. The sky's clear as anything here. I'm driving with the top down.'

'Really? Wow, that's weird.'

'Yeah, well I thought I'd let you know, so you wouldn't be worried.'

'Uh… yeah, thanks Dad.' But the call had had the opposite effect. Zach was watching Pepper who was sitting on the bed now, holding the stone, a strange expression on her face, something that hovered between excitement and pain. Purple light shimmered and swirled beneath her palms.

'You still there, Zach?'

'Er… yeah, sorry. Have a… have a good trip.'

'You all right? You sound funny.'

'No, I'm fine. Don't worry about me.'

'OK. I'll phone you tonight, before I turn in. Ciao for now!'

The line went dead. Zach slipped the phone back into his pocket.

'Who was that?' asked Pepper, but her eyes were

249

closed and she sounded odd, as though half asleep.

'It was Dad. He says the weather's fine just a few miles down the road.'

'Oh, that's good.'

'No, Pepper, that isn't good. *Weird* is what that is. It's exactly what happened the night Grandma vanished.'

She opened her eyes then and once again anger flared in them. 'Will you quit with all that?' she snapped. 'It's all you can talk about today. Your Grandma! Christ sake, everyone knows she just got fed up and ran off with somebody else!'

Zach stared at her, dismayed. 'Who told you that?' he cried.

'It's what my dad says.'

'Oh yeah, and we all know how much you trust *his* word, right?' He thought for a moment. 'Pepper, how did you get his permission to come here for the weekend?'

She stared at him. 'I just asked nicely, and...'

'Tell the truth!'

'I *made* them say it was OK.' She grinned, excited by the idea. 'They couldn't help themselves. It was funny. They wanted to say no and they *couldn't*. I just told them "thanks" and walked out the door. My dad stood on the path, looking really angry and shouting after me, but all that came out was, "Have a nice time! Have a nice time!"'

'But... what if they come after you?'

'Oh, I didn't say I was staying *here*. I told them I was going to a girl's house in the village. A sleepover.'

She rolled her eyes. 'Like I'd be interested in that.'

'And they didn't even want you to go to a sleepover?'

'They don't want me to do anything,' said Pepper. 'They don't want me to have a life.' She leaned forward and pushed the stone into his hands. 'Don't you see, Zach? We get to do whatever we want now. *Anything*. The stone puts us in control. Nobody will ever tell us what to do again.'

'But, Pepper, don't you think maybe that's a bad thing?'

'How is it a bad thing?' she protested.

'Like, maybe we *need* to be told things sometimes.'

'Oh, stop being such a wuss! Here, let me show you something.' She took her hands off the stone and lowered her head for a moment as though concentrating. Then she reached out her hands as if about to conduct a symphony. 'Begin,' she murmured.

One by one, every item in the room that wasn't anchored down rose slowly into the air and floated effortlessly in space. Zach looked around open-mouthed. His books, his games, his laptop, his hockey stick, his shoes, his clock, his bedside cabinet, his table lamp, his clothes, everything he owned was floating in the air. Then Pepper made a few simple gestures and the smaller items began to perform an intricate ballet, swooping backwards and forwards, in and out, looping the loop and spinning around, none of the objects ever quite touching each other. Zach sat there watching in amazement, knowing that Pepper was right, he *wouldn't* be able to do this, not if he practiced for weeks. Pepper was somehow much more adept at it than he was. He found himself wondering if that was why she was resisting giving the stone back so tenaciously; because she understood it better; because she knew how to use it to its full potential.

She gave a last little gesture and everything floated effortlessly back to its original position and sank back into place. She opened her eyes and gave him a wicked grin.

'Right,' she said. 'See, that's what I'm talking about! Now… tell me. What have you got to drink?'

TWENTY-FIVE

THE SLITHERS

The day wore on towards evening and the weather got steadily worse. By twilight, gusting winds were rattling the windows, swaying the branches of the trees at the top of the garden. Pieces of detritus flew through the air and pockets of drizzle spattered the french window.

Zach sat at the kitchen table, staring through the glass as the last light faded from the already grey day. He sat waiting. Pepper was still up in his room, holding onto the stone, unable it seemed to tear herself away from it for one minute. She'd consumed a couple of cans of lager by now, but Zach had stopped at one, telling himself that he needed to stay sharp, just in case anything happened. He'd come downstairs on the pretext of wanting another can, but instead had taken up position in the dining room where he could keep watch. He felt keyed up inside, absolutely convinced that something was going to happen, and he wanted to be ready for it when it did.

Darkness gathered outside, so he switched off the

kitchen light and resumed his seat watching, waiting.

And then he heard it. A sound rising and falling on the wind, a long, formless wailing, faint at first but growing stronger with every gust, a shrill animal sound that seemed sad and lonely and threatening, all at the same time. Zach swallowed hard but kept his gaze fixed on the garden. After a while he became aware of footsteps on the staircase as Pepper finally tore herself away from the stone and came down to investigate.

'What's that noise?' she asked him.

He turned to look at her scornfully. 'You *know* what it is,' he said quietly.

She shook her head. 'No way,' she said, but then a particularly shrill note sounded and he saw a look of doubt ignite in her eyes. 'It can't be,' she reasoned.

'It can,' Zach assured her.

He turned back to look at the garden and now he saw the first signs of movement out there – dark glistening shapes were coming up from the holes in the lawn. First he saw two or three, then more, until it seemed to him that the whole garden was alive with them. The toad-things. They were coming in force this time. He knew exactly what to do, had already rehearsed it in his mind and had even checked earlier on to make sure that the old key still fitted the locks. He got up, went to the corner, grabbed the key and got the hooked pole from behind the curtain.

'What are you going to do?' asked Pepper, grimly.

'I'm going to close the shutters,' he said, with a

calmness that surprised him. He unlatched the french window and slid it aside, already aware that the toad-things were turning in his direction and hopping towards him. He stepped out and the wind greeted him, more powerful than ever. He reminded himself that he needed to pull down all the shutters on the ground floor. He ran around the side of the house to the front. Reaching up with the pole, he engaged the hook in the catches and pulled down the shutters on each of the two windows and the front door. They clicked smoothly into place, automatically locking shut. There were no ground floor windows at the ends of the house, so he ran around to the back and got there just as the first of the toad things came flopping up onto the patio. He paused long enough to launch a kick at it, sending it tumbling back towards the garden, then began to turn away with the intention of pulling down the big shutter on the french window, but he froze at the sound of a shout from Pepper, who was standing by the opening. He turned to look at her and she was pointing into the garden.

Zach turned back and his heart lurched in his chest. Something different was coming up out of the ground, something much bigger than the toad creatures. It was hard to see properly in the dim light, but he got an impression of a long, glistening slug-like body, a shape that narrowed to come out of the football-sized hole and then swelled as it emerged, like an obscene balloon. The head was hideous, completely featureless apart from a set of wide gaping jaws and a cluster of writhing tentacles sprouting from where its eyes ought to have been. The thing came oozing up, rearing some six feet into the air and just when Zach thought there couldn't be any more, it kept on coming, twisting around and flopping forward onto the ground, sliding along on its pale ridged belly, its tentacles twisting this way and that as it searched for its prize. In that instant, he knew why Granddad Alistair had christened them 'The Slithers'.

Zach knew he should run back into the house, but for the moment he was mesmerised and when he saw a second large creature bursting up through the soil further down the lawn, terror overcame him. He was only dimly aware of something flopping wetly onto his feet, but he couldn't tear his eyes from the garden to look at what it was.

Then there was a shout from right beside him and Pepper was there, lashing out with her Doc Martens boots, and a couple of toad-things went skittering away with shrieks of pain. 'Zach!' she bellowed in his ear. 'Wake up!'

He shook himself and remembered that he was still holding the hooked pole. He brought it into play and thwacked another of the hopping shapes back towards the garden, but there was a whole mass of them advancing now, flopping up the steps onto the patio like an obscene wave. The nearest of the Slithers seemed to become aware of him. It lifted its hideous head, opened its jaws and howled, the same howl they had heard before but closer now, and so shrill that it was almost deafening.

'Come on!' gasped Pepper and she ran back towards

the french windows. Zach followed, as though in a dream, and so panicked was he, so terrified, he almost went in without lowering the shutters, but he remembered at the last moment and stepped out again. He paused and reached up with the pole, but the hooked end was now slippery with slime and he was having trouble inserting it in the catch. Pepper stood in the open doorway, pale-faced, staring out at him. 'Hurry,' she said, her voice toneless. Zach glanced over his shoulder and his heart nearly stopped because the nearest Slither was already dangerously close, gliding forward on a river of slime towards the patio.

Zach shouted something, he wasn't sure what. He turned back, renewed his efforts to get the hook into the slot, panic making him clumsy. Sweat ran down his face as he struggled.

'Come on, Zach!' Pepper urged him.

The hook finally slotted into position with a click and Zach started to pull the shutter down – but then something whizzed through the air and wrapped around the pole with a slapping sound. He looked around in dull surprise to see that the Slither had shot out a long, purple tongue, something that had unfurled like a party streamer from its open jaws. Then the pole was whipped out of his hand with prodigious force and went whirling back into the garden as though it had no more substance than a matchstick.

'Forget the shutter!' yelled Pepper, but Zach knew that if he did that, the glass of the french window would be shattered in an instant. He flung a desperate glance up to the bottom edge of the shutter, which had stopped around three feet above his head and knew that he would only have time for one attempt. He steeled himself and crouched down, aware as he did so that the Slither was coming up the steps to the patio and was doubtless preparing to fire off that tongue a second time. Zach gritted his teeth and leapt upward, right arm extended. He seemed to hang in the air for a long, terrible moment and then his fingers connected with metal and his weight brought the shutter rattling down. He ducked under it at the last instant, heard a loud thwack as the Slither's tongue connected with metal and then the lock clicked into position. He slid the french window shut, then dropped to his knees and locked that too. He sank to the floor with a gasp of relief, his heart pounding in his chest.

Pepper stood there looking down at him. 'That was close,' she said.

'Do you believe me now?' he asked her, then winced as something crashed against the shutter, causing it to buckle inwards towards the glass. He imagined the huge bulk of The Slither connecting with the metal and wondered how long the shutter could hold back that kind of weight. Zach got to his feet. 'We'd better head upstairs,' he said grimly. He hung the shutter keys back on the rack where they were always kept and led the way.

Up in his room, they kneeled on the bed and looked out onto the garden. It was like looking down onto a sea of hopping, coiling, squirming motion. There was a sudden flash as lightning ripped the sky apart and an instant later the bedroom lights went off, leaving them sitting in darkness. There was a silence so deep that Zach thought he would fall into it.

Then thunder seemed to shake the bed on which they were kneeling. The heavens opened and heavy rain cascaded down onto the squirming mass of creatures below them.

'Oh my God,' whispered Pepper. 'What do we do now?'

Zach pulled his mobile from his pocket. 'We phone for help,' he said. He pressed the button and looked at his screen, aghast.

'What is it?' she asked him fearfully.

'No service,' he said.

TWENTY-SIX

UNDER SIEGE

They sat on the bed, barely able to breathe, terrified. Pepper had instinctively picked up the stone and was hugging it to her, the strange purple light the only illumination they had. Zach kept hoping that the power failure would be only temporary, that the lights would suddenly click back on again, but time passed and they didn't. The two of them sat, listening to the creaking, buckling sound of the shutters being assailed by the Slithers.

'What are we going to do?' whispered Pepper. She was staring straight ahead, her eyes wide and unseeing, her head tilted to one side as though listening. The wailing sound had changed now. It had dropped back to a weird, whispering noise that seemed to be all around them.

'We can't do anything but wait,' Zach told her. 'And hope they can't get through those shutters.'

'We can't just sit here,' she cried. 'What if... what if they break through?'

Zach shook his head. 'If it looks like they're going

to get in,' he said, 'we'll have to give them what they want.' He placed a hand on the stone and grimaced at the shuddering power within it. 'I'll just throw the stone out of the window. Maybe if I do that, they'll leave us alone.'

Pepper glared at him in dismay and hugged the stone tighter. 'No,' she whispered, shaking her head. 'No, you can't do *that*!'

'I think we have to,' he told her.

'No,' she said. 'No, no, no! It's ours now. It belongs to us.'

'But it doesn't, Pepper. It never did. It was always theirs, don't you see? Granddad Alistair found that out the hard way. We can't make the same mistake.'

There was a sudden crash from downstairs and then a shattering sound as the buckling metal shutter connected with the glass of the french window and smashed it out of its frame. 'They're going to get in,' Zach told her. His mind was made up now. He placed a hand more firmly on the stone. 'Pepper, it's the only thing we can do. Give me the stone.'

'No. No, you can't... you mustn't!'

'Pepper, we're running out of time. Give it to me!' He went to pull it forcibly from her arms and then, unexpectedly, a powerful force slammed into him, sent him reeling back from the bed and up against the wall. He slid down into a sitting position, dazed. Pepper got to her feet now and her eyes blazed with a kind of feral madness. She glared down at him, her mouth twisted into a grimace.

261

'You're not to touch it,' she cried.

He felt anger surge within him and he pointed a finger at the stone, imagined it being wrenched forcibly from her arms. It started to come towards him, then stopped abruptly, hovering in midair, shuddering as she willed it back again. Zach grunted, feeling her superior strength gradually overwhelming him. Realising he could not beat her this way, he let her have the stone and concentrated instead on her ankles, sweeping them sideways in his mind. Her feet slid out from under her and she fell, losing her grip on the stone. It hit the floor and rolled back towards him.

He flipped onto his knees and reached out a hand to grab it – then pulled it away with a bellow of pain as the stone glowed red hot, burning the flesh of his palm. He let go and the stone whipped up into the air and curved back into Pepper's grasp, but when he looked at his hand, it was unharmed. Pepper had made him imagine the pain.

Downstairs there was a grinding sound as metal began to buckle under extreme pressure.

'Pepper, we have to throw that thing out!' protested Zach. He got to his feet and stumbled towards her. 'I don't want to fight you any more. If we don't let them have the stone, they'll come in here and take it. Please, just give me…'

But she had turned suddenly aside, as though dismissing him. She was listening intently to something only she could hear and her gaze was fixed upon something in the hallway. Zach looked but he could see nothing out there. Pepper nodded, as though responding to a voice. 'Yes,' she said. 'Yes, of course. Of course, I'll come with you.' She started walking towards the open bedroom door, her expression blank.

'Pepper, where are you going?' He reached out a hand to try and stop her but she shrugged him off.

'I'm going outside,' she told him, calmly.

'Pepper, don't me stupid. Give me the stone!'

'Can't you hear? They're calling me. They want me to meet them.'

'What are you talking about? Pepper, please! The stone!'

He tried to pull it from her arms and she whipped suddenly around, her eyes blazing with an unnatural light. In that instant something hit him in the face and chest, something that felt like a giant fist, something that lifted him clear off his feet and sent him sprawling. The world exploded in front of his astonished gaze like the biggest firework display ever and he tumbled headlong into darkness.

He opened his eyes and a blurred face was peering at him from a distance of a few inches. At the same time he became aware of a bad smell filling his nostrils, making him gag. It was the rancid smell of rotting meat. He gagged, blinked his eyes back into focus. Granddad Alistair wasn't looking any better than the last time Zach had seen him. In fact, if anything, he looked considerably worse. One of his cheeks had fallen away completely, revealing the bones beneath.

Zach realised that he was stretched out on his bed, fully clothed. Granddad Alistair was leaning over him, staring into his eyes. Zach glanced frantically around. There was no sign of Pepper and more ominously, no sign of the stone. 'What's happening?' he gasped.

Granddad Alistair shook his head. 'It's a mess,' he said. 'Whichever way you look at it. Why didn't you listen to me, laddie? I tried to warn you. I *told* you what would happen.'

'Yes, but… I couldn't help it, Granddad. The stone was… really cool.'

'Is that what it was?' Granddad Alistair gave a long sigh. 'But didn't I say that there would be a price to pay for taking it?'

Zach tried to sit up but Granddad Alistair reached out a hand and pushed him back again. Even through his T-shirt, Zach could feel that the old man's hand was as cold as a hunk of refrigerated meat. 'Where's Pepper?' he asked.

'Gone,' said Granddad Alistair, with what sounded like genuine regret. 'Gone to pay the price. In the end, they'll have the stone *and* they'll have your greatest treasure. That way they know you'll never dare to challenge them again.'

'But… the stone *is* the treasure. Isn't it?'

Granddad Alistair chuckled, showing yellow misshapen teeth. 'Is that what you thought?' he asked. 'Funny. I made the same mistake. But we never really know what we have until it's gone.'

264

Zach lay there listening. Apart from the tumult of the storm outside, the house had fallen strangely silent. No sounds of buckling metal, no smashing glass. He began to get a very bad feeling. He tried to sit up again, but Granddad Alistair still had his hand pressed against his chest.

'You have to let me go!' gasped Zach. 'I've got to find Pepper.'

'Too late,' murmured Granddad Alistair. 'You should have thought about that before. Why don't you go back to sleep, boy? There's nothing you can do for her now. Nothing.'

'LET ME UP!' bellowed Zach and suddenly, he was alone in the dark room. No sign of anyone else. Not a trace. He got himself upright and swung his legs off the bed, realising that he couldn't afford to waste any more time. He stood up and for reasons he wasn't entirely sure of, he grabbed the old hockey stick from where it stood, propped against a wall. He went to the door and out onto the dark landing. No sign of Pepper. He descended the stairs and hurried through to the kitchen, then stood for a moment, staring in mute disbelief. The shutters were open and the kitchen floor littered with broken glass. The frame of the french window had been slid aside, even though there was hardly any glass left in it. The keys lay discarded on the floor nearby. Out in the garden the rain continued to bucket down and a flash of lightning briefly illuminated a scene from somebody's worst nightmare.

A long straight path had been formed through the

midst of the squirming horrors on the lawn. About halfway along it was Pepper. She was walking down the path, the stone tucked under one arm like a glowing purple rugby ball. Beside her walked somebody else, the skinny, shambling figure of a woman with lank white hair. She was dressed in a rotting nightgown. As Zach stared in horror the woman turned her head to glance back towards the house and another flash of lightning lit up her face; a face almost completely denuded of flesh, a gaunt, cadaverous nightmare with empty eye sockets and grimacing teeth. As Zach watched, Grandma Mary slipped a bony arm around Pepper's shoulders and led her onwards. At the top of the garden the old wooden shed stood waiting, its door wide open.

'No,' whispered Zach and knew in that instant, that he couldn't allow this to happen. 'NO!' he bellowed and launched himself through the shattered window and out onto the patio. His appearance seemed to instantly galvanise the nearest toad-things into frantic motion. One of them hurled itself towards him, but he met it with a swing from the hockey stick and batted it away, sending it tumbling over its companions. He kept running, the rain soaking through his clothes in seconds and streaming into his eyes, half-blinding him, but he was determined not to slow his pace. More of the creatures hurled themselves at him, but he swatted, kicked, pushed them away, felt their soft bodies squish beneath his running feet as he began to close on the two figures ahead of him.

And then the ground away to his left, where the pond site was located, exploded in a fountain of dirt as something new came thrusting up from under the ground, smashing open the metal grille. It wasn't like the other Slithers. This thing was huge, it towered above him as it reared into the air, a great quivering mass of translucent skin, inside which, multi-coloured organs throbbed and quivered. It was somehow shaped like a horse and somehow like a human rider, as though the two elements had inextricably fused themselves together. The man-shaped thing had a huge vestigial head from the middle of which a single eye glowed bright red. Two impossibly long, serpentine arms hung from its broad shoulders, twisting and writhing like tentacles. An open mouth bellowed in anger. And Zach knew in an instant what he was looking at. The *Nuckelavee* had finally come to claim its prize.

The creature hung in the air a moment, while Zach stared helplessly up at it and then it started to come down on top of him, threatening to crush him flat. For an instant he hesitated, mesmerized, but at the last moment he flung himself frantically to one side, and ran through the ankle-deep creatures on the lawn, kicking them aside, slipping, sliding on the slime of them. The *Nuckelavee* crashed to the ground, mere inches from him and he felt the earth shake beneath the sheer weight of it, but he ran onwards, around its thrashing tail, and headed back towards the two figures he'd been pursuing. He overtook them and came around to block their progress. Grandma Mary registered his presence and gave a shrill shriek of anger. She leapt at him, her bony fingers outstretched to claw at his face but he lifted the hockey stick to bar her way. Her hands clamped around it, wrenching it from his grasp with supernatural power. He let her take it, spun quickly around and ducked behind her, aiming to grab the stone from Pepper's arms. She barely registered him, her expression blank, but nevertheless she hung on tightly to her prize and he had to use every ounce of strength he had in order to tear it from her arms.

He gathered it to him and turned to race back towards the pond site but the *Nuckelavee* seemed to guess his intention and oozed forward to block his path. It reared upwards again and its mouth opened. A long tongue shot out and the sinewy purple length of it wrapped tightly around Zach's waist and began to draw him in towards those open jaws. For an instant, panic claimed him and a vivid flash of lightning showed the glistening maw into which he was about to plunge, a pulsing red orifice fringed with jagged yellow teeth. Terror rippled through him and he almost gave in to it, almost allowed himself to be swallowed – but at the last moment something deep within him rebelled.

He grabbed the tongue in his left hand and pulled it to his face. Then he bit into it, using all the power he could muster. The purple flesh parted, a fishy gloop rushed into his mouth and a great bellow of pain and rage filled the air. All of a sudden Zach was released. He tumbled downwards and hit the ground. In that instant, he remembered that he still had some powers and, though he knew they'd have no effect on the Nuckelevee, he might still be able to use them to achieve his objective. So he concentrated and imagined himself rising into the sky. Suddenly, magically, it happened.

He hovered for a moment, then pictured himself gliding in an arc towards the place where the pond used to be and that happened too. He was still holding the stone under one arm, keeping it tucked in like a rugby ball. As he closed on his goal, he saw the twisted remains of the metal grille hanging open and beneath it, the narrow opening between the rocks that led down into darkness. It occurred to him that he couldn't afford to miss this shot so, as he lifted the stone in his right hand and came drifting down, he pictured the path it needed to take even as he flung it with all his strength. It curved as it hurtled through the air and went straight down the shaft. It disappeared from sight and Zach dropped to the ground. He stood there, staring at the opening, horribly aware of a great shadow gathering over him, as the *Nuckelavee* turned and prepared to crush him beneath its glistening body.

And then green fire blossomed in the shaft, the earth shook beneath Zach's feet with enough power to send him sprawling to the ground. The air around him filled with the sound of unnatural screaming. He rolled onto his back, bewildered, to see the *Nuckelavee* writhing and twisting as if in unspeakable agony. It fell towards him and he rolled desperately aside. The creature went thundering straight past him, its body narrowing as it forced itself into the opening and went squirming down into the inferno below. Zach sat up and looked across the garden, turning his head this way and that as he tried to make sense of what he was seeing. The toad-things were scrambling back into their holes, shrieking as they went, plumes of smoke billowing from their warty backs, as though they were being consumed by the same fire that was blazing down in the shaft. Those that didn't make it to their holes in time lay writhing and wriggling frantically on the ground, before bursting open in gouts of slimy blood and finally lying still. In what seemed like moments, the lawn was completely devoid of life.

The rain stopped falling as suddenly as if somebody had flicked a switch. There was a last low rumble of fading thunder and then a deep, impenetrable silence.

The lights in the house clicked on.

Zach sat there, stunned, hardly believing the nightmare could be over quite so suddenly. Everything seemed so calm, so *normal*. And then a thought flashed across his mind. Pepper! Where was Pepper?

The instant the thought registered with him, he was back on his feet and running up the garden, ignoring the last dead monstrosities that burst and spread beneath the soles of his shoes. He reached the open shed door and ran inside. He looked desperately around. Empty. The shed was empty!

'Pepper!' he screamed. 'Pepper, where are you?'

And then he heard a gasp, somewhere down at floor level, and he dropped to his knees, looked under the cobweb-festooned workbench. She was there, lying on the ancient boards, curled up in a fetal position, her hands to her head as if to ward off an attack. He reached in and took hold of her, felt her flinch at his touch, but managed to pull her out from under the bench and help her to her feet, noticing as he did so that there was no hint of any extra power in his muscles. He was, quite suddenly, an ordinary boy again. He got Pepper upright and helped her out into the night air. Gazing up into the heavens, he could see that the clouds were already rolling away, revealing the clear night sky and a scattering of stars. In Zach's pocket, his mobile phone pinged as a text message came in. He started back towards the house, one arm still supporting Pepper. She took some stumbling steps as her senses gradually came back to her.

They came alongside the ruin of the pond site, where black smoke was now billowing out from the opening, bearing the disconcerting smell of burnt fish. Pepper sniffed the air, stared at the smoke for a moment. 'The stone?' she whispered, looking yearningly into his face.

He shook his head. 'Gone,' he said, and saw her face crumple into an expression of pure misery.

'It can't be,' she whispered. 'Please don't let it be.'

'I'm sorry,' he said, and left it at that. He helped her back into the house and got her seated. He went to the sink and poured her a glass of water, then brought it to her and urged her to take a drink.

'What do we do now?' she asked him, forlornly. 'Zach, now we'll be… we'll just be ordinary.'

'We'll be *alive*,' he assured her. 'That has to count for something.'

Her shoulders began to move then and he held her tightly against him, while she cried.

EPILOGUE

Zach was still filling the pond with the hosepipe when Dad's car drove in through the gate, late on Sunday afternoon. It had been quite a struggle getting everything done in time for his return, but Zach hadn't mentioned what he and Pepper were doing, the two times that Dad had phoned, wanting it to be a complete surprise for him.

Saturday morning had involved an early trip to the big garden centre in Cullen, driven there in a van that belonged to one of Pepper's friends. Zach had bought everything he thought he'd need and he hadn't stinted on anything. In the end, it had taken most of the money that he'd had hidden in his bedroom, but he figured it would be worth it. They'd got Pepper's friend to drop all the stuff at the front of the house to avoid embarrassing questions about the state of the garden out back and Zach had paid him in cash. The last of his money had gone on getting the french window replaced. Zach had blamed it on the storm and the guys from the emergency team who'd fitted it,

273

told him that there'd been a few problems in the area last night. 'There's been chimneys blown down and all sorts,' one of them said, as he handed over a hefty bill. 'Your dad can probably claim the money back on his insurance.' But Zach didn't plan to mention it, not unless Dad noticed anything different. He'd managed to get the battered-looking shutters closed again. He'd blame the damage to them on the storm, which wasn't so very far from the truth. And it wasn't as if they were ever going to be needed again.

Once the glaziers had left, Zach and Pepper had gone to work in earnest. First they'd cleared away the remains of any of the toad-creatures that hadn't made it back underground, wrapping them in bin bags and burying them in a pit they'd dug behind the shed. Then, while Pepper concentrated on cleaning up the kitchen to the best of her ability, Zach had started work, digging out the pond and laying the liner. That was Saturday pretty much taken care of, but they were up first thing Sunday to continue the project.

After chatting with somebody at the garden centre, Zach had chosen a selection of suitable plants and he and Pepper had placed them in a shallow section at the pond's edge. Unlike Granddad's effort, *this* pond had an air pump that would keep the water clear and weed-free. Zach had even buried electric cable under the turf and run it back to the patio where there was an outside socket. All in all, it looked pretty amazing.

Topping up the pond had been the final job and

Zach couldn't have left it any later. He was just finishing up when the BMW cruised in through the gate.

Dad got out of the car and wandered over, staring in open-mouthed astonishment. Zach looked up at him and smiled, savouring the moment.

'Well, what do you think?' he asked.

'Zach, what the…? How did you…? Wow! It looks amazing.'

'It was what we talked about, right? You said you wished you could make the pond like it used to be. I used Granddad Alistair's old photographs as a guide. This is as close as I could get it.'

'But how… how did you *afford* this? It must have cost a bomb.'

Zach waved a hand. 'Actually, I got all the stuff on sale. I had a few quid put aside. Some money I… I won on the slot machines, a while back.'

Dad shook his head, laughed. 'It looks amazing,' he said. 'But Zach, there was no need to go to all this trouble. You must be exhausted!'

Zach shrugged. 'I *am* a bit tired,' he admitted. He looked at his blistered hands, telling himself that this time they'd have to heal the natural way.

Pepper came out of the house carrying a can of lager. She handed it to Dad. 'Hi, Mr Hamilton. Welcome home. How was your trip?'

'It was really useful, thanks. Made a lot of good contacts.' Dad set down his briefcase and smiled at her. 'This is really nice.' He popped the ring pull and took a swig, 'I guess you must have helped with all this,' he said. 'It looks brilliant. Thanks so much.'

Pepper smiled and Zach noted that there was still a certain sadness in the smile, but he thought she was coming to terms with things now. They'd spent a lot of time talking it through while they worked. He knew how she felt but he also thought that they'd been really, really lucky.

Dad was beginning to notice other things now – the terrible state of the lawn for a start.

'Oh, by the way, we got those moles sorted out,' Zach told him, noticing his expression. 'A guy came on Saturday and put down some poison. He says we won't be bothered by them again.'

'Really? How much did it cost?'

'Nothing,' Pepper assured him. 'A friend of my dad's. He did it as a favour.'

'Oh,' said Dad. 'That's great.' He was noticing other things now. There were tree branches lying on the ground and a wooden post was leaning over at a crazy angle. 'That storm must have been fierce,' he said. 'I passed a couple of fallen trees on the way up the hill.'

Zach nodded. 'It was unreal,' he said. 'But Granddad's shutters came in pretty useful. They took the worst of it.'

Dad looked impressed. 'Good thinking,' he said. 'You know, I would probably never have thought of using them.' He looked at Pepper. 'You going to stay for something to eat?' he asked her.

'Actually, I really should get going,' she said. 'My mum and dad will be expecting me.'

'OK. Well, another time maybe. See you later. And thanks for all your hard work.'

'I'll walk you out,' Zach told her. He dropped the hosepipe into the pond and went with her to the gate. They stopped for a moment and he gave her an encouraging smile. 'You going to be all right?' he asked her.

'I guess I'll have to be,' she said. She sighed, rolled her eyes. 'Time to head home and face the music. It's not going to be pleasant.'

'If they're too hard on you, just come back,' he advised her. 'I'll clear it with Dad.'

She nodded. 'It's going to be tough,' she told him. 'Whatever they say to me now, I'll just have to take it. It was so much easier when I could *stop* them.'

'You'll just have to talk to them,' said Zach. 'Tell them what you want.'

'You make it sound easy,' she said.

'I didn't say it would be easy.' He leaned forward and kissed her. 'But ring me if you need any help. See you tomorrow,' he said and stood watching, as she strolled off along the lane. When she had turned the corner out of sight, he walked back to Dad, who was standing there, gazing thoughtfully into the clear cool depths of the pond.

'I'm going to love this,' he said. 'Sitting out here in the sunshine, drawing up my plans for the future.' He looked at Zach. 'It's weird. I've only been

277

gone a couple of days and it feels like so much has happened.'

'I know what you mean,' said Zach. 'It feels like that for me, too.'

'Well, I think I'll go in and change my clothes. Hey, maybe we should go out to eat again. It's the least I can do after all your hard work. A bit of a reward. We could try that Indian place again, you know, the one where they gave us a free meal?'

Zach grinned. 'I doubt that'll happen a second time,' he said. 'But yeah, that'd be nice. You go in,' he suggested. 'I'll just finish up here.'

Dad picked up his briefcase and wandered into the house. Zach watched him apprehensively, waiting to see if he noticed anything different about the glass, but he didn't seem to. Zach pulled the hosepipe out of the pond and saw that it was close to full now. The guy at the garden centre had told him to leave a few inches to allow for rain. He went to the patio to switch off the tap. On his way back to collect the hose, something caught his attention, something lying on the grass, catching the light and gleaming gently.

He stooped and picked it up.

It was a jagged shard of stone, about the size of a conker. He held it in the flat of his hand, noticing the way it glowed with a pale green light that seemed to ripple and swirl, aware of the gentle thrum of energy that seemed to be pulsing out of it. It must have been flung upwards, he decided, from the explosion in the

278

shaft and against all the odds, had passed through the narrow opening at the top. He had a momentary impulse to fling it away, to throw it as hard as he could and never bother to look for it again.

But at the last moment something stopped him. Almost of its own accord, his hand went to his side and slipped the stone into the pocket of his jeans.

Then humming softly to himself, he strolled back to the house to change his clothes.

More Philip Caveney Titles
by Fledgling Press

The Crow Boy Trilogy:

Crow Boy

Seventeen Coffins

One for Sorrow

The Calling

The Calling

I enjoyed this book enormously ... Fledgling Press
are onto something good here, I reckon.

--**The BookWitch**

This is a splendid book which manages to combine
adventure with a painless sprinkling of facts.

--**www.thebookbag.co.uk**

This is a stonking good read for anyone of 10+.

--**Historical Novel Society**

One for Sorrow

The story plays engagingly with the tropes of fictional
time travelling: are the people of the past ghosts or
truly alive, can events be changed without affecting
history, and is time linear or circular? [...] Caveney
negotiates these pitfalls with a sure foot, and produces
an exciting read which somersaults with increasing
chaos between an endangered present and a threatening
past.

--**Historical Novel Society**

This is a stunning story, brimming with moments of
heart-stopping terror, tender scenes when Tom meets
an old friend ... and quite a lot of gentle humour.

--**www.thebookbag.co.uk**

Seventeen Coffins

It's a dark and scary tale . . . Don't miss it, though: it's
well-written, thrilling and thoroughly convincing!

--**www.thebookbag.co.uk**

Crow Boy

The book is both intriguing and thrilling . . . It is a
rich, satisfying book, with lots of layers and plenty to
think and talk about, and it deserves to be as popular
with readers as Mr Caveney's other excellent books.

--**The BookBag**